Lost Goodbyes

M. Wright

M. WRIGHT

Rebel Publishing

ISBN: 978-0-578-23193-8

PRINTED IN THE UNITED STATES OF AMERICA

This book is dedicated to all the people affected by Human Trafficking. The lost ones who never came home, the ones who came home and are making progress toward a better life, and for those who investigate, educate, and rescue those who find themselves trapped in this life. I recognize numerous organizations across the country are educating people and helping to find freedom for those affected. I applaud their efforts in being on the front lines of such atrocities. Human trafficking is an estimated $32-billion industry and the second-fastest growing criminal industry. Drug trafficking is the number one. It is estimated that every two minutes, a child is bought and sold for sex in the United States.

If you know of someone who needs help, or you need help for yourself, please reference the sticker below with the phone number.

Call the National Human Trafficking Hotline **888-3737-888**

HUMAN TRAFFICKING
IN OUR BACKYARD
www.InOurBackyard.org

Human Trafficking Indicators

- Victim may appear fearful or anxious.

- Victim may avoid eye contact or social interaction.

- Victim may appear malnourished or show signs of physical abuse.

- Multiple female victims may be together and may have similar tattoos.

- Victim may be controlled by traffickers and not be able to speak for themselves or make purchases without the traffickers consent.

- Victims of human trafficking can be of any race, ethnicity, gender, age or socioeconomic status.

- A large number of sex trafficking victims are domestic born and a large number of labor trafficking victims are foreign born.

- Traffickers use force, fraud or coercion to profit off some type of labor or paid sex act.

What To Do If You Suspect
Human Trafficking

- Write down a physical description (age, race, height, tattoos, scars, identifying characteristics).

- Write down a description of vehicles involved (color, make, model, license plate and state).

- Note time of day to help authorities search video to identify the traffickers and victims.

- Do not confront a suspected trafficker directly or alert a victim to any suspicions. It is up to law enforcement to investigate suspected cases of human trafficking.

- Immediately after traffickers and victims have left, call the National Human Trafficking Hotline at 888-3737-888 and report what you observed. Make a call in a private area sooner if possible.

- Don't worry about being wrong - report anything that may be human trafficking. The trained advocates at the hotline are available 24/7 to receive your calls.

PREFACE

This book is a work of fiction. No real names of people or circumstances were used in the creation of the book. Any similarities to situations or incidents are unintentional.

Human trafficking is a real problem within our communities, and the author hopes that through this book, the reader will be able to identify with or identify signs of human trafficking. With the help of the organization, In Our Backyard, an indicator sheet and phone number have been provided if the reader feels they need to call.

Human trafficking is not only sex trafficking, but it is also labor trafficking as well. Sometimes, trafficking is happening right before our very eyes, and we fail to recognize the signs. Here are the definitions of both provided by the organization, In Our Backyard.

Sex Trafficking: Commercial sex act induced by force, fraud, or coercion, or in which the person performing the act is under the age of eighteen.

Labor Trafficking: Using force, fraud, or coercion to recruit, harbor, transport, obtain, or employ a person for labor or services in involuntary servitude, peonage, debt bondage, or slavery.

Education on what human trafficking is and how to recognize the signs is one of the most important actions we can do to stop this atrocity that happens within our communities.

CHAPTER 1

Rachel stood holding the handrail to the subway car as it rambled down the tracks. Her mind was a thousand miles away. She was tired and ready to enter the sanctity of her apartment and relax in a hot bath. Her day had started like any other day at the *New York Times*. Her job as an investigative reporter had her hopping from one story to the next. There were two stories she had been handed, and one was starting to take precedence.

She had spent most of the day trying to verify the incoming information about a child prostitution ring operating out of a warehouse on the Lower East Side. Her source had been vague about the location of the operation and any names involved. As with anything of this subject matter, the source did not want to be identified. Rachel had taken a particular interest in this story. She didn't like to think of her past, but this story was hitting a little too close to home.

She had experience with being a child prostitute. She knew the fear and pain that children would be going through as their abductors and handlers were preparing them for their eventual "customers." The life was horrible, and she wished these adults would treasure children instead of abusing them and hurting them in ways from which they would never recover.

She had been six years old, and her sister, Maggie, had been nine years old when they were abducted. They had been asleep when the abductor came in through the open window. Rachel heard the man before she saw him. He was whispering to Maggie while he had his hand over her mouth. Rachel sat up in bed and was about to scream when she felt the blow. The man hit her in the head, and all she remembered after that was waking up in a dark, smelly room with duct tape over her mouth, and her hands taped behind her back. Maggie had been there too. She was on the little bed by the window. She had tape on her mouth, and her hands were taped behind her back as well. Rachel ran over to her, and they hugged each other the best they could, each crying silent tears and wondering where they might be.

Rachel closed her eyes briefly and willed the images from her mind. She hated reliving that night. She also knew she should have told someone once she and Leslie had escaped, but she hadn't. She was too embarrassed by what she had had to do with the so-called customers. Plus, Leslie had been the one to help her with the escape. She didn't want Leslie to be in trouble too. Then Leslie had disappeared, and she had been left on her own. She had been too scared to reach out. She didn't want to disappear, as well. Leslie had been the older girl who had taken care of her and Maggie. The only one who had seemed to care when all else was going wrong.

The subway car rumbled to a stop, shaking Rachel from her thoughts. She watched as the doors slid open and was startled to see three men wearing masks and hoodies entering the car ahead of hers with guns drawn. The screams from the passengers echoed through the station. Everyone in Rachel's car sat or stood silently, watching the tragedy unfold in front of them. Rachel could not believe what she was witnessing. These three men stormed toward a woman and a young girl. The little girl looked to be around eight years old. She had long, blond hair and was wearing the cutest royal blue dress. The girl was ripped from the woman's grasp by one of the men, while the other man bashed the woman across the face with the butt of his pistol. The third man waited by the door holding everyone at gunpoint.

The men exited the train as quickly as they had entered, and the little girl was gone.

Why was no one helping or trying to stop this madness? It seemed that everyone in the car ahead of her had been frozen in place. Terror was no surprise in this city. The past had proven this with the Twin Towers. The reality of violence was always present in everyday life of all New Yorkers. She knew everyone's reaction to violence was different, but this little girl was taken away at gunpoint! No one was helping!

Rachel stood holding the bar, battling her own fear. The screams of the little girl pierced through the paralyzed state she found herself fighting. The present had just collided with her past . . . a past Rachel thought she had overcome. Fighting the urge to get away from the scene and the memories that were rushing back to her, Rachel stepped from the subway car and flipped open her notepad and started writing down what she had just witnessed. Some of the other passengers were trying to console the woman as best they knew how. Someone had called 911 because Rachel could hear the sirens as they were getting closer. Transit police were already starting to process the chaotic scene as passengers scurried away to their next destination. A few of the passengers were sticking around to give their statements.

As Rachel approached the woman, she heard her telling a transit officer, between sobs, that the little girl's name was Skylan Marie Winslip. She was seven years old. Making a quick mental note of that information, Rachel stepped beside the woman and asked if she were all right. The gash above the woman's eyebrow was bleeding, and the thin scarf she was holding to the wound was doing little to stop the blood flow. Rachel reached into her bag and pulled out a T-shirt and handed it to the woman. "Put pressure on the wound. It will help to stop the bleeding," she said. The woman briefly looked into Rachel's eyes and took the T-shirt and applied it to her head.

"Thank you," the woman said between sobs. Holding her head with one hand, the woman reached out with her other hand, and asked, "Would you stay with me?"

The relaxing evening was not meant to be. "I will," Rachel answered. "My name is Rachel. What's yours?"

"Abigail Winslip," she said. "Thank you."

The first officer on the scene was Sergeant O'Shea from the Fifth Precinct. Rachel stood by as Abigail answered his questions, and the EMTs bandaged her wound. As the officer was finishing up, Abigail's husband, Eugene Winslip, came rushing to her side. As the two embraced, Rachel was asked by Sergeant O'Shea if she would stick around and provide a statement. Rachel knew she didn't have a choice; she had had a front-row seat to all the chaos. She nodded her head and waited patiently as Sergeant O'Shea readied his clipboard for her statement.

Sergeant O'Shea looked up to see Rachel pulling out a news reporters' notebook. His dark eyes narrowed as he asked, "News reporter?"

Rachel knew the tone and responded quickly, "Yes, sir, Rachel Denton, *New York Times.* Investigative journalist."

The sergeant was not surprised. "Were you a witness to this incident?"

Rachel held up her hands as if to surrender and said, "I was. I was standing at the head of my subway car and witnessed the whole thing unfold in the car ahead of me. I've written down a few notes if you'd like to have a look."

Sergeant O'Shea agreed and took down all the information Rachel provided. "Thank you," he said. "I'll pass this on, and one of our detectives will probably be in touch. As a professional courtesy, can I ask that you not run this as your top story in tomorrow's paper? We need to get our investigation underway, and it's all going to be a bit complicated with an investigative reporter as one of our eyewitnesses."

Rachel knew the routine. She also knew this might be the break she needed on that lead about the child prostitution ring. She hoped that by being cooperative, she might gain a valuable asset within the NYPD with insight into the crimes that were being alleged. Rachel handed him her business card and said, "I'll hold off for now, but I have a job to do too. I hope you understand." Relations between reporters and police officers were tenuous. Rachel knew the game, and this game had just begun.

Rachel left the station and hailed a cab. She had no desire to board another train. All she wanted now was to go home to her apartment and process the events that she had witnessed. Her heart ached for the little girl, Skylan. She got into the cab and said a prayer for both Skylan and her parents. This was going to be hard on them. Rachel prayed the girl would be safe and not harmed. A special request was sent up in prayer for Skylan that she would not be subjected to the prostitution life.

Rachel knew this was probably a part of the prayer that wouldn't be granted. Her relationship with God had been tenuous since her own abduction. She had prayed every day after her first encounter with Darius. She was subjected to the evil and horrendous acts that would never leave her memory. Still, the prayers continued, and eventually, her escape seemed to be an answer to all her cries for help.

As the cab pulled up to the curb, Rachel ended her prayer. She hoped this would not be one of those sleepless nights.

CHAPTER 2

Rachel stepped into her dark apartment. It was after midnight. All she wanted to do was take a hot bath and go to bed. Tomorrow was going to be another busy day, and she knew she'd have to divide her time between being an eyewitness and being a reporter. Her editor would be chomping at the bit to get something out for the next paper. As for now, all she wanted was a hot bath.

The water was hot as she relaxed back against the curve of the tub. Her glass of wine balanced on the little shelf was just within arm's reach. She kept thinking about the subway, the way those men were so confident in their target, and how they knew where the mother and little girl would be. It had all happened so quickly. Maybe these three men were part of the child prostitution ring. Their methodical approach to the abduction led Rachel to believe they had done this before. She would have to look into the other reported abductions to see if there were any similarities.

She wondered how many children that had been abducted in the past year had been found safe and how many had been found at all. All these questions . . . She reached for her wineglass and prayed Skylan would be kept safe. Memories were starting to filter back into her mind, so she let them play out. She really couldn't stop them anyway.

Rachel thought back to Maggie's and her abduction. The little house they called home was in Arvonia, Virginia. It sat on the edge of town near the railroad tracks. Their mom worked the day shift down at the local diner and picked up odd jobs when she could for a little extra money. Their dad was in prison for armed robbery and murder. He had tried to rob a bank in Richmond, Virginia, and in the process, had shot and killed a guard. Life was tough for Rachel and Maggie, but their mom was doing her best. The girls were happy, for the most part. Maggie would help with the cooking and house-work when their mom had to work late. Rachel did what she could to help, as well. Rachel missed her mother and found herself feel-ing angry with her mother for never trying to find them after they had been abducted. That's what she believed anyway because she never saw her mother again.

That night before bedtime had been normal. The girls had fold-ed their clothes and put them away. Their mother had come in and tucked them into bed with a kiss and hug good night. She told them to sleep tight, and she'd see them in the morning. Of course, that never happened. The guy had been calm. He knew how to get their cooperation without making a lot of noise. Rachel started to tear up, thinking about her mother. That night was the last night she and Maggie had seen her. They were taken under cover of darkness and whisked away to someplace where neither Maggie nor she was familiar with.

The bathwater had gotten cold. Rachel stepped from the tub and grabbed the nearest towel. Slipping on her oversized T-shirt, she headed for bed. Just as she was snuggling in, her cell phone rang. The number was one she wasn't familiar with, but she knew in her line of work it could be a lead for a story or a source who had just changed phones again. "Rachel Denton," she answered. The female voice on the other end was muffled and barely audible.

"Hello? I have information on a little girl who was taken this evening."

Rachel sat straight up in bed. Her heart racing, she replied, "Go ahead, I'm listening. Do you know where she is?" Rachel listened intently to the silence on the line.

Finally, the voice said, "She wore a pretty blue dress."

Rachel tried hard to contain the excitement in her voice. This was the best lead she had had in a while. "Please," Rachel said, "tell me where she is." The line went dead.

Rachel sat in stunned silence. Questions were racing through her head. *Who was that on the phone? How did that person get my number? Why call me and not the police?* Rachel decided she would try calling the number back. The phone rang and rang. No answer. She flipped open her laptop and did a quick reverse phone number lookup and found nothing of value there. It was just a cell phone, no name. Rachel knew she wouldn't be able to sleep, and she needed to report this to the NYPD as soon as possible. She quickly got dressed and was on her way. She decided she would take a cab. The thought of going back to the subway gave her the chills.

Rachel called ahead to see if Sergeant O'Shea was still on duty but was quickly informed by the dispatcher that Detective Andrews was now in charge of the case. She would have to meet with him.

Detective Andrews was a rough, tough dinosaur of a detective. Rachel had dealt with him a year ago when she had been investigating an elder abuse case in one of the care homes near Brooklyn. He was not the most pleasant of detectives to work with, but she had managed then, and she would manage now. Only this time, she had the advantage since she had been an eyewitness to the crime. She still had no idea if this case were related to the child prostitution ring on the Lower East Side, but she wasn't going to rule it out just yet. Her gut instinct told her this was going to be the story of a lifetime. She would follow every lead—no matter what.

Rachel sat in the waiting room until Detective Andrews finally burst through the door, looking disheveled and tired. He quickly looked around and honed in on his target, Rachel. She stood up and said, "Hello, Detective Andrews. My name is Rachel Denton."

"I remember you. You're that journalist. I have no comment," he said as he turned to go back into the hall.

Rachel quickly responded, "I have information on the little girl who was abducted from the subway."

The detective turned around and looked her way again. "*You're the eyewitness?*"

"Yes," Rachel said, "but I also was contacted by someone awhile ago who knew of the abduction. She didn't say much, but I thought you should know."

Detective Andrews was quiet. "You're not here to get a story?" he asked.

"We can worry about that later," Rachel said. "We need to help the girl if we can."

Detective Andrews nodded and said, "Follow me." Rachel shared the phone number with the detective and then gave her eyewitness statement again. Detective Andrews took notes and seemed to be nonchalant and distant. It was as if this were just one of ten thousand statements he took every day, and this too would lead nowhere in particular. Rachel knew that finding this little girl should be the top priority, but the reality was that this case was just one more that was added to the ever-growing pile on this man's desk. "Thanks," Detective Andrews said. "I'll be in touch if there is anything I might have missed."

Rachel was frustrated as she left the police department. Her gut was telling her to keep after it, but her boss would be expecting something on his desk this morning. She caught a cab to her office and quickly went to work on a short, but interesting story about the possible child prostitution ring located within their great city. The piece was a teaser to what Rachel hoped would be a massive story uncovering the people behind the abductions and putting them away in prison for a very long time.

After completing her teaser story, Rachel headed back to the NYPD to do some research on the other child abductions that had happened in the past. Getting to the core of the child prostitution ring would be difficult, but knowing the how, when, and where of the other abductions might prove to be very beneficial. Detective Andrews would probably be of no help, so Rachel decided she'd try talking to Detective Martinez in the Child Crimes Division. He was much more helpful in the other stories she had done.

Detective Martinez was just walking out of the NYPD as Rachel got out of her cab. She waited until he was within earshot and then said, "Hi, Detective. I was wondering if I could speak with you for a moment."

Detective Martinez smiled and said, "Sure thing, you're welcome to tag along this morning." Rachel knew an opening when she saw one, so she quickly got in step with the detective and followed him to his car. "Hop in," he said. "I've got some errands to run this morning, so we can talk while I drive. Are we on or off the record?"

Rachel smiled. "We are on the record. I'm doing some research for a story I'm working on."

"Let me guess," he said. "The child abduction from yesterday?"

"Well, sort of," Rachel said. "I really would like to know about any other abductions that have happened either here in New York or surrounding areas."

Detective Martinez glanced over at Rachel, and an air of seriousness enveloped them both. "How many do you want to know about?"

Rachel looked up from her notepad and said, "How many are there?"

"A lot," he said. "Not at liberty to say exactly how many."

Rachel nodded. She knew the game and didn't press him on the exact number. "What can you tell me about the other abductions?" she asked.

"I can't tell you a whole lot. Most of the girls were abducted from public places. For example, walking to and from school, a park, and a few from an area arcade. I'm currently looking into some of the out-of-state abductions to see if there are any similarities in the methods of abduction. This girl from the subway is the first that I know of that was taken in such a forceful and violent manner."

Rachel couldn't believe what she was hearing. Detective Martinez hadn't given her details, but by the way he was talking, there were numerous abductions. How many girls were out there? She couldn't help but think what these girls were being subjected to—mental and physical abuse. Rachel had stopped taking notes and sat in the passenger seat of the patrol car seized by the images that were filling her mind.

She was back in the room with Maggie. Sitting on the floor listening to Maggie tell her about the man with the long, blond hair and blue car. She was telling Rachel never to go with him because he would take her to other men who would touch her and make her do things that weren't right. Rachel remembered Maggie saying that the man smelled like cigarettes, and he always tried to act nice and buy things for her after she had been with his friends. Maggie would always cry when she was done being brave with Rachel. Rachel knew because Maggie would go into the bathroom and turn on the shower. Rachel could hear her sobbing quietly. Rachel knew the man with the long, blond hair was not a nice man, but at the age of six, she had no idea . . . until the day that he came to get her.

Detective Martinez glanced over and saw her and quickly asked, "Everything okay? Rachel, Rachel, earth to Rachel."

Rachel snapped back to the present. Detective Martinez had stopped the car and was looking at her very intently. "I don't know where you went just now, but you look as if you've seen a ghost. Are you okay?"

"I'm fine," Rachel said. "I just remembered something from

when I was a kid."

"Care to share?" he asked.

Rachel shook her head no. "Not now. Where are we going?" she asked.

Detective Martinez pulled back into traffic and said, "Headed over to talk with a woman who might have some information on a possible abduction. She claims a young girl approached her at the local market and asked if she would take her home with her."

Rachel was intrigued. "How old was the girl?"

"Here we are. I guess we'll find out," he said.

Mrs. Tonya Franklin, a stout black woman in her fifties who had a kind face and friendly demeanor, greeted them. "Come in, come in," she said. "Can I get you anything?"

"No, thanks, Mrs. Franklin. This is Rachel Denton, a reporter with the *New York Times*. She's riding with me as an observer today," Detective Martinez said.

"Call me Tonya," she said. "Mrs. Franklin sounds way too formal."

Detective Martinez pulled out his notepad and began the interview. "Mrs. Franklin, Tonya, can you start at the beginning and tell me what happened?"

Tonya sat up straight and began telling about the run-in with this young girl. "I was down at the local market on Houston Street. I was almost done shopping when this white girl came up to me and asked if I'd take her home with me. I couldn't believe what I was hearing. I asked the girl where her mom was, and all she did was put her finger up to her mouth and shushed me. I told her not today. I feel bad now because I came home and turned on the television and saw where there was an abduction of a little girl from the subway. This girl that approached me wasn't her, because she was older, but she could have really needed help, and I did nothing."

Detective Martinez quickly reassured her, "Mrs. Franklin, you *are* helping. If you can, will you describe the girl that approached you?"

Mrs. Franklin wiped away the single tear that was sliding down her cheek. She smoothed her dress with shaky hands and then said, "She was white and had brown hair that was tied back in a ponytail. She was wearing blue jeans and a purple shirt. She was sad looking. She stood about up to here, pointing at her shoulder, and I'd guess she was probably around eleven years old."

"Did the girl seem afraid of anything or anyone?" Detective Martinez asked.

"Not really, but she was quiet and kept looking around, like she was looking for someone," Mrs. Franklin replied.

"You say she was about eleven years old. Did she have any unique features, like scars or acne? Did she appear too thin or too large for her size?" the detective asked.

"She looked normal as could be. Looked healthy. Her clothing looked clean, and she appeared to be like any other little girl that could have been out shopping with her mom or dad," Mrs. Franklin said.

"Thank you," Detective Martinez said. "I appreciate you calling in, and I assure you we are actively working every tip that comes in. If you remember anything else, please feel free to call the precinct. Here's my card with my direct number."

Walking back to the squad car, Rachel found herself remembering the day she had escaped. It was a day that she relived in her dreams whenever she found herself overly stressed. She wished Maggie could have escaped with her. She had made it out, but she wondered what might have happened to Maggie. She just disappeared. Rachel didn't even have a chance to say goodbye. Rachel secretly hoped Maggie was still alive and had found a way to escape on her own. She had been looking for her since she had entered college. No clues had been revealed, but Rachel knew she had to be out there somewhere.

Detective Martinez closed the door of the squad car and pulled out his notepad. He made a few more notes and then looked over at Rachel. "Well, I'd like to know what's going through your mind right now. The look on your face is very curious, to say the least."

Rachel looked over at the detective and said, "I was thinking about the day I escaped my abductor."

Detective Martinez sat in stunned silence for a moment before he said, "I think you and I need to go have a cup of coffee somewhere. Looks like you need to talk."

Rachel swallowed hard and nodded. "I think that might be a good idea."

Rachel hadn't talked to anyone about her abduction, and she knew she should have a long time ago. Maybe she wouldn't have been haunted with dreams had she sought help. But she had been too afraid Darius would find her and take her back. She had vowed a long time ago that Darius would never find her, and she made sure her appearance was changed enough that no one would recognize her. She had cut her hair and had kept it colored. Her appearance resembled a hard-core rocker chick with ever-changing hairstyles and colors. She no longer resembled the All-American girl with long, dishwater blond hair with a wholesome look. She was the person you saw walking down the sidewalk with a sense of purpose and an air of confidence. Someone you didn't want to mess with. Her tough exterior was her shell of protection from the cruel world she had once known. Inside, though, she was the same All-American girl with a ton of insecurities.

CHAPTER 3

Detective Martinez parked the car at Norm's Café. He and Rachel walked in and sat down in the back booth, just opposite the kitchen.

"This should give us some privacy," he said.

Rachel slid into the booth, and Detective Martinez ordered two coffees. "OK." He started. "First thing, call me Joe, and second, start from the beginning."

Rachel looked across the table, and for a minute, she felt as if she had been transported back in time to when she was fourteen years old. She should have gone to the police then, but she had been scared, and Leslie had forbidden her to tell anyone of their plight. She felt the same fear well up inside her and try to silence her from within. The coffee arrived and proved to be the catalyst that gave her the courage to start talking. She couldn't explain it, but she knew she had to tell her story.

"I was six years old," she began. "My sister Maggie was nine years old. Our mom had tucked us in for the night, and everything seemed normal. Sometime later, I woke up and saw a man with long hair holding his hand over Maggie's mouth and whispering to her. I started to scream, but something hit me, and I blacked out. I woke up later and was in a dark room with duct tape over my mouth, and my hands were taped behind my back. Maggie was there too. She had tape on her mouth and hands as well."

Detective Martinez looked across the table at this young lady who seemed to have it all together with a great job and couldn't believe what he was hearing. "Where were you living at the time?" he asked.

"In Arvonia, Virginia, on the edge of town by the railroad tracks. We lived there with our mom, Jennifer Denton. Our dad, Lloyd Denton, was in prison for murder. He had tried to rob a bank in Richmond, Virginia. He shot and killed a guard in the process. I haven't seen my mom or my dad since the night Maggie and I were abducted."

"Rachel, do you mind if I take some notes while we talk? Did you ever report this?" he asked.

Rachel felt a wave of courage flow over her and sat up straight with a newfound conviction and said, "You can take all the notes you want. My story might help someone else. And, no, I never reported any of this. I was afraid Darius would find me and take me back."

Detective Martinez quickly ascertained this was not going to be a short talk about getting something off her chest. This was an afternoon of misery that was just starting, and he knew he should proceed with caution. If this guy, Darius, was still out there, he wanted to know everything he could learn from Rachel. Her story was starting to sound like another abduction case he had worked on a couple of years back.

"Go on, Rachel. I want to know the whole story. You are right. Your story might help someone else. What happened after the man got you back to the house?"

Rachel took a sip of her coffee and said, "We were introduced to an older girl, Leslie, who was supposed to help take care of us. Leslie took the tape off of us and told us to be quiet and listen. She gave us some clothes and told us that we were never going to see our mom again, so we better quit being babies and get with the program. I started to cry, but Maggie took my hand and told me it would be okay. So, I believed her. She was older, and she was the only one there I could trust. We got dressed, and Leslie went and got Darius, who came in to look at us. When he came in, he yelled at Leslie, pointing at me and told her he didn't want to see me. I was not right for this one. Leslie apologized to him and sat with me as he started looking at Maggie. He turned her around in a circle and said, 'She'll do.' Then he turned around and left the room. I asked Leslie what was going on, and she just told me not to worry about it.

"I remember falling asleep after eating our dinner that night, and when I woke up, Maggie was gone. I started to cry, and Leslie came over and hugged me. She told me everything was going to be all right. I asked her how old she was, and she told me sixteen. I asked her where her mom was, but she just looked away and said, 'I don't know.'

"Maggie came back the next morning. She had bruises on her legs and back and a red mark on her cheek. I tried to talk to her, but she just went to her bed and cried herself to sleep. Leslie tried to reassure me, but I was scared. When Maggie got up later, she cried and cried. Leslie told her the pain would go away and just to rest. I tried to talk to Maggie, but she wouldn't talk to me. After a few days, Maggie did start talking to me again. She told me that Darius was a bad man, and that he made her do things that weren't right. She also told me she would try to protect me from him. We both said our prayers that night and hoped God would protect us."

Detective Martinez sat in stunned silence. He was getting a first-hand account from someone who had daily lived the horror he was investigating. He was curious about how this girl had escaped with her life. Most of his cases were recovery based. The children never made it out alive.

"Can you tell me how long you were held in the house?" he asked.

"Eight years," she said. "I escaped when I was fourteen."

"How did you escape? Did you have help?"

"I did have help. Leslie became like my second mom. She and I escaped one night after things got really bad. I had just come back

---

17

from one of my so-called dates that Darius had set up. My dress had been torn, and the guy had been really rough with me. I was bleeding. There was blood, and the pain was unbearable. I had managed to keep it together until I reached the so-called safety of the house. Leslie helped me clean up and told me, 'If things go right tonight, we'll be out of here.' I knew Leslie wasn't being treated right either, but I felt helpless. Maggie disappeared when I was thirteen, so all I had left was Leslie," Rachel stated.

"When did your abuse start?" he asked.

Rachel's head bowed. She took a deep breath before she began. "It started when I was ten years old. Maggie had told me lots of stories about what to expect. It started with touches, then some oral sex. It was something Darius kind of eased me into. After that, things got more horrible. I was forced to have sex in all manners imaginable. The so-called dates that Darius set up were terrible. The men were mean, and a lot of them liked to hit me before they had their way with me. Can I stop now?" she asked. "I don't want to talk anymore about that."

"Sure, Rachel," Detective Martinez said. "So how did you and Leslie escape?"

"We waited until the house got quiet, and then, we climbed down through a hole in the floor that Leslie had been working on. When I was twelve, part of the floor in our room started falling apart, so Leslie convinced Darius to fix it for us by placing an old stop sign over it. He screwed the sign to the floor with his drill, but Leslie worked at getting those screws loose so the sign would move. After she got it loose, she climbed down beneath the house and found that she could get out by crawling toward the small outlet where the guys got under the house to fix the pipes. It was just a mobile home, so it wasn't that hard. After we got free from the house, we went to a place that Leslie said we'd be safe. It was an abandoned house near the park. I don't remember the address. We stayed put for about two weeks, and then Leslie found or made a friend who drove us to Pittsburgh, Pennsylvania. That's where we blended in, and I finally was able to start living a somewhat normal life." Rachel paused and took a sip of coffee. She was really spilling her guts, but it felt good. She had needed this.

Detective Martinez ordered sandwiches and said, "You're doing great, Rachel. Tell me more."

"For two years we made ends meet by doing odd jobs, and I think Leslie prostituted for the rent money. She never let me go back to that lifestyle. I wanted to help, so I spent my time doing part-time jobs like cleaning houses, yard work, and general labor. Jobs where people didn't require me to be sixteen. Shortly after I turned sixteen, Leslie got sick. I got up one morning, and she was throwing up bad. She told me she was going to the doctor, but she never came back. That was the last time I saw her. I don't know if she died or just ran away. I couldn't afford to keep the apartment, so I moved in with a friend of mine, Kori. She was a runaway and had been on the streets since she was fourteen. She had met a nice guy when she was eighteen, and they had gotten married. She was going through classes to get her GED, and she told me I had better get enrolled as well. I wasn't going to be able to get much of a job without one, so I enrolled. Kori helped me get my information from the elementary school in Arvonia, plus she helped me send off for my birth certificate. After that, I was registered and well on my way to getting my GED. While I was taking classes, I got a job at the local pizza joint. When I turned eighteen, I finally received my GED. Three years to get my degree seemed like a lifetime, but I am thankful for Kori and the opportunity she and her husband gave me. By working part-time those three years, I managed to save enough money to start out on my own.

"I was able to enroll at the Community College of Allegheny

County, where I graduated with my associates'. I had applied for a four-year scholarship at Temple University in Philadelphia and received that scholarship, where I went on to complete my degree in journalism. After graduating from Temple, I applied to become a reporter for the *Sun* and got the job. An opening came up at the *New York Times*, and I went for it. And here I am, investigative journalist spilling her life story to one of New York's finest."

Detective Martinez smiled and downed the last of his coffee. "You are one courageous and brave woman! I admire you for all you've been through. How're you feeling now?" he asked.

Rachel sipped on her coffee and then looked up. "I'm doing okay. I feel surprisingly better. Who knew talking about everything would feel so freeing! Thank you for listening," she said.

"No problem, Rachel. Happy to help. Would you be opposed to talking to me another time about some of your experiences in more detail? I have a few cases that have some similarities to yours, and I'd like to see if anything intersects."

Rachel's ears perked up. He was telling her there were still active cases that might be related to hers? How could that be? It had been fourteen years since she escaped. Could this still be happening all these years later? She knew the answer but didn't want to admit it. She had tried to push out the memories and pretend it had never happened—only to realize that this current assignment she had been given was going to be the unraveling of her memories and maybe one of the longest-running child abduction/child prostitution rings of all time. Was Maggie still alive? Maybe she could finally find her sister!

"Sure," Rachel replied. "I'd be glad to as long as I get exclusivity on the story as it unfolds."

Detective Martinez smiled and said, "You got it! In fact, you *deserve* it. I can't think of a better person to write the story."

CHAPTER 4

The next day, Rachel woke up with renewed energy. Her curiosity was sparking over the possible intersections of cases that Detective Martinez had mentioned. She really wanted to go and talk to him, but she knew her editor was chomping at the bit to get a story on the abducted girl from the subway.

Rachel headed down to the precinct to see if there had been any new press releases on the case. Upon entering the precinct, she was met by Detective Andrews. He didn't look happy to see her. His narrowed eyes and flushed face were evident as soon as she saw him. "Young lady, I need to talk to you, *now*, in my office!" he all but shouted.

Rachel hurriedly put her notebook back in her bag and followed him to his smelly office. The odor of cigarette smoke nearly choked her as she walked in and sat in the chair opposite the desk. "How can I help you?" she asked.

Looking at her across the desk, he pulled out a cigarette and lit it, his eyes narrowing all the more. "Your name is Rachel Denton?" he asked.

"Yes," she replied. "Why are you asking my name? You know who I am." She wondered why this man was allowed to smoke in what was supposed to be a nonsmoking building. Nonetheless, maybe seniority had its perks.

"Why would the mother of the girl abducted from the subway want to talk to you?" he asked.

"I don't know. Maybe because I witnessed the crime?" There

was only a hint of sarcasm. She had to keep her cool.

The reddish tint in Detective Andrews's face was getting darker, and it looked as if he were going to swallow his cigarette.

"Precisely," he roared. "She wants your help in finding her daughter. She thinks if you run a story, it will help. I told her there was no way I would allow that to happen because being so reckless would probably—no, most likely—endanger her daughter's life. I hope you agree."

Rachel knew she had to pick her words carefully. She didn't want to lose this story. There had to be a way to get on this detective's good side.

"Detective Andrews, I'm not about to endanger that little girl if I can help it. I want to help if I can, and if a newspaper story can be of some benefit, I'd like to be the one to write it. I know the television crews have been relentless in their coverage, but I know how delicate a situation this is," she replied.

Detective Andrews sat silently. It seemed she had touched a soft spot. Finally, he put out his cigarette in the ashtray that was beyond overflowing and said, "I appreciate that. I didn't expect you to reply like that, but I respect you for doing so."

Rachel remained still, her eyes locked on the man that seemingly had had the wind just knocked out of his sails. She was preparing for the second round, but it never came. He reached for a file on his desk, opened it, seemed to hesitate, and then he closed the file.

"I'm going to put you with Detective Joe Martinez and give you the story you want. He's working on a child prostitution ring on the Lower East Side. I'm not saying this abduction on the subway is related, but there is always that possibility. The subway case remains my case, so I don't want you pestering me for any information. I'm allowing you access to minimal information with Detective Martinez, and he will need to review anything you take to print. Do you understand?" he said.

Rachel nodded and silently thanked God for watching over her. "Thank you, Detective Andrews. You won't be disappointed."

This opportunity was huge, and she wasn't going to lose this story. She would play by his rules. There was a distinct possibility that this could be the breakthrough story that she had been waiting on. This could propel her to the next level of investigative journalism.

The rest of the day was spent reviewing the public records to see if anything stuck out. She would much rather be talking to a detective doing an active investigation, but that would have to wait until tomorrow. It seemed she was always waiting on the story.

CHAPTER 5

etective Martinez called early the next morning. Rachel was in the middle of a meeting with her editor, so she let it go to voicemail. The two had been going toe to toe on when Rachel was going to have enough for a full-blown story on the prostitution ring. Rachel explained the unprecedented access she had been given and the opportunity this was going to provide. She explained that Detective Martinez and Detective Andrews would need to see her pieces before publication to ensure that pertinent information didn't get published before it was necessary and some-how interfere with apprehending the suspect or suspects. In addition, the detectives didn't want to put any potential children in harm's way. Rachel assured her editor that she had exclusivity on this story, and he would be pleased with the outcome. This time, though, he would have to trust her to bring the story in as it unfolded and with the blessings of the detectives.

Her editor finally gave in and said she could run with it only if she worked on other stories as well. Although this would mean an increased workload, Rachel agreed.

The warm sunshine soaked into her and gave her a renewed sense of purpose as she stepped from her office building. Her editor hadn't been happy at first about the arrangement with Detective Andrews, but he had conceded in the end with some conditions. The story was hers, and although it wasn't exactly how she hoped it would be, it was hers. Rachel dialed Detective Martinez, and he quickly answered. "Hi, was wondering if I'd get a callback."

"You knew you would. I'm not going to let this one go. So, what's next?" she asked.

"Meet me at the precinct tomorrow morning. I've got some things I need to do today, okay?"

"Sure," Rachel said, "see you tomorrow."

Detective Martinez was knee-deep in verifying bits and pieces of Rachel's story. He had found her father and learned he had been murdered in prison. Tracking down her mother was proving to be a challenge. It seemed there was no trail after the girls had been abducted. It was as if the family, the mother and two girls, had simply vanished. He wondered if something could have happened that night to the mother as well. It was the only logical explanation he could think of since the mother never reported the missing girls to the police. He didn't want to think of the other possibility . . . that the mother actually knew of Rachel and Maggie's abduction. She could have allowed it for a monetary payment.

There had been a newspaper article in the Arvonia area about the family going missing, but nothing else. Phone calls to the local police department netted nothing. The only file that they had on the case had been closed due to a lack of evidence and no next of kin. The only progress he was able to make was the information he obtained from the elementary school. He was able to get copies of both birth certificates and their Socials.

Rachel didn't show up in any system until her GED was obtained. Maggie wasn't showing up at all. Nothing was coming up on the mother, either. The police report and crime scene photos didn't show anything out of the ordinary in the tiny home. Nothing out of place and no indication that there was even a struggle. It simply looked as if the occupants had vanished into thin air.

He knew that one man couldn't have accomplished taking two little girls and a mother without some commotion. There had to be more people involved in the abduction. He would need to look over those crime scene photos again. There had to be something. Maybe Rachel could even take a look at them. Seeing the photos might jog her memory, or even better, she might see something out of place that other people wouldn't recognize. He had to make sure she was ready to look at them, though. As far as he knew, he was the first person that Rachel had opened up to about her abduction. She was tough, but he wanted to make sure she was in a good place emotionally before he showed the photos to her. The time would present itself; he just had to be patient.

Focusing on the man Rachel referred to as Darius was his next step. He had to get a better description, but, in the meantime, he would just try to do a first-name match to as many Darius's that were in the system. He also spent some time going over all the abductions that had been reported over the last fourteen years. His search included Pennsylvania, Ohio, West Virginia, Virginia, Maryland, and New York. He knew the enormity of the information he would receive back would be overwhelming, but he had to try. Focusing on children who had been found alive, he combed through the cases looking for anything that was similar. Methods of abduction, description of the abductor, age, gender, and finally, any man the children might have referred to as Darius.

He found that all the eyewitness accounts were vague because of the ages of the children. Their recollection of the abductor was sketchy and often just as general as someone describing their uncle. One case, though, caught his attention. It had occurred very near the time that Rachel and her sister had been abducted.

There was a girl out of Harrisburg, Pennsylvania, that had escaped the grasp of her abductor and had reported the man was a white man who smelled with long, blond hair. He had a tattoo of a star on his hand. Apparently, she had been playing at the park across the street from her house, and the man had approached her from behind, grabbed her, and started carrying her to his car.

She bit the man on the hand, which caused him to lose his grip. She ran, screaming across the street to her house. Her mother had stepped out to see what the commotion was and saw her daughter running toward her, crying. The man had turned his back and was getting in his car by the time the mother saw him. All the mother could tell the police was that the man was white, with long, blond hair. She described the car as an older green model car. Maybe a Chevy.

This hadn't been a night abduction, but the little girl had described the man as having long, blond hair. Finishing out his day, he pulled the file from his desk from two years ago where Sophia Lepaste, a nine-year-old girl, had been abducted from her home on the Upper East Side of the city. The nanny had tucked her in bed for the night and gone to the living room where she had fallen asleep on the sofa. When the parents arrived home around 1:00 a.m., they went to check on their daughter. She was gone. The window was open, and the nine-year-old had never been found. No trace evidence had been found, and the trail had gone cold.

Detective Martinez knew he was grasping at straws, and he needed to have Rachel give him a few more details before he could investigate much further. Things were starting to make a little more sense, but he knew he was still a long way from solving the mystery.

Whoever these people are, they are extremely well organized. The sheer audacity to go into someone's home and take someone's child made him angry. These girls had been right where they were supposed to have been . . . in the safety of their own home. The likelihood of Rachel and Maggie's abduction being connected to this prostitution ring was very high. He didn't want to let Rachel know his thoughts too quickly. She was just now opening up about the ordeal, and he didn't want to spook her. He knew that Darius, or whatever name he was going by now, could still be out there, and he could still be in the business. The dark web was a Wild West of horrific crimes.

CHAPTER 6

Rachel arrived at the precinct at about 8:00 a.m. She waited in the lobby for a few minutes until Detective Martinez came to get her.

"Good morning, Rachel," he said as he opened the door. "Glad you could make it. I've got a full day planned. Are you able to stay the entire day?"

"I am. I'm hoping I can get enough of a story by day's end to appease my editor. It was a battle to get him to agree to this way of telling the story, but I convinced him to let me have a go at it."

"Well, today should give you enough for a short story, no doubt. I was hoping to get a few more details on your story as well."

Rachel tensed as she heard his request. She knew he would naturally want to know more, and she also knew she needed to tell him. The day before, when she had told him about her abduction, it had served to be a type of pressure release valve. It surprised her at how much better she had felt after getting it out in the open.

"No problem," she replied. "As I said before, my story might help someone else."

Detective Martinez nodded and said, "Let me grab my stuff, and we'll get the day started."

As Rachel got up, she noticed the mother, Abigail Winslip, from the subway abduction come through the door. She recognized Rachel immediately. "Hi, Rachel, isn't it? I'm glad to see you. I wanted to thank you for your kindness the other night."

"I was glad to help, Mrs. Winslip. Have they got any leads on your daughter? I've been praying they find her soon."

Mrs. Winslip struggled to keep it together as she shook her head. The tears were welling up, and Rachel felt terrible for even asking. She put her hand on Mrs. Winslip's shoulder and said, "I know the police are doing everything possible to find her. Don't give up hope."

"I'll never give up hope," she said. "She's my only daughter, and I will find her and bring her home."

As Detective Martinez approached the door, he saw Mrs. Winslip though the glass. He turned back toward the interior offices and paged Detective Andrews. Coming through the door, Detective Martinez said his greetings. "Good morning, Mrs. Winslip. I've paged Detective Andrews for you. He should be with you shortly. Now, if you'll excuse us, we have to get going."

"Thank you, Detective," she replied. The lack of makeup and sleep accentuated the sadness in her eyes. Rachel waved as her, and Detective Martinez stepped out into the parking lot. Rachel knew the probability of finding the girl. It made her all the more ready to expose this prostitution ring. Maybe, just maybe, Skylan's abduction was tied to the prostitution ring. She silently prayed for Skylan, and all the others she knew were being forced to do unspeakable things.

"Had your coffee yet? I'm ready for a cup," he said. Rachel smiled. She knew coffee was the main staple of all cops' diets.

"I could use a cup," she replied.

After getting coffee, Detective Martinez started driving to the Lower East Side. He wanted to check out a few warehouses. Plus, the drive would give him time to ask Rachel a few more questions. Before he had time to formulate his first question, Rachel had her notebook out and asked, "Do any of the previous child abductions have any similarities to the Skylan Marie abduction?"

Detective Martinez smiled. He had to hand it to her . . . She was good. This was going to be a challenging day. "The only similarity is that the girls are all within the age range of eight years old to eleven years old," he replied. "Race, location of abduction, family status are all over the map. It appears the abductions are random. Our Internet Crime Unit is working on the dark web, trying to locate possible clubs or venues where these girls might be."

Rachel hurriedly took notes. She didn't want to miss anything. "Can I ask where we're going?"

"Down to check a couple of warehouses on the Lower East End," he replied. "Hoping I'll find something that will help break this case wide open."

Rachel sat quietly for a few minutes and wondered why this prostitution ring was working out of a warehouse. It just didn't seem practical, and, in her experience, she was always delivered to her customers.

"Spill it," the detective said. "I can see those wheels turning."

"I was thinking," she said, "why are they supposedly working out of a warehouse? Doesn't seem practical. I was always driven to my customer." Rachel's face flushed with embarrassment and shame. She really didn't like talking about this.

"Go on," he said, "I'm listening."

"Leslie would always dress us and get us ready. Darius would come and pick us up, then deliver us to our customer. We lived in a mobile home in a pretty decent neighborhood, so I guess from the outside, it must have looked normal to other people. They probably thought Darius was my dad and Leslie, an older sister. Anyway, he'd drive us to other houses where our customers would be and drive us back to the mobile home when we were done."

"Do you know where this mobile home is that you lived in?" he asked.

"Somewhere near Manassas, Virginia. I know when Darius drove me to a customer, we would always go to Maryland. I saw a lot of Maryland tags on the cars. Then as I got older, I realized we were always going into Washington, D.C., to meet our customers. On the way back, I'd always see a sign for Manassas."

Detective Martinez sat silently while he drove. Everything she had just told him made sense. This was a pretty elaborate prostitution ring she had been a part of. It was very probable that this prostitution ring in New York was a part of an original setup that had manifested into a much-larger operation. New York wasn't that far from Washington, D.C. It was possible.

Rachel broke the silence with two more questions. "So, how many abductions are we talking about here in the city? Have you inquired about any out-of-state abductions?"

The detective took a deep breath and then responded. "All total, I have thirty-nine cases on my plate. Eighteen of those girls have been found deceased. They all have been between eight years old and eleven years old. The twenty-one remaining missing girls have never been found. My oldest case is from two years ago."

Rachel was shocked but interested, to say the least. This was the type of information she was hoping for. She also knew that Detective Martinez was not the only detective with a caseload. "How many other detectives have abduction cases?" she asked.

"Detective Andrews and I are the only ones right now in our precinct," he replied. "He has about the same number of cases. We're working with other precincts and trying to keep everyone in the loop. Some of the missing girls are from other precincts, so it's a bit complicated. The precincts are neighboring, so the police commissioner thought it would be best if he had a small group of detectives dedicated to the abductions. He felt it would prove more effective in solving the cases.

"Rachel, can I get you to sit down with a sketch artist and describe Darius and Leslie for me?" he asked.

"I can," she replied, "but it's been fourteen years. I know their appearance has changed."

"That's okay. We can do an age progression on the sketches and get pretty close to what they would look like today."

"So, are you thinking my story has something to do with what you are investigating now?"

"It's a possibility."

Rachel wondered if there were any possibility that Maggie was still alive. If Detective Martinez thought Darius could still be around, then why couldn't Maggie? The thought of seeing and talking to Maggie again made her smile.

"How can my story, which happened primarily in Washington, D.C., be tied to New York City? We're talking about two hundred or so miles," Rachel said.

"Prostitution rings are big businesses, especially on the dark web. If one ring was established fourteen or so years ago, and they were successful in avoiding detection, then they would logically expand to other areas to increase their revenue flow," he explained. "Major cities are their bases for operation, and with the advancement of the internet, I can see where the prostitution ring could have expanded their operations. Four hours away isn't all that far, Rachel. Besides, if the business was booming in D.C., then I bet they could have started up a ring here in NYC."

The possibility was there, and Rachel could feel herself becoming overwhelmed with the enormity of the story she was charged with writing. Although the local media had termed these types of crimes as human trafficking, which it truly was, the term was not as shocking as child prostitution. She knew the story would need to be even more shocking for her readers to take notice. Her focus would be on using the term "child prostitution." This was going to be more than a story. This was going to be personal.

They found nothing of value at the warehouses they investigated. The buildings were empty except for the rats and other animals that inhabited the large spaces. Rachel gave the descriptions of Darius and Leslie to a sketch artist back at the precinct. The final sketches were amazing. It gave her chills to see their faces again.

Rachel finished her day by researching a few more abduction cases that Detective Martinez had given her access to. She made notes on the approximate numbers of abductions and possible similarities. She decided she would incorporate the latest abduction of Skylan Marie into her story with minimal details. She didn't want to cross Detective Andrews. With all the information she had been given, the one case that caught her attention was the Sophia Lepaste case. The little girl had been abducted from her bedroom two years ago. She had never been found.

CHAPTER 7

Skylan was scared. Her world as she had known it had been ripped apart. She sat on the bed with the blindfold sagging just enough to see the room out of her right eye. The room was dark except for the sliver of light that came in through the opening of the black curtains as they fluttered from the breeze coming out of the air vent in the floor.

She heard a man and a woman talking in the other room. The man was angry with the woman about something, but Skylan couldn't tell what. She bowed her head and prayed that God would keep her safe. She had learned in Sunday school that God could do great miracles, and that He was always with you if you believed. She believed and had asked God to be with her always. She believed with her whole heart that He was. As she finished her prayer, the woman came into the room. She took the blindfold off and sat on the bed beside Skylan.

"What's your name?" Skylan blurted out before the woman could speak. "Mine is Skylan."

"Ruth," the woman said. "Just call me Ruth." Ruth admired this girl for being so brave. She hadn't expected this.

"Where am I? Where's my mom?"

"You don't need to worry about your mom. You're going to live here with me now," Ruth stated with a forced smile.

Skylan's eyes started welling up with tears. She wanted to cry, she wanted her mom, she wanted to go home. Ruth saw the tears and quickly assured her it was going to be okay. But Skylan could tell by the false tone of Ruth's voice that something was not right. Something was definitely wrong.

Skylan was an only child, and although she was seven years old, she was very mature for her age. Her mother homeschooled her, and she was already doing fourth-grade work. Her mom and dad had talked to her about strangers and how to get away if someone tried to grab her, but these men had had guns, and Skylan didn't know what she should have done. The man had hit her mom with the gun and then dragged her away. Skylan knew her mom wasn't dead, just hurt bad. She also knew she had to get back to her mom. These people were not going to get away with this. She quickly dried her tears and decided she would do her best to get away.

Ruth stood up and walked over to the closet. She picked out an outfit and tossed it on the bed, "Put that outfit on, and I'll be back to check on you in a minute," she said.

Skylan looked at the outfit. It was a red dress with white leggings. The dress looked like a cowgirl's dress because of the shiny pearl snaps on the shirt part. The skirt was red, like a bandanna and had a lot of ruffles. There was a pair of black cowboy boots to wear as well. She put the outfit on and was pulling on the last boot when Ruth came back. Ruth smiled and stood there with her hands on her hips. "You look adorable. I think he'll be pleased."

Skylan was confused. Who was "he"? She didn't have time to think too long because "he" came into the room.

"Hi," the man said. "You look like you're ready for a rodeo."

The man was tall and had medium brown hair. He didn't look scary, but Skylan could tell something wasn't right. She stood in front of him and didn't say a thing.

"Turn around for me, sweetie. Let me see that dress," he said.

Skylan slowly turned around and silently prayed that God would take this man away.

"Okay," he said, "let's go. I'm taking you to a cowboy birthday party."

Skylan didn't want to go with this man. She looked over at Ruth, and she said, "Go ahead, honey. You'll have a good time."

Skylan reluctantly followed the man to his car. She made a mental note that it was a green car with tan seats.

"Get in," he said. "We've got a little way to go."

Skylan got in and put her seat belt on. The man did the same. They drove for what seemed like an hour. Pulling up in front of an old house, the man looked over his shoulder and said, "We're here!"

They got out and went inside the house. Skylan thought it was strange that the man did not knock on the door. Once inside, she saw that there were no balloons, no other people, and no party. She knew she was in trouble. The man closed the door and picked her up and put her on the sofa. As he squatted down to her eye level, he said, "Today is the first day of school for you. What you learn today will be of great importance. So, pay attention! Do you hear me?" he said in a stern tone as he put his hands on her thighs.

After about an hour with this man, Skylan was returned to the house where Ruth was waiting. She walked into the house and went straight to the little bed in the room with the black curtains. She crawled up on the bed and started praying out loud.

"Dear God, why did you let that man touch me like that? It wasn't right because I'm little, and he's not. Please, God, keep me safe until my mom and dad find me. Help me to be brave, and please don't let that man do that to me again. Amen."

Ruth stood in the doorway as Skylan prayed, tears sliding down her cheeks. This girl was different. She had faith; she had a will to survive beyond the abuse. She reminded her of herself so very long ago. Skylan looked at Ruth and asked, "Why are you crying? Did he touch you like he touched me?" Ruth nodded and then walked over to the bed. The two hugged and cried together. Skylan pushed back slightly from Ruth and wiped her face. She took a deep breath and said, "We have to get out of here."

Ruth wiped her own tears and slowly began to stand. She turned her back on Skylan and said, "I don't think we can."

Skylan couldn't believe what she was hearing. Here was an adult who supposedly could do what she wanted, and she was saying she didn't or wouldn't help get away from this man. She may be only seven years old, but in two weeks, she would be eight, and she would figure out how to escape. The teacher in Sunday school talked about a man named Daniel who had been thrown in the lion's den, and the lions hadn't eaten him because he asked God to shut their mouths. That's what she would do. She'd ask God for protection, because if God could do that, then He could stop this man from touching her again.

Skylan looked up at Ruth and asked, "Do you believe in God?"

"I do, but I haven't talked to Him in a very long time. I heard you talking to Him, though. Do you think He will help you?"

Skylan was excited that Ruth believed in God. "Yes, He will," she said enthusiastically. "I just have to believe with all my heart."

"I hope He helps you," Ruth said. "I hope He helps all of us."

Skylan was startled when a girl about ten years old shoved past Ruth and bounded into the bedroom. She had on jeans and a T-shirt with her dark brown hair tied back in a ponytail.

"Hi, Ruth, I'm back," she said.

"Hi, Sophie, glad to see you again," Ruth said.

"Who's this?" Sophie asked.

"New girl. Her name is Skylan," Ruth replied.

Sophie looked at Skylan, gave her a sneer, and told Ruth, "She'll never last; too little."

Ruth chuckled softly and said, "I don't think you should count her out just yet. She's one tough cookie, and she talks with God."

Sophie swung around and stuck her tongue out at Skylan. "Tell your God to get you out of here then," she taunted.

Skylan was intimidated but softly replied, "He will get me out, and He'll get you out too."

Sophie laughed. "Yeah, right."

"You just wait and see," Skylan replied.

"Okay, girls," Ruth said, "time to eat our dinner, and then it's off to bed with you."

Ruth went into the kitchen and pulled out the frozen pizza that had been baking. She thought about the time when she was nine and had burned her hand getting a pizza out of the oven. Her little sister Rachel had tried to wrap her hand and be the little nurse, but the bandage had fallen off. She missed Rachel, and she had found her recently while reading the paper. One of the bylines was Rachel Denton. It had to be her. Ruth was happy that Rachel had made it out. She knew Leslie had been killed after running away. She had helped to bury the body.

What a twist of fate because she was now playing the part of Leslie with these new girls. She hated the life she had, but there was no escape. Darius had only gotten stronger and more powerful as he went from abductor to district administrator. Ruth had seen the results of the girls who thought they could escape. She shuddered at the thought of Skylan being murdered and hoped she could convince her to stop talking about escape.

After the girls were in bed, Ruth sat down on the sofa and bowed her head to pray. It had been a long time since she had prayed, but Skylan had sparked the fire with a renewed sense of hope for a better life that still smoldered. She also said a prayer for Rachel.

She knew Rachel was working with the police after being an eyewitness to Skylan's abduction. One of the news channels had shown a picture of Rachel as being an eyewitness. Her appearance was so drastically different than what Ruth remembered, but she knew that Rachel was only protecting herself. The rough rocker chick appearance was not who her little sister was. The jagged hair-cut and the pink highlights did well to cover the blond locks of silky hair that Ruth remembered.

She thought of writing Rachel a letter, but the probability of Rachel being found out would be devastating. Ruth had no desire to see any more of Darius's handiwork. He was a ruthless killer with a very violent temper. Besides, he would not only kill her for writing the letter, but he would also kill Sophie and Skylan. She couldn't bear the thought of her being the reason that they would be killed. She knew there had to be a better way.

Noticing a small cell phone on the table, she quickly picked it up and put it in her pocket. Darius would be furious if he knew there was a cell phone here. Sophie must have gotten it somewhere in her jaunts. Ruth suddenly thought, *I can call Rachel!* She quickly went to the phone book and got the phone number to the *New York Times*. After a very nice girl on the other end of the line gave her Rachel's number, she dialed the number. She wouldn't tell Rachel it was her. She would just say she knew about the subway abduction and the little girl in the blue dress. Rachel was smart. She would find a way to follow up on the phone call.

After making the call, Ruth took the phone apart and destroyed everything about it that she could. She left the house and walked the pieces down the alley to the dumpster. Darius would never know.

Sophie would never ask about the phone because she knew she was not supposed to have it anyway. Ruth would act normally, and maybe, just maybe, Rachel would be able to find them without any more direct contact.

CHAPTER 8

Rachel stared at the age progression sketches in total silence. She was stunned to see Darius with short hair staring back at her from the page. A chill ran up her spine. Rachel had guessed his age to be around twenty with long, dirty-blond hair when she had been abducted. Fast-forward fourteen years, and the sketch had him closer to thirty-five years old with a conservative haircut. He looked like any other thirty-five-year-old walking around the city.

Detective Martinez was excited to get these composites out but was cautious because he wasn't sure how relevant they would prove to be. The backstory on the release of the sketches was going to be from a past abductee who had escaped years ago and had just now come forward with her story. He knew this would put Rachel in danger, but he had to try.

Rachel looked across the desk at the detective. "They got the eyes right," she said. "They still give me the chills."

"This must be hard for you. Are you okay?" he asked.

"I am," she replied. "I'm a little concerned about Darius still being out there. Do you think he's involved with the subway abduction? Are you going to release this to the public? Are you going to say I gave you the description?" Rachel was firing off questions out of nervousness and fear.

"Slow down, Rachel," he said. "I've talked to our commissioner, and he has agreed to keep your name out of this for the time being. I'm also going to assign a detail to you for your safety in the event that Darius is involved, and he tries to reach out to you. To answer your other question about him being involved in the subway abduction, it's highly probable. I need to get some additional information on this dark web group that our Internet Crime Division uncovered. According to their research, there is a service called 'Forever Young.' This service claims to be able to provide their customers with whatever their fantasy desires. All their girls are ready to have a good time. They are working up a profile for me so I can get in and see if this group is prostituting young girls. Maybe this will be the break we need. I know you and I would like to see this prostitution ring shut down for good."

Rachel understood all too well. "Detective, do you think my sister, Maggie, could still be alive?"

The detective exhaled slowly, then said, "I don't know. If she's half as tough as you are, then I say there's a pretty good chance. Have you ever tried to find her or your parents?"

"Yes, I found out my dad died in prison. I never found out what became of my mother. I never knew what became of Maggie either," she stated. Rachel knew he had probably pulled up her past, checking out her story, so she asked, "What have you found out?"

"About as much as you have," he said. "I still need to get with the State of Virginia and see if they have any Jane Does."

Rachel inhaled sharply, "Do you think my mother is . . . dead?" she asked.

"It's the only thing that makes sense," he said. "What mother doesn't look for her children? There wasn't even a missing person's report filed after you girls were abducted."

Rachel knew he was probably right. She hadn't wanted to think that her mother might have been killed. If that were the case, then the night of Maggie's and her abduction, there would have been more than one person perpetrating the crime.

She pulled out her laptop and began working on the story she was going to turn in to her editor. This week's piece featured the two-year-old abduction case of eight-year-old Sophia Lepaste. Detective Martinez had even provided a two-year-old photo of Sophia, along with an age progression sketch of what she might look like at the age of ten. Her main focus would be on the methodology of the abduction in contrast to the violence of the subway abduction involving Skylan Winslip. She wanted her readers to be aware that these cases may or may not be related. She implored her readers to be mindful of their surroundings while out and about because you never know when you might spot a missing child or some clue that would help the police in solving these abductions. She ended her piece by providing the tip line phone number. There was always hope.

Detective Martinez gave her the thumbs-up after reading the article and disappeared into the inner sanctum of Detective Andrews's office. After about thirty minutes, Detective Martinez returned and, with a smile, said, "You have his blessing. Take it to print."

Rachel's editor was thrilled with the article and fast-tracked it to print. It would appear in the next paper.

The following morning, Rachel grabbed a paper on the way to the precinct. She was shocked and excited to see her article had made the front page. As she made her way up the steps and back to Detective Martinez's office, she could hear other officers talking about the subway abduction case and Sophia Lepaste's case. The detective was standing in the doorway of his office when she rounded the corner. He had a smile on his face and appeared to be in a great mood.

"Good morning," she said. "You look happy."

"I am," he replied. "We got a phone call this morning from Ms. Tonya Franklin. She is 100 percent positive that the age progression sketch of Sophia Lepaste is the same girl who asked her to take her home."

"That's great!" Rachel said. "What's the next step?"

"Finding Sophia!" he stated. "We need to go back to the neighborhood market and start asking more questions. Surely, someone else saw the girl at the store."

"I'm ready," she replied.

"I need to get some things together before we head over to the market. Meet me back here at 2:00 p.m."

"Sounds like a plan," she said. "I've got a story to work on anyway. Is it possible to use one of the empty offices to work in?"

"Sure. I'll let Detective Andrews know you're working on the next story."

CHAPTER 9

Ruth woke up the next morning to the sounds of Sophie and Skylan talking. Darius hadn't called the night before with any appointments for either girl, so today would be a good day. Breakfast was Pop-Tarts with juice for the girls and coffee for Ruth. Darius never provided too much, so she made do with what was given.

Lately, Ruth felt her time was running short. She was the oldest female caretaker in the organization. Darius had always catered to her since she had been his personal favorite, but now, she felt ignored and left out. A year ago, after turning thirty, Darius had commented that he needed some "younger blood." Ruth knew what had happened to other girls who didn't fit the bill anymore. They wound up dead. Bodies stuffed in suitcases or barrels, weighted down, and thrown into the Hudson or buried in remote lots. She didn't want that to happen, so she had made sure she was needed in some capacity. Taking care of the girls seemed ideal. She didn't have to entertain customers and endure all their filthy fantasies. On the other hand, she had to console the girls when they returned to the house. She didn't know which was worse. The thought of escaping crossed her mind now and then, but she had seen the aftermath of failed attempts. She had even helped clean up after some. It scared her. The fear alone kept her doing the very thing she despised.

This time around, she had been given the job of taking care of two very different girls. Sophie was tough. Her mental aptitude for dealing with the abuse was commendable. She never cried after the first time, and she always played along perfectly. She was prone to sneaking off and going down to the corner market to shoplift candy or soda, but she always returned. Ruth had warned her not to get caught by Darius. She told her of the consequences, but Sophie was confident and chose to ignore her warnings. Ruth prayed Sophie would be kept safe.

Skylan was young and special. She seemed to have angels sitting on her shoulders. Her faith in God was outright contagious. It was as if she had a direct connection to God. Ruth wanted to be around Skylan. She wanted to protect her from Darius and all the other creeps. The reality was she couldn't. Customers never stopped calling, and Darius was always bringing in new girls to take the place of those who didn't make it. Ruth had decided the world was an evil place. Skylan had reminded her of the good, and this had her thinking . . . Was escape possible? Ruth prayed for Skylan's safety, and for the one day that escape would be possible. She also prayed that her anonymous call to Rachel had proven successful. Rachel had to find them.

As Ruth sipped her coffee, she was surprised at how easy it was to pray again. For years, she had felt hopeless and trapped. Now, Skylan had come into this house, and it seemed like there was light again. She knew darkness would still come, but at least now, she felt like she had a chance. There was renewed hope that one day she would be able to see Rachel again. Leaving her that night so long ago had been hard. Darius had come by around 9:30 p.m. and said he had a special customer. Maggie Denton ceased to exist that night. She had gone with Darius to his apartment, and that's where she stayed until she was seventeen. She was his. Darius preferred the name Ruth, so she started going by her middle name to please him. He had also told her if she messed up even once on a job that Rachel would be killed. This kept her on the straight and narrow.

Rachel was all she had left. Darius had killed their mom the night they were taken. She was so scared that night. She remembered Darius holding his hand over her mouth while he whispered for her to stay quiet. His other hand had slid under her nightgown, and he had touched her where he shouldn't have. She started to squirm, and that's when Rachel had sat up in bed. She was about to scream when someone else in the room hit her on the head. She had fallen back down on the bed in a heap. Ruth squeezed her eyes shut and remembered her mom opening the bedroom door. Darius nodded to the other man, who hit her mom with something, then dragged her into the kitchen. She never saw her mother again.

Ruth and Rachel were bound and carried off in a smelly, old car that night. They had been put in a room where Ruth held vigil until Rachel woke up. Their lives had been forever changed.

Sophie and Skylan came bounding into the living room. Each had dressed in blue jeans and a T-shirt.

"What are we going to do today, Ruth?" Sophie asked.

"I don't know, Sophie," Ruth replied. "I need to get some extra clothes for Skylan so we may make a trip to the warehouse."

Skylan was wearing Sophie's clothes, and they were a bit large on her. She had rolled up the pant legs, and the T-shirt hung on her like a nightshirt.

"This was all I could find to wear," Skylan said. "I didn't want to wear that dress again." She wrinkled up her nose as she remembered yesterday.

"That's okay, Skylan," Ruth said. "We have a whole warehouse of clothes and shoes for you to pick from."

"Just don't choose too much," Sophie said, "because Ruth will have to dress you for your customers."

Ruth shot Sophie a look. "Now, don't you worry about that, Skylan," Ruth said. "We'll work that out later."

The warehouse was huge. There was a lot of trash lying on the floor and scattered around the outside of the building. Skylan didn't think there could be any clothes in this place. As they entered the side door, they walked up a flight of stairs. The room opened up, and there were racks of clothing and shoes for as far as Skylan could see. There were packages of brand-new socks and underwear, jeans, dresses, and tons of hair bows, ribbons, and barrettes.

Ruth went to work, gathering the right size clothing for Skylan. She chose dresses and pretty outfits of all types. Skylan felt uneasy and asked, "Where did all these clothes come from?"

"Darius keeps the warehouse full for all the girls," Sophie said.

Ruth looked at Sophie again and shook her head. "Not the time, Sophie," she said.

Sophie shrugged her shoulders and ran over to the table where the shoes were and started trying some on.

Skylan looked at Ruth and said, "I'm not ever going to see my mom again, am I?"

Ruth knelt and looked Skylan in the eyes and said, "I don't know. I hope one day, you'll see her again. Until then, we all have to do what Darius tells us to do."

Skylan could see the sadness in Ruth's eyes, and she knew that she would have to be brave. Brave enough to endure this man they called Darius and smart enough to figure out a way to escape. She would just need to be patient and keep saying her prayers.

Skylan was able to choose some clothes, but Ruth was careful not to let her have too many. Darius would be furious if the girls had too many clothes at the house. Customers preferred certain outfits, and that was what the girls were expected to wear. She did allow her to have several pairs of jeans and a few T-shirts for the days when her services weren't needed or when she wasn't with customers.

After gathering the things they needed, the girls headed back to the house. Ruth was sure that Sophie would disappear in the afternoon again like she always did, so she would need to make sure that Skylan didn't go with her. This job was getting more precarious by the day.

CHAPTER 10

Rachel arrived at the precinct to meet Detective Martinez at 2:00 p.m. She was anxious to hear if they had uncovered any other good leads in the Sophia Lepaste case. The detective met her at the door and said, "Follow me. We're going to go meet with the market manager, where Ms. Franklin saw this girl."

Rachel smiled and quickly fell in step with him as they made their way to his car. As she shut the door and started putting her seat belt on, she asked. "Is this something I can release in my story?"

"We'll see," he said. "Let's hear what the manager has to say first."

It wasn't a definite "no," so Rachel was excited to get her story. Of course, it would need to be approved by Detective Andrews. As they turned the corner to go to the market, they were both surprised to see the local news channel there with one of their reporters.

"I guess someone let something slip yesterday," Detective Martinez said in a sarcastic tone.

Rachel looked over at him and said, "Hey, it wasn't me. I was knee-deep in a story about whether this new product that came out last week claiming to get rid of wrinkles was worth the money. So, it must have been one of *your* people."

The manager met them as they came in the front door. "Let's talk back in my office," he said. "It's pretty crazy out here. My name is Matt, by the way."

After introductions were made, Detective Martinez got right down to business. He handed Matt the sketch of the age-enhanced

Sophia Lepaste and said, "Have you seen her around here?"

Matt carefully looked at the sketch. "It's possible," he said. "I've had trouble with a girl who's been shoplifting in here. She's fast, and she's good. Never takes a whole lot, maybe a soda or a candy bar. I've got her on tape from a couple of weeks back. Didn't have a chance to catch her because I wasn't here that day. After seeing her on the security tape, I decided to go back and see if she'd been in before. Sure enough, she's stolen from me a total of five times that I can prove."

"You mind if we take a look at those tapes?" Detective Martinez asked.

"Knock yourself out," Matt replied. "I've got them right here."

Rachel pulled up a chair and pulled out her notebook. Detective Martinez started the first tape—the images were grainy, and the camera connection seemed to be intermittent. A lot of static sounded. The second tape was better, and the image of the girl was a bit clearer. Her face was never fully seen by the camera, but the physical description seemed to match. She had stolen a candy bar and soda that day. The fifth tape was the tape that appeared to identify the thief the best. She briefly looked toward the camera before she stole a cell phone from a customer while standing in line at the checkout. The cell phone had been lying on the woman's groceries in her basket next to her purse. The girl had distracted the woman with something on the floor, and before the woman stood back up, the girl had stolen the phone. She calmly walked out of the store and headed north. Rachel looked at the detective's face and could tell that he thought this might be Sophia as well. He continued to watch the tape one more time before he spoke.

"I think that could be her. She looks to be about ten years old, and she resembles the age-enhanced photo. We need to see if our forensic guy can get this image enlarged. I'll take it to Mrs. Franklin and see if this is the girl that approached her," he said.

"Anything I can do?" Rachel asked. "I'd like to do a canvas of the neighborhood going north to see if I can get someone to talk to me about who this girl might be."

"I think you better leave that to us. My guys will be on it as soon as we get a better photo to start showing around. Thanks, though, I know you want to help. Just be patient. I'll get you that story you've been waiting on," he said.

All the way back to the precinct, Rachel sat silently in the car. She wondered if this girl could possibly lead them to Skylan. As soon as they walked into the precinct, the detective that always sat across from Detective Martinez met them with a handful of messages. "All for you, Joe. Have fun!" he said with a laugh.

"Thanks, Ed. I'll need you to get the group of detectives together for a meeting. I'll have a photo of a young girl that will need to be followed up on. We'll need at least six detectives so we can do a door-to-door canvas. We'll start first thing tomorrow morning," he said.

"No problem, I'm on it!" Ed replied.

"I guess I'll have to wait for the results of the canvas before you give me anything for a story?" Rachel queried as Detective Martinez was calling the forensic lab.

"You got that right. Don't worry, though. I'll keep you in the loop as much as I can. You've proven you're here to help, not hurt, so we've got your back," he said.

Rachel waved and left the precinct. She had other stories that needed her attention, so she would focus on those while there was some downtime.

CHAPTER 11

Keeping up with the "fluff" stories, as she referred to them, was somewhat difficult. Her heart wasn't into writing about whether a particular product worked or not. She wanted to stay in her lane of investigative journalism. She knew these stories were a form of investigative journalism, but she preferred the criminal division over the consumer product division. It seemed the consumer stories were some form of punishment being doled out by her editor. Rachel knew that sometimes a person had to do what they didn't want to in order to do the one thing they really wanted to do. She would persevere, and she would make a difference. She hadn't gotten this far to quit, and she wasn't going to be a quitter now.

The cab ride to her apartment seemed short. Her mind was a million miles away. Her thoughts were with her sister, Maggie. Where was she? Was she still alive? Did she escape from Darius too? All these questions were filtering through her mind as the cab pulled up to the apartment. Her thoughts were interrupted by the cabdriver. "Miss, miss. We're here," he said.

"Thank you. Keep the change," she told him as she handed him the money and exited the cab.

As soon as she got settled into her apartment, she started organizing all her notes. She had a whiteboard, a corkboard, and a massive coffee table that served as a desk. She started a timeline for the Sophia Lepaste case and focused on that since it was the one case that seemed to be making some headway. Before the day was over, Rachel had Sophia's case on one side of the room and Skylan's case on the other. In the middle was her makeshift coffee table desk that served as the intersection point between the cases. There wasn't much to intersect yet, but Rachel had a gut feeling that these two cases were going to.

She stepped back to look at her progress. She was pleased with the number of notes she was able to produce. Now, if only she could have access to more case files. She would have to ask Detective Martinez if she could work at the precinct tomorrow, reviewing more cold case files.

Her cell phone rang as she was preparing her evening meal. It was Detective Martinez. "Hi," she said, "what's going on?"

"I need to talk to you. Can I come over?" he asked.

"Sure, no problem. Come on over," she said. There was an air of professionalism about his request, so she was beyond curious to see what the formality was all about. Could he have found the girl from the store security tape? Or was this about something else? Detective Martinez arrived at her apartment in less than an hour, so she didn't have to wait long for her answers.

Rachel opened the door. "Come on in. I've been working from home today, so it's a little bit of a mess in here," she said.

"I'd say. Looks like you've turned into an NYPD detective," he said as he walked over to look at the boards. "Pretty impressive!"

"Thanks. I try to be thorough when I'm reporting a case," she replied. "So, what was all the seriousness about on the phone about coming to see me?"

"The Pittsburgh Police Department gave me a call today. They say they have a case they would like me to take a look at. It involves a young woman that was found deceased about the time you say that Leslie disappeared. The description they gave of the body closely resembles your description."

Rachel stood still, her heart pounding wildly. *Is Leslie dead?* She knew she hadn't been feeling too well before she disappeared. Had she been *that* sick? Why had she not seen how badly off she had been?

"Rachel, are you okay? Rachel?"

"I'm fine. Just shocked. Last time I saw her, she wasn't feeling well, but I didn't think she was *that* sick," she replied.

"It wasn't an illness that killed her," he told her. "The Pittsburgh PD has her case listed as a homicide. It appears she was beaten and stabbed before being buried in a vacant lot. I'm sorry."

Rachel looked at him and seemed to digest the information quite calmly. He was hoping she wouldn't break down in tears, and he wasn't disappointed. She had referred to Leslie as being her second mom, so he was surprised there wasn't more emotion.

"Darius must have found out we were in Pittsburgh. But how?" she asked. "We covered our tracks well. Changed our appearances. How did he find her and not me? Are you sure it's her?"

"Not totally," he said. "I need to make a trip out there and get the particulars on the case and see what evidence they have. Was wondering if you would like to tag along. You're the only one who could possibly identify her since you were with her so long. Keep in mind that they do not have the body any longer and autopsy photos are what we will be looking through."

"I'll have my bags packed and ready," she said. "What time do we leave?"

"I'll pick you up in the morning. It will be a road trip, so pack accordingly. Budget is tight. My boss won't spring for a plane trip."

"Not a problem. I'll let my editor know that I'll be working from the road for a week or so."

CHAPTER 12

The night seemed to drag by, and sleep was not possible. Rachel couldn't stop thinking about Leslie and the last time she had seen her. Leslie had been down with some sort of illness for about a week, and she had told Rachel she was going to go to the doctor. When Rachel returned home that evening, Leslie never returned. She had stayed a week at the home with no word from Leslie. Rachel knew she couldn't afford the rent, so she packed her things and left. She had no way of knowing where Leslie was or even which doctor she had supposedly gone to see.

Luckily, her friend Kori had suggested she come live with her and her husband for a while. It was the best thing that could have happened to her. Kori was able to help her get her GED and eventually move out on her own. She had never confided in Kori the details of her sudden homelessness or past with Darius. Kori seemed to understand the need for her to break away from the past and never asked any questions. Kori understood the street since she had been homeless once before as well. She knew some people didn't talk about the details of their past. They just wanted to move forward, beyond them.

Detective Martinez was prompt. The doorbell rang, shaking Rachel from her stroll down memory lane. She grabbed her bag and laptop and silently prayed that this road trip would be a productive trip with some long-awaited answers to some questions she had had for years.

"Good morning, Joe," Rachel quipped. "I hope you're going to stop somewhere for coffee."

Detective Martinez was shocked at her using his first name. Since he had told her to, she had refused, continually referring to him as Detective Martinez. This was a welcome sign. He smiled and said, "Morning, Rachel, coffee is in the car. I have yours as well. Two creams, right?"

"Perfect! So glad you remembered."

"We've got a bit of a road trip ahead of us. Are you ready?"

She smiled and said, "Are we there yet?" laughing as she saw the look on his face.

"All right, smarty-pants," he said. "We'll be there soon enough. The ride will give us an opportunity to talk some more."

Rachel knew he would naturally want to know more details about her past and possibly Leslie. So, she braced for what was going to be a long ride. Her lack of sleep was going to be a factor. Hopefully, her emotions wouldn't get the better of her, and she could be of some help in filling in some of the gaps of her past.

"Fire away, Joe," she said. "I'm ready when you are. And just remember, I'll be asking questions of my own for the next installment for my editor. I'll need to have something for him by the time we return."

"I'll see what I can do," he said. "Let's wait until we get out of the city, and then we can get down to business."

Rachel was relieved and sat back to enjoy her coffee. It would take at least an hour, maybe more, to get outside of the city. She tilted her head back on the headrest and closed her eyes. Before she knew it, she was asleep. The sleepless night had caught up with her.

Detective Martinez knew she probably hadn't slept at all since he had broken the news to her about the woman the Pittsburgh PD had retrieved . . . possibly Leslie. He would let her sleep. She needed it. The autopsy photos were not pleasant, and he needed her to be at her best. He hoped he could prepare her for what she was going to see. Whoever had killed this woman was brutal.

They were an hour outside of the city when Rachel finally woke up. "Morning, again," he said. "How was the nap?"

As she stretched and reached for her coffee, she said, "Sorry. Didn't sleep last night. Couldn't stop thinking about this body being Leslie." She took a sip of her coffee and made a face instantly. "Wow, cold coffee. Not my favorite."

He laughed and then said, "We can stop at the next place I see for a fresh cup. I need another anyway."

"Thanks. You're the best," she said as she reached for her laptop. "I guess we should get started on those questions.

"Is there anything you can tell me about the canvas your detectives did yesterday? Did they find out anything?" she asked.

He let out a sigh because there wasn't much he could tell her yet. He knew she would be very disappointed. "I'm afraid I haven't received any news yet. I do know they completed their canvas, but I haven't received their reports yet. I'm sure they'll have something by the time we get back."

Rachel knew she was premature with her questions concerning the canvas, but she had to try. "Okay, I guess I'll have to be satisfied with that. My editor won't be thrilled, but I'll have something for him."

"You can always write about the possible sighting and direction the girl was going when last seen. Give another description, and I'll give you a still photo from the security tape. That should suffice," he said.

Rachel pressed her lips together and knew that was all she was going to get. "Okay, sounds good."

"Are you sure you're ready to see the autopsy photos?" he asked. "They're pretty gruesome."

"I'll be fine. We don't even know if this is Leslie," she said. "I've seen some things in my lifetime. Believe me, it hasn't been all roses and rainbows."

Pulling into the fast-food joint, he gave her a quick look of understanding and said, "Let's go get that second cup of coffee."

"Sounds good," she replied. "Can I grab something to eat as well?"

"Sure, I'm hungry too," he said. "Sit down, or you want it to go?"

"To go is fine. I'm ready to be there and get this done."

Back on the road, they traveled the rest of the way, each lost in their own thoughts. Detective Martinez was hoping this wouldn't be too hard on Rachel if the body did turn out to be Leslie. She was tough, but he knew from experience that sometimes the rough exterior was only hiding a very vulnerable interior. Even some of the most seasoned detectives had their breaking points. He knew how to handle those times, and he was ready for whatever the Pittsburgh PD was going to unravel for Rachel.

Rachel sat quietly as they drove. She knew Joe was deep in thought, and she was still tired from the sleepless night before. She lay her head back and closed her eyes. Then she started to pray. She prayed that this body would not be Leslie. All these years, she had told herself that Leslie had just left and made a life for herself. The disappointment of being left behind had turned into a form of gratitude after getting her GED and graduating from college. Leslie had given her the opportunity to move beyond the terrible nightmare of prostitution. She thanked God for Leslie and the opportunity that she had been provided before falling asleep once more.

Arriving at their hotel in Pittsburgh, Rachel was relieved to have a little time to gather her thoughts and work on her next consumer product piece. She wrote the article and emailed it to her editor. She had an hour before she had to meet up with the detective for a late dinner. He had gone ahead to meet with the medical examiner and collect whatever evidence and photos they had. They would meet with the detective from the Pittsburgh PD tomorrow morning. She was finally ready to see if this woman they found was Leslie.

The restaurant in the hotel was pretty nice. Rachel arrived early, so she was seated and given a menu while she waited on Joe. The trout sounded good, so she decided that was what she would order. Joe arrived and sat down opposite her and had a serious look on his face.

"Why so serious? Hard time getting what you needed from the medical examiner?" she asked.

"Not really, just a lot of details that weren't so pleasant. Let's just wait until tomorrow to talk about all this. I'm ready for some good food."

"Sounds great," she said. "I'm famished."

CHAPTER 13

The ride to the Pittsburgh Police Department was quiet. Each was lost in their own thoughts. Rachel was ready. She had seen a lot of bad things, and whatever she was going to see today was not going to surprise her. Darius was a ruthless, evil, and violent man. She had seen his handiwork. He was a murderer, and he always made his victims suffer. Her knowledge of this had her changing her appearance regularly, and photos of her were nonexistent. She purposefully never had her photo taken for any college graduation or any other purpose. She felt that using her real name was risky enough. She didn't want to change her name because she secretly hoped one day her sister, Maggie, would see her byline and try to make contact. Darius never called her Rachel anyway, so he probably forgot her real name. He had always called her "Little Bit." She truly hated that nickname!

Arriving at the station, Detective Martinez glanced over at Rachel and said, "So, our day begins. Are you ready?"

"More ready than you know," she replied. "Let's get this day started."

Sitting at the conference table, she readied herself for the photos that Detective Jargonsky was pulling out of the case file. He had explained to them that the body had been found in the area of California-Kirkbride buried in a shallow grave. California-Kirkbride was a neighborhood in Pittsburgh's North Side. According to the detective, it was located on a flat river plain that comprised the majority of old Allegheny City. A significant portion of the neighbor-hood's buildings was owned by absentee landlords who often rent-ed to subsidized tenants through Section 8 and similar programs. The vacant lot where the body was discovered was one of the lots where one of the row houses had been.

The dozer driver had unearthed it when making the pad for the new construction. The grave was approximately three-foot deep and contained the body that appeared to have been wrapped in a blanket. A purse was found next to the body. No other items were in the shallow grave.

The medical examiner determined the cause of death to be blunt force trauma with multiple stab wounds.

Detective Jargonsky said he had seen the sketches that Detective Martinez had faxed to the department and realized the possibil-ity that this might be the woman in the sketch. The body showed signs of extreme brutality. The head had been severed off almost completely. The murderer had gouged her eyes out. The marks on the spinal column confirmed whoever murdered her was trying to dismember the body. There were saw marks on the legs and arms. Each of the marks looked as if the murderer had gotten only so far and then stopped. Torture was the main objective for whoever had done this. Detective Martinez flipped through the case file and said, "I notice the medical examiner didn't give an opinion as to whether the victim was alive when these injuries were perpetrated. Is there any way to tell?"

"Not really," Detective Jargonsky said. "My guess is that some of the injuries were done while she was alive. The amount of torture is horrendous. We are dealing with one sick son of a bitch, if you ask me!"

"No doubt," Detective Martinez said. "He may be sicker than you could have ever imagined."

Rachel had been sitting quietly across the table from Detective

Jargonsky. The body was so distorted and gruesome that she thought it could be Leslie, but she wasn't a hundred percent. Once she saw the purse and its contents, though, she knew it was Leslie. The purse had a secret compartment which the photo showed with a fuzzy pink troll doll inside. This had been Leslie's. She had taken it out once to show Rachel when she was first abducted. She said it had been in her hand when Darius abducted her. It was the only thing she had from her past life. It had been a sort of good luck charm while Leslie had been with Darius.

As for the torture, it told a gruesome story, which was no surprise to Rachel. She knew Darius dismembered girls and put them into suitcases. He then buried them or threw them off a bridge somewhere. She had even helped with one. It was one of the worst days of her life. The lesson it proved to teach was never to cross Darius. He was evil. Rachel considered him the devil incarnate.

Detective Martinez had been watching her reaction. He finally said, "You want to add anything, Rachel? Do you recognize anything?"

"It's Leslie," she stated rather flatly. "The purse with the troll doll confirms it. She carried it everywhere. It was the only thing she had from her past life. She told me she had it in her hand when Darius abducted her."

She pushed her chair back and got up to leave. "I'll be back. Need to find a ladies' room."

"Down the hall, second door on the right." Detective Jargonsky said.

Rachel walked into the restroom and washed her face. The cold water felt good. The next part of this meeting would be the tough part. She knew the detectives would have more questions. She would have to tell them about Darius and his murderous rages. The evil torture and about her firsthand knowledge of one of the murders. Would they consider her an accomplice? She secretly hoped not, but she had helped. Darius had threatened her with her life and Maggie's life if she didn't. She bowed her head and began to pray. Her prayer was for the safety of the girls that were still out there. She prayed for Maggie, hoping she was still alive. Her final prayer was for the courage to tell the detectives what she knew. Gathering herself, she went back down the hall to the conference room.

The detectives had secured some snacks from the vending machine. The coffeepot was brewing along the back wall, and there was bottled water out for the taking. She raised her eyebrows slightly as she entered. They were anticipating a long talk. She took a deep breath and let it out slowly. This was going to be a long day.

CHAPTER 14

R achel unscrewed the cap on one of the bottled waters, took a sip, and then said, "Okay, I'm ready. I know you have a ton of questions. Let's get to it."

Detective Jargonsky had a look of amusement on his face. He had never encountered someone like her. She was tough, and he was curious about her backstory, to say the least. Detective Martinez had given him the short version, so he was ready to hear the rest.

"You're certain this is Leslie? Can you give us her last name so we can get some type of verification from the DMV or birth records?

"I only knew her as Leslie Knowles. She said she was sixteen years old. That's what she told me when I was first abducted. She never said anything else about herself to me. I only know her last name from a bill I saw on the cabinet when we moved into our own place here in Pittsburgh. I know that isn't much to go on, but that's all I know."

"So, that would make her . . . The detective quickly did the math to approximate her age. That would make her around twenty-six years old when she was killed. That fits the approximate age the medical examiner put in the report.

"This guy Darius you spoke about, who was he?" Detective Jargonsky then asked.

Rachel wasn't surprised the Pittsburgh detective knew her story. Detective Martinez would have had to tell him. Surprisingly, she wasn't upset. She sat up straight and let out a sigh, "Darius is the man who I believe abducted my sister Maggie and me. I was six, and my sister was nine. He was also the first man who introduced me to the business of prostitution." She had a look of complete disgust on her face as she proceeded. "He started setting me up with customers when I was ten. My sister Maggie had disappeared by then, but she had prepared me for what was to come. She told me all about the disgusting things I would be expected to do and what I would be expected to take. I'm hoping my sister is still out there, but I also know that if you crossed Darius or tried to escape, you'd wind up dead."

"Did you personally witness Darius killing anyone?" Detective Jargonsky asked.

"I was thirteen when another girl came to live with us. Her name was Asia. Anyway, that's what she said her name was. Asia was about nine, small for her age. She was Asian and very pretty. She went with Darius to have her first 'lesson,' sex 101." Rachel wrinkled up her nose and then continued.

"When they got back to the house, Asia was holding her arm. Darius said she had broken it. Leslie wanted to take her to the hospital, but Darius refused. He said it would draw attention to them. Asia was really hurting, so she and I went into the bedroom while Leslie and Darius argued about what to do with her. We could hear them arguing, and I had heard Darius say we need to just take care of her. Nobody will ever know. I had heard him say this before, and I knew what it meant. They were going to kill her."

Rachel stopped for a moment and took some deep breaths. What would come next would be hard, and she knew that these two detectives wouldn't be expecting what she had to say.

"You're doing great, Rachel," Detective Jargonsky said. "What happened after that?"

Detective Martinez gave her a nod and said, "Take your time, Rachel. I know we haven't talked about this part of your story, but it needs to be told. It might help us find out who killed Leslie. It might lead us to Darius."

Rachel bowed her head into her hands and began rubbing her temples. This was harder than she had thought it would be. Finally, she looked up and said, "Darius came into the bedroom and got Asia and me. He took us out to his car and told us to get in. We did. Asia thought we were going to the doctor. I knew the doctor probably wasn't in the cards. Darius drove for a while until we were out of town. He turned down this country road. I hadn't seen a house in a while. There was no one around. I knew this was going to be bad.

"He got us out of the car and walked us through the field over to where there was a bunch of trees. There was also an old barn that looked like it was going to fall down at any moment. Darius shoved Asia ahead and told her to go into the barn. He took ahold of my arm and whirled me around so that I was standing in front of him. He told me this was going to be the biggest test since coming to be with him. He told me I was going to kill Asia. I shook my head no, and he slapped me across my face and told me if I didn't, then Maggie would be next. He said he would kill Maggie and that I would have to watch. He then said after Maggie was dead, he would kill me. I knew he was serious. Leslie had told me about how girls ended up gone."

Rachel closed her eyes and took a deep breath. The smell of the old barn was permeating her nose, and she knew that in the next few moments, she would be reliving the entire day over again. This was intense. *God,* she prayed silently, *help me to continue with courage.*

The detectives gave her time to continue. They knew this had to be hard on her. The time elapsed since the incident hadn't softened the effects, and they knew she would be forthcoming and honest. The tough inner core of this young woman was commendable.

Rachel looked at both of them, and then with a strong resolve, continued. "We walked into the barn. Asia was by the back wall. Darius had her come over to him, and then he nodded for me to grab the shovel that was leaning up against the other wall. I closed my eyes and grabbed the shovel. Darius began to hug Asia. He was fondling her beneath her dress. This caused Asia to stiffen up. I wanted to hit Darius in the head with the shovel, but I knew I probably couldn't swing the shovel hard enough to kill him. Asia began to cry the rougher he got with her. I was terrified. I swung the shovel as hard as I could and hit her on the back of the head. She crumpled into a heap on the ground. I closed my eyes and prayed God would help us. Darius finished the job by slitting her throat.

"There was blood everywhere. I ran to the door of the barn and threw up. I'd never seen so much blood coming out of someone. Darius yelled at me to get back in there, that he needed help. I reluctantly went back. He used his knife to cut her up. He was putting her body parts in a small suitcase. I wanted to kill him so badly. His words of warning kept ringing in my head. He would kill Maggie and then kill me. I didn't want that to happen. After he put Asia in the suitcase, he brought out a wheelbarrow from the corner of the barn and poured a bag of cement in it. He told me to get the shovel and stir when he poured in the water. I stirred the cement, and he poured it into the suitcase and shut the lid. We then put the suitcase into a black trash bag. After loading it into the trunk of the car, we drove back to the city. We stopped at some bridge on the way back and dumped the suitcase over the edge. I didn't say a word to anyone, not even Leslie. I'm sure she knew, though."

Both detectives sat silently for a moment. The weight of her words struck emotions that neither wanted to show. This girl was sitting here talking about murder and prostitution like it was an everyday occurrence. In all reality . . . it probably was.

Detective Martinez was mentally going through every Jane Doe child death he could think of. Asia was a little girl whose parents deserved to know the outcome. She needed to be laid to rest properly. None of the cases he could think of seemed to fit, but there was one out of West Virginia that just might be this girl. Her name was Lily Ashita. She was nine years old and had been found by a fisherman inside a suitcase that he had snagged while out fishing. The location was just outside the city of Manassas, West Virginia. It was in the cold case file in the basement of the precinct. He'd have to look into it further when he returned.

"Well," Detective Martinez said, "I appreciate your honesty. I know that must have been very difficult. Are you okay?"

"I will be. I know Darius is responsible for Leslie's murder," she said. "When are you going after him?"

"We need some hard evidence. Something tangible to give the district attorney," Detective Jargonsky said. "I'll need to get a written statement from you. Is that possible?"

"Sure," Rachel said. "I'll get right on that." With no hard evidence, she knew proving Darius was the killer would be difficult. She went to work on her statement. She knew Detective Martinez would be looking into Asia's murder, and hopefully, someone had found her and reported it to the police.

She had opened herself up and poured out her experiences without crumbling. She was proud of herself. She knew by being strong, the possibility of finding Maggie was there. She had to find her. She was all she had. Plus, there was still the abduction of Skylan Winslip. Finding her before Darius did something terrible to her was critical.

After finishing up the statement, Detective Martinez and Rachel returned to their hotel. Both were quiet on the ride, lost in their own thoughts.

"I'm going to order room service tonight," Rachel said. "Hope that's okay. I'm exhausted and really need some time to myself."

"I understand," he said. "I need some time as well. Enjoy the evening. We'll head back in the morning."

Rachel nodded and stepped onto the elevator to go to her room. "Thanks," she said. "I'll see you in the morning."

"Coffee at eight?" he asked.

"Sounds good. See you then."

Detective Martinez called the precinct when he returned to the room. He had the intern that was working to pull the cold case on Lily Ashita. He wanted it on his desk when he returned.

It was going to be a sleepless night for him as he rehashed the day's events. He had had no idea that Rachel had helped to murder one of these girls. He wondered what else she had been exposed to while being held by this man they called Darius. He shuddered at the very thoughts that filled his mind. He had reviewed some of the cold case files, and there were horrific findings by the medical examiner on the bodies of the missing that had been found. He hoped Rachel hadn't been exposed to some of those tortuous acts that he had read about. It had been a true miracle she had survived and escaped. It sounded more and more like this Leslie Knowles had been Rachel's guardian angel of sorts.

Whoever had killed Leslie had been violent. The killer's murderous actions demonstrated familiarity with the victim. This killing was personal. He silently prayed that Leslie hadn't suffered too much at the hands of this coldhearted monster.

He found himself thinking about Sophia Lepaste. If she were the one shoplifting, why hadn't she tried to escape? She was being allowed to leave whatever place she was being held to walk to the local market? Why didn't she just walk to the nearest precinct and ask for help? He remembered Rachel saying that Darius used her sister Maggie as a sort of bargaining chip to get Rachel to do his bidding. So, maybe this girl was being held by the same method. But who was she protecting? Maybe no one knew she was leaving.

There were so many questions that he wanted to have answered. Could Skylan Winslip be tied to the Sophia Lepaste case? Maybe they even lived in the same place. He had to figure this out. Too many young girls were being abducted, and too many were being found dead.

This prostitution ring was complicated and widespread. It seemed that there were numerous sects within the main group, with each sect operating on their own for the common good of the whole. Who could be the head of the organization? Finding the head of an organization like this could take years. Heck, they had been in business for years. He rubbed his head and leaned back against the pillow. He'd get a little shut-eye before daylight. There wasn't going to be an easy solution.

The Internet Crime Unit had been working on a profile for him, so he would check with them when he got back to the office. If he could go online and pretend to be an interested customer, he might have a chance at curing this cancerous blight from his city.

CHAPTER 15

Darius hadn't been around for a while, and Ruth was grateful. Sometimes, he would go out of town to set up a new house for a new handler and be gone for a few days or even a few weeks. She secretly liked the downtimes. The girls didn't have to have customers, either. That was always a plus.

The only downside was she never had any money to buy groceries. Darius was always the one who brought them groceries and toiletries. Having Sophie around had helped because she was always shoplifting things. Ruth hated to ask her to help, but there had been times if it hadn't been for Sophie, they would have gone without.

The girls came into the small living room and sat on the tattered sofa. Both seemed to be still sleepy from the night before. Ruth looked at them and smiled. The innocence was still there. She hoped it would remain in them, even though she knew Darius would soon snuff it out just like he did with all the girls. This life wasn't for the weak. Sophie and Skylan were strong girls, and she knew that one day they would get out. She just hoped it wasn't by Darius's hand.

"You girls want something to eat?" Ruth asked. "I've got one package of Pop-Tarts you can split. Sorry, but the food is getting pretty low in the pantry. I'll see what I can round up today."

Skylan looked at Ruth and could see the pain in her eyes and the regret that she couldn't offer them anything more to eat. "Sounds good," she said. "Maybe we can split the package three ways today."

Sophie understood all too well and got up and went to the

bedroom to get dressed. This was her chance to help Ruth out and get another phone. She had misplaced her other one and hoped that Darius or Ruth hadn't found it. "I'm not hungry this morning. You girls can split it. I need to take a walk down the street to wake up. I'll be back in a few," she said.

Skylan looked curiously at Sophie as she disappeared into the bedroom, then turned back to Ruth. "Why does she get to go on walks by herself? You told me I couldn't leave unless I was with you. I think I'll go with Sophie this morning."

Ruth quickly and sternly said, "No, you won't be going with her. She isn't supposed to go out by herself, either, but I can't stop her anymore. She always returns, and I haven't told Darius she goes out, so you better keep your mouth shut too."

Skylan was taken aback and sat on the sofa in silence. She understood the cruelty that Darius could bring into the situation just by the tone that Ruth had used in her response. She wasn't going to say anything. At least not to him. Skylan decided she would stick to the straight and narrow and find another way to break free.

"How about that Pop-Tart?" she asked. "I'm a little hungry. You want to share?"

"Sure, I'll go pop it in the toaster," Ruth said. Sophie bounded past the two as they sat eating their Pop-Tart. She skipped out the back door and down to the little alley. She seemed happy. Skylan couldn't figure out why she was so happy. Sophie had told her last night about some of the things that Darius had made her do. The customers were harsh, and they made her do things that she knew wasn't right. Little girls should not have to do things like that. The most frightening thing Sophie told her was about the actual sex act. Skylan knew about this but had never heard about it in such detail. It scared her to think that this was what Darius was going to have her doing. It hadn't happened yet, but Sophie said it would. She also said it would hurt really badly and that there would be blood.

Skylan was terrified to have Darius come back, so she kept praying that God would find a way to help her. So far, her prayers had been answered because she hadn't seen Darius for almost two weeks.

"What are we going to do today, Ruth?" she asked.

"I don't know. Is there something you would like to do?"

"Can we go for a walk? I really would like to get outside and see the sunshine for a change. Plus, I think it might be my birthday!"

"Happy Birthday!" Ruth said. "Let's celebrate and give you a new haircut and color today. I think you would look good with red hair."

Skylan was shocked and scared. Her mother had never talked about coloring hair or getting a haircut. All she had ever done in her short life was getting a trim. Her long hair was beautiful. She didn't want to lose it. Her eyes filled with tears as she looked at Ruth. "Why?" she whimpered. "I like my long hair. Besides, I don't like that for a birthday celebration."

"It's what Darius said I should do. I have to do what he says. It's not going to hurt, and who knows. You might actually like it," she said as she forced a smile.

Skylan knew she was helpless about the news. She would just pray that someone would help her. Without her long, blond hair, she wouldn't look the same. She was afraid she would be lost forever. She wanted her mother. She wanted to run into her arms, feeling the love and warmth surround her as her mother hugged her. The reality was she would just have to survive in this terrible place a few days longer. She didn't want to think past a few days. Her mind couldn't comprehend the reality of never seeing her parents again.

"I guess it is what it is," she said. "Let's get it over with."

Ruth got up and went into the bathroom and got the scissors out of the drawer. She came back into the kitchen and got things ready to cut Skylan's hair. As she was putting a towel around Skylan's neck, she felt the girl shiver. It broke her heart to have to do this to the child, but she knew her life and Skylan's depended on it. She ran the brush through the long, blond hair and decided a pixie cut would probably be the best to start with. The drastic change would alter Skylan's appearance so she wouldn't be recognized. The media was probably having a field day with this abduction. All-American, blue-eyed, long blond-haired girl gets abducted from the subway . . .

It didn't take long, and Skylan went from long, blond hair to short, red hair. The transformation was just what Darius would want. She looked completely different.

Ruth held the mirror up for Skylan to admire her new look. Skylan looked at her reflection through the tears that were silently streaming down her cheeks. The girl she was seeing looked older with short red hair. The pixie cut accentuated her face more and defined her cheekbones. She knew she was the same girl inside, but the outside was sure different.

"Well, how do you like it?" Ruth asked.

Skylan wiped her tears with the back of her hand and then quietly said, "It's okay."

Sophie walked through the back door with a smile on her face and a bag in her hand. She noticed Skylan's new look and said, "Wow, cool! Looks like a totally different girl."

"Just what the day ordered," Ruth said. "You weren't gone long. How was the walk?"

"Fine," Sophie said. "I managed to panhandle a twenty-dollar bill from some old lady, so I went and got us a few things."

As Ruth put away the items Sophie had brought, Skylan watched quietly, wondering how Sophie could have gotten such a great deal on all she brought home. There was cereal, milk, eggs, bread, and lunchmeat. She had been shopping with her mom and knew that all that would have cost way more than twenty dollars.

Sophie slipped the phone she had stolen into a cubby behind

the Pop-Tarts. She was certain Ruth had found her other phone, so she secretly hoped she would find this one too.

Sophie went back to the bedroom, and Skylan decided she would follow her. "How did you buy all that with twenty dollars?" she asked. "I know it costs more than that."

"If you can keep a secret, I'll tell you," Sophie said. Skylan was surprised and happy that Sophie was going to have a little trust in her.

Skylan nodded and said, "I'll keep your secret."

Sophie gave her a look and then said, "I ask people for money when I go out on the street. Sometimes they give me their loose change, and then there are times they actually give me the greenbacks. I keep a stash here in the bedroom. Here, I'll show you." She went over to the closet and pulled out some shoes and got on her hands and knees. She proceeded to pull up a corner of the carpet, and underneath was a little stash of money. There wasn't much there, but it was enough to get a few things. Sophie quickly put the carpet back down and piled the shoes back in the closet. "Now, you know," she said. "So, if something happens to me, you can have it."

Skylan was shocked and pleased. Sophie was pretty smart. But her comment about something happening to her had Skylan wondering what that might be. She was afraid to ask, so she just nodded her head in agreement.

This little hiding place could prove very helpful for Skylan if she could just figure out how to get away from this house and out from under the watchful eyes of Ruth. There had to be a way. She wasn't going to give up.

With her new look, she would see if Ruth would be up for that walk. Skylan needed to find out where she was being held. The surroundings weren't familiar. The trip to the warehouse hadn't sparked any familiarities either. Maybe she would suggest a trip to the local park. The name of the park would more than likely be posted, and she hoped she would recognize the name.

CHAPTER 16

Skylan sat straight up in bed after hearing a loud knock on the front door. She could hear Ruth getting up to answer the door. She strained to hear who was at the door. Then the familiar voice of Darius reached her ears. She cringed at the thought of him being here. It meant that she or Sophie would be called to be with a customer. She pulled the covers up over her head and prayed that it wouldn't be her.

The door to the bedroom opened. Skylan feigned sleep and prayed even harder. She heard Sophie getting up. Ruth was helping her get dressed. She heard Ruth tell Sophie, "Don't make him mad, honey. He's been drinking." Sophie didn't say a word. The room grew quiet after the two left. Skylan heard the front door close.

Getting out of bed, she crept to the door and opened it slightly. She could see Ruth sitting on the tattered sofa with her head in her hands. She could tell she was crying. Skylan went back to bed and prayed that God would protect Sophie and help her. She was scared. She had this awful feeling that her life was going to be changed forever if Sophie didn't come back.

Sophie slid into the backseat of Darius's car. She was scared. Darius was unusually quiet. She knew this was different than the other times he had come to get her for a customer. There had been no mention of a customer, yet Ruth had made her dress up for one. She decided she would play it out—she had been in sticky situations before. He hadn't been around for a while, so maybe she could bluff her way through whatever he had planned.

Darius drove to a secluded lot somewhere on the East Side and stopped the car. He turned around in his seat and looked at Sophie. The evil in his eyes seemed to penetrate her skin. Sophie became very uneasy. She had never seen him like this before. She swallowed her fear and asked, "Are we meeting my customer here?" Darius continued to stare at her. She smoothed her dress with her hands and pretended to fix her hair. Then he spoke quietly.

"You've been a busy girl, haven't you? I saw on the news a picture of a girl who looks just like you. The news says the girl was asking a lady at a local market to take her home with her. Would that girl be you?" His voice had continued to grow louder as he spoke. She could tell he was trying to contain the anger that was rising steadily.

Sophie was unfazed. She had been expecting this at some point. She had gotten brave that day, and she knew she would draw some attention. But she was undeterred and confident when she replied. "Wasn't me, Darius. You know we can't leave Ruth's side. You would have us killed. I want to see my parents again, so I'm not going to mess up like that."

Darius got out of the car and walked around to the backseat door where Sophie was sitting. He grabbed the door handle and swung open the door. Sophie sat still with her hands clasped together in her lap. She appeared uninterested and not the least bit scared. Darius reached in and yanked her out of the car. She stumbled out, trying to keep on her feet. He whirled her around to the back of the car and slammed her against the wheel well. The impact was harsh. Sophie knew this wasn't going to be easy.

Sophie stood straight after her impact and asked, "Why would you think that girl was me? I've been nothing but perfect for you. I entertain your customers, and I get top dollar whenever I do. I even do things for you that you like. Why are you so mad? It wasn't me."

The clarity with which she was talking and the confidence she exuded was commendable. Darius was questioning his first assumption. He also knew this girl could tell you she was Miss America and make you believe it. He didn't want to mess up that pretty face. He did have customers who were very eager to get her booked, and he knew the money she would bring in would be tremendous. His two-week stint out of town had taken a serious toll on his finances. He had made some great contacts and even started setting up another ring in the Chicago area. But he had to prove to this girl he was in control. If it were her, he wanted her to never think about doing this again.

He lit a cigarette and paced back and forth while he puffed. Sophie was anticipating a blow at any minute. She remained calm, however. The blow never came. Darius threw the cigarette on the ground and toed it into the dirt with his shoe. Sophie braced herself for what was to come. Darius came back over to her and lifted her dress. She closed her eyes. He pulled down her underwear and said, "It's time for you to make me happy." She bit her lip and knew what was coming. He must have believed her. She was relieved in that regard, but what he had in mind would change her forever.

After four hours of intense molestation and rape, Sophie walked back through the door of the little house. Ruth and Skylan were on the sofa. Sophie ran to the bedroom and shut the door. Ruth looked at Skylan and said, "You stay put. I'll be back in a minute." Skylan nodded her understanding.

Sophie was stripping off her dress when Ruth entered the bedroom. She started to pull out Sophie's favorite jeans and a T-shirt from the dresser. Sophie turned around and said, "No, I don't want to wear anything for a while. I just want to take a shower and go to bed."

Ruth was sickened by the appearance of Sophie. The child's stomach had slash marks made by a knife. They appeared to be superficial, but Ruth knew they would probably leave scars. Her pubic area was angry red and bleeding. Her buttocks were bruised. She had been broken. Ruth wanted Darius dead. She had to help these girls. She helped Sophie get her shower, dress her wounds, and put her into bed. Skylan had seen it all. She had tiptoed over to the bedroom door and witnessed the aftermath of Darius. She was horrified by the sight of her new friend, Sophie. She knew she needed to figure out a way to escape—and soon.

Sophie slept most of the day, and Skylan kept to herself. She stayed in the bedroom with Sophie and quietly sat on her bed and prayed. She wanted to talk to Ruth, but she didn't know what to say.

Ruth finally came in and motioned for Skylan to follow her. Once in the kitchen, Ruth said, "Have a seat, Skylan. I think we need to talk. I need to tell you a little bit about Darius and why we have to do what he says—always."

Skylan listened intently and then said, "I saw her, Ruth. I saw the blood and bruises. I won't be a problem. I promise."

CHAPTER 17

After getting back to New York, Rachel hit the story hard. She had seen Darius's brutality. She wanted to stop him. Leslie hadn't deserved the beating she took, not to mention the other torture she endured. The only problem was she didn't know how to stop him. She needed to know if her sister, Maggie, were still alive. Her prayer was that Maggie had secretly survived and escaped. If she had been in the business this long, it wasn't out of the question that her fate might have been the same as Leslie's. She shuddered at the very thought and prayed it wasn't so.

Rachel stopped by the deli on the corner on her way to the precinct. She was hungry this morning and wanted a breakfast sandwich to go with her coffee. She ordered at the counter and then sat in the booth by the back door. She was lost in thought when she heard a familiar voice at the counter. Her heart was pounding wildly, and her breathing was constricted as she heard, "I'll take a ham, egg, and cheese sandwich, to go." She quickly tossed her hair so that she was looking through the long bangs that previously had been tucked behind her ears. It was Darius. He was here. She struggled to keep her breathing even as she placed her phone on silent and texted Detective Martinez. She gave him the address and the message, "Darius is here!" She quickly shut the phone screen off and prayed her sandwich order would not be called before his. Finally, she decided she couldn't take the chance, so she got up slowly and quietly slipped out the back door.

Once in the alley, her phone lit up with a text from Detective

Martinez. "ON MY WAY!"

Rachel decided to wait for Darius to leave and follow him, if possible. She didn't have a car, but maybe she could get a tag number, or even a cab so she could at least tail him inconspicuously.

Darius walked out of the deli and got into his car. She quickly snapped a photo of the vehicle and tag number. Then he pulled away from the curb and was gone. She stepped out from the building and walked over to the street. Detective Martinez screeched to a halt in front of the deli. She quickly got in and told him which direction Darius had gone. She also showed him the photo of the car and tag number. They drove off in the direction Darius had gone. The traffic was terrible, so the chase was quickly abandoned. "We'll just go back to the precinct and run the tag," he stated. "Find out where he's been staying, if there's a good address on file."

Rachel was disappointed but knew the chase was futile in this traffic. "Okay," she said. "Just seeing him was a shock. The sketch you guys have is dead-on!"

The tag came back to a Darrin Potswell with an address in a borough of Manhattan, the Lower East Side to locals. Rachel was beyond excited about the possibility of capturing the man who had abducted her and Maggie. She wanted him to rot in jail for the things he had done. Detective Martinez was quick to point out, though, that sometimes addresses didn't pan out and often were empty lots or empty buildings.

Rachel knew he was right, but she was determined to catch him. Bring him in to face the horrible things he had done. Detective Martinez had been gracious enough to let her tag along on the ride to the Lower East Side to check out the address. She was grateful for this and prayed that Maggie would be there . . . alive and well.

They pulled up next to a warehouse and parked. Additional officers were staking out the building from all sides. Rachel didn't see any activity around the building. It looked abandoned and neglected. She knew the address had been a dead end. She took a deep breath and looked over at the detective. "I guess it's just another dead end," she said.

"Not necessarily," he replied. "I'm going to get out and do a walk around. See if there is any way into the warehouse. Want to come?"

Rachel looked at him incredulously and said, "I sure do! What made you think I wouldn't?"

The door of the warehouse was open slightly as they approached. Detective Martinez motioned for her to stay while he and the others cleared the building. She waited with another officer until the all-clear had been given.

She entered the warehouse and was met by the disgusting smell of rat excrement and whatever else was all over the floor. Detective Martinez was upstairs, and his voice had an excited tone about it. Rachel walked up the stairs, and to her amazement, was met with the sight of clothing hanging from racks, new packages of socks, underwear, and shoes. The items were all new. She also noticed the clothing items were all smaller sizes. Her hair on the back of her neck stood up, and chills ran up her back. This was the central hub for all the girls to get their clothing. She had heard about these places. Supposedly, they were strategically placed around in the cities where they worked so they could get new clothes and shoes without going out into the public to shop. It was another layer to the organization to protect them from drawing too much attention.

She walked by the tables of new shoes and hair bows, then stopped and picked up one of the hair bows, feeling the soft velvet of the ribbon. Detective Martinez saw her reaction and went over to her. "Are you okay?" he asked. "You seem to be remembering something again."

"I always knew we got new clothes from somewhere. I thought for a long time that Leslie would buy them for us. When I got older, one of the other girls told me there were warehouses full of brand-new clothing, shoes, and accessories. I had never seen one until now. It's eerie to think these clothes are all for girls who are forced into the prostitution business."

Detective Martinez was quick to say, "Right now, we are not sure that this is what you think it is. We need to do some research and stake out the place to see if we can catch anyone coming in here. I hope you understand you can't write anything about finding this place. We have to have an ironclad investigation if we're going to put Darius away for good."

"I understand completely," she said. "You can count on me to keep the lid on this. Is there any way I can sit with the officers that will be doing the stakeout?"

"Sorry, Rachel," he said. "Regulations won't allow for that to happen. I'll keep you informed, though. You can bank on that."

Rachel put the hair bow down and walked down the stairs. She was disappointed she couldn't be on the stakeout. She would find a way to be in the right place at the right time, though. She had to find out who was using this building.

The stakeout would start in a couple of days, and in the mean-time, she could do some snooping of her own. Especially since she knew this place existed.

CHAPTER 18

Darius didn't return for a couple of days. Sophie was starting to get around a little better. Skylan would help her when she let her. Sophie had been very explicit when relating to Skylan what had happened to her. Skylan had listened to everything she had to say. It upset her to think that a grown man had done that to Sophie, who was still just a little girl.

Sophie came into the bedroom and sat beside Skylan. "I'm not sure how much longer I'll be here. I have made Darius really mad. He believed my story, though. That's why I wasn't hurt any worse. I'm going to cut my hair and color it blond. Don't be too shocked when I get done," she said with a little laugh.

"Why do you have to change your hair?" Skylan asked.

"I made the mistake of asking some woman to take me home one day while I was out. She told the police. There's a sketch going around. Darius saw the sketch and thought it was me. I lied to him and told him it wasn't me. I convinced him for now, but he'll find out the truth before long," Sophie explained.

"Is that why he did those terrible things to you?" she asked.

"Yes," Sophie almost whispered, remembering the torture. "Don't you ever tell anyone about what I've told you—especially Darius."

"I won't," Skylan said. "God is going to get us out of here. I know He will. I've been praying, and He brought you back the other day, so I know He'll help us."

"Don't count on it," Sophie said. "I think we're all doomed to a bitter end. Including Ruth."

"God won't let that happen," Skylan protested. "He takes care of His children. I know He does."

"I hope you're right," Sophie said as she rolled her eyes.

Ruth came in with a hollow look in her eyes. It looked as if she had lost her best friend. She looked over at the girls and said, "I'm going down to the warehouse to get a couple of outfits for Skylan. You girls stay in the house and don't answer the door for anyone. You understand?"

Sophie understood all too well. Skylan was going to find out firsthand what this business was all about. She was not going to be the same little innocent girl when her first customer was done with her. "We understand," Sophie said. "Don't be long."

Sophie looked over at Skylan and said, "You're going to have your first customer. You remember what I told you. Play along and don't get all crybaby on them. You'll just make them mad, and things will only go bad."

Skylan felt a knot in the pit in her stomach and nodded her head. She closed her eyes and prayed. "Please, God, not now. Not me. Be with me and protect me."

Ruth got into the car with Darius, and they went over to the warehouse. When they pulled up, nothing looked out of the ordinary, but she felt like something was different. It was a feeling that someone other than Darius or her had been here. She kept her feelings to herself as she stepped out of the car. Walking up to the door, she felt like someone was watching her. Was she crazy? Darius followed her, shoving past her to the door. "Come on," he said. "This client wants something special, and we're going to deliver."

Watching from the warehouse across the lot was the one person who could positively identify Darius. Rachel was crouched down, covered with an old painter tarp she had found in the building. She had made sure that only her camera lens was able to see the warehouse across the way. If anyone were to look her way, they would see nothing but what appeared to be a heap of trash. When the car drove up, she started taking photos. It was the same car!

Her heart was racing as Darius stepped from the car along with a woman. The woman was looking down, and Rachel couldn't make out any facial features. They both disappeared into the warehouse, only to return after a few moments with two outfits. As the woman exited the warehouse, Rachel saw her clearly. *Maggie! It's Maggie!* She couldn't believe her eyes. She cried silent tears of joy as she kept taking photos. She willed herself to stay still until the car had been gone for at least twenty minutes. She didn't want to be coming out of her hiding place and be seen—especially if they forgot something and came back.

Climbing out from her hiding place, she was met by one of the detectives who had been sent to stake out the warehouse. She was surprised to see him and said, "Thought you guys were going to wait to set up on the warehouse."

"Well, we didn't," he said. "I'm sure Detective Martinez would like to see you in his office. Like now!"

Rachel swallowed hard. She knew she had messed up, and she would have to hear all about it. She hoped she hadn't messed up so much that they would pull the story from her. "I guess you are going to give me a ride?" she asked.

"You got that right, young lady. Get in."

When they arrived back at the precinct, Detective Martinez met Rachel. He didn't look happy. He held the door for her, and she followed him back to one of the interrogation rooms. She sat down at the table and waited. Detective Martinez held out his hand and said. "I need your camera. I need all the photos you took."

"But wait," she said." I can explain everything."

"No explanations!" he said in a little louder voice. "I have questions that I'll have to be answering when this gets out. I want all the evidence you gathered. I'm going to try to smooth this over, so you don't lose your story. Do you understand where I'm coming from?"

"Yes," she said. "I understand. I will tell you that it was Darius, and the woman with him was my sister, Maggie. She's aged some, but I would know her anywhere."

"I need you to go home and stay there until I can clear the air around here," he said. "Do you understand?"

Rachel was frustrated and replied, "Did you hear me? That was my sister, Maggie! She's alive!"

"I heard you, and we'll get a positive identification before proceeding," he said. "I know you want her to be your sister, and honestly, I hope she is, but we won't know anything if we spook them, and they run."

"Fine," Rachel said. "I'll go home. Just keep me informed."

"An officer will drive you," he said. "I'll call you later."

Rachel felt all the frustration and excitement of the day as she stepped from the patrol car. Darius hadn't discovered her, and she had got the confirmation she thought the police would need. In her mind, the proof was already discovered.

She walked up the stairs to her apartment and entered into her space. All she wanted to do was go and get her sister, but she also knew that it was not possible at this time. She had to be patient. She had to grateful and positive. This case was more than just finding her sister. It was about all the missing girls who were being subjected to the horrors of prostitution.

She decided she would spend her time going over the case one more time, adding the new information she had acquired today. Detective Martinez would smooth things over. She was involved, and she was going to help bring this ring down.

CHAPTER 19

Skylan looked at the outfits that Ruth presented to her when she got back to the house. They were cute, but she knew they were for one of the customers, not her. She picked up the little sleeveless royal blue dress. It was pretty. It had small white anchors all over it. Ruth had even brought little white sandals to go with it. It made Skylan scared to even think about putting it on. The other outfit was a white dress with a navy-blue sash belt. Navy shoes matched it with white socks.

Ruth looked at Skylan and said, "I think the one with the anchors will work the best. It will go well with your hair. The customer has a boat he'll be taking you out on, so the theme on the dress will be perfect."

Skylan nodded and went and put on the dress. She was quiet and subdued. Ruth was worried she would mess this up, so she said a prayer for her. "Please keep her safe, dear Lord. She's only eight."

Skylan returned, wearing the dress. She was adorable, but Ruth knew this day was not going to be a good day for her. "You look fantastic," she said a little too enthusiastically. "The customer will love you."

Darius arrived then and took Skylan to meet her first real customer. The ride to the marina was quiet. When Darius parked the car, he turned in his seat and said, "I want you to do just as the nice man says. You will be going out on his boat, so be a good little girl and make him happy."

Skylan nodded her head. She couldn't bring herself to say

anything. She was dreading what was about to happen, and it scared her to think she would be hurt like Sophie.

Just then, a tall, white man with bushy blond hair came up to the car. Skylan looked at the man and determined this was her customer. He didn't look scary. He looked like a normal man. Like someone's dad. He had boat shoes on and was tan, like he was outside a lot.

"Thanks for dropping her off," he told Darius. "What's the little darlin's name?"

"Taylor," Darius said as he looked at Skylan and gave her a sharp look. "You can call her Taylor."

"Okay, Taylor," he said. "Are you ready? We're going for a little boat ride today. We should return in about two hours. Your ride will be here when we're done. Come on."

Skylan got out of the car and looked back at Darius. He was giving her that sharp look again, and she knew she was trapped. This was really happening. The man held her hand as they walked to his boat. Other men were getting their boats ready, and they paid no attention to them as they walked past.

"Here we are," he said as he motioned for her to step on the boat. "Her name is *Mermaid*, see?" He pointed to the side of the boat.

Once the man got the boat underway and headed down the river, he came back to where Skylan was sitting. "How are you doing?" he asked. "Have you ever been on a boat before?"

Skylan felt a wave of peace flow over her as she answered, "I've been on my dad's boat. I'm doing fine. My dad's boat is really big."

"Well, I'm glad you're familiar with boats," he said. "Let's go down to the cabin for a while. There are some things down there I'd like to show you."

"Who's going to be driving?" she asked. "I don't want to crash into someone else."

"My driver will take care of that," he said. "We can go have a little fun."

Skylan reluctantly went down into the cabin with the blond-haired man. Once down there, she noticed that there was a statue of a whale on a shelf inside one of the cabinets. She walked over to the cabinet and admired the whale for a moment. The man came over to her and slid his hand up her leg. She turned around and abruptly blurted out, "Do you know the story of Jonah and the whale?"

The man was taken aback. He had never been asked that by anyone, and here was this little eight-year-old girl, asking. "I have," he said. "I learned the story in Sunday school when I was a little boy."

Skylan felt emboldened and asked, "Do you believe in God?"

The man was flabbergasted. He rubbed his mop of blond hair and looked at this girl. "I guess I do believe in God. It's been a long time, but I guess I still do. Now, can we get back to why we're here?"

"Jonah didn't do what God wanted him to do, so he was swallowed by a whale," she said. "Aren't you afraid you'll get swallowed by a whale if you don't do what God wants you to do?"

"I don't think there are any whales that would swallow me here in this part of the country," he said. "Now, come here. I want to see that pretty little dress."

"God can do anything He wants," she said. "If He wants to send a whale to swallow you, He will. Besides, you don't really want to see my dress. You just want to do things to me that God says is bad. He will know what you do to me. He will send a whale to get you."

The man sat on the bed in the cabin and stared at this little girl who was full of knowledge beyond her years. Jonah had been a favorite story of his as a child, and it hurt to hear her bring up the fact that he wasn't acting as he should be. No one had been around him for many years that held him accountable for his actions. He had been doing this sort of thing with young girls for quite some time. Not one of the girls or any of his so-called friends had challenged him by bringing in the moral aspect of his actions. What was he going to do with this little ray of sunshine? She had touched a nerve, and he no longer wanted to harm her in any way. He knew he could complain to Darius, and he would take care of her. There wouldn't be any question as to the evil that Darius would bestow upon this little girl. He quickly pushed those thoughts away. He did not want to see this child harmed. He couldn't believe the thought process he was going through. He looked up at her and asked, "If we talk about Jonah for a while, will that be okay with you?"

"That would be great!" Skylan exclaimed. "Jonah must have been scared inside that whale. What do you think?"

They talked about Jonah until their two hours were up. The boat docked, and the blond-haired man walked her back to the car where Darius was waiting. As they approached the vehicle, the man felt the little girl stiffen and knew the fear she was probably feeling. "It'll be okay," he said. "Just you wait and see."

"Hi, we had a lot of fun," he told Darius. "Was wondering if we can do this again the day after tomorrow?"

Darius was glad to see the customer was so happy and replied, "Sure. You want to meet here again or somewhere else?"

"Here would great," he said. "I've sent the payment to you. I think I'd like a standing appointment every other day with this one. Can I have that kind of access? I'll send you a payment for one month."

Darius was shocked, "I guess, but don't you think you need to give her more rest than that?" he asked.

"Taking it slow with this one," the man said. "I know what I'm doing."

"Okay," Darius said. "I'll keep her for you if you're willing to pay the premium. See you the day after tomorrow."

Skylan got in the car and silently thanked God for protecting her and giving her the courage to speak about Jonah.

When they arrived back at the house, Sophie and Ruth were waiting for her. They were both thinking the worst and prepared to give her the comfort they knew she would need. Skylan came through the front door, smiled, and went to her room. Darius looked at Ruth and said, "She'll have this same customer for a month. He wants her every other day. Have her ready."

Ruth was shocked. Never had any customer wanted a girl for that often for that length of time. "Okay, I will," she said.

After he left, Sophie and Ruth went into the bedroom. Skylan was sitting on her bed with her head bowed and hands folded in prayer. When she said amen and looked up, she saw them standing there and asked, "What's for dinner? I'm hungry."

"Are you okay?" Sophie asked. "You aren't hurt? What did that man do to you?"

"Nothing," Skylan replied. "We talked about Jonah and the whale."

Ruth and Sophie could not believe what they were hearing. Ruth motioned for Sophie to go in the other room. Ruth then came over to the bed and sat beside Skylan.

"Are you sure the man didn't hurt you in any way?" she asked.

"No. He did touch my leg once, but then we started talking about Jonah and the whale. It was his favorite story when he was a kid. He said he learned about Jonah in Sunday school. He also said he believed in God. God took care of me today. He will take care of me always, Ruth."

Ruth hugged her and cried tears of joy. This little child had not been harmed. She had even managed to help this child molester remember his upbringing. It was a miracle for sure. She hoped that the day after tomorrow would bring more miracles.

"We're having meat loaf this evening," she said. "Let's go eat."

"Ruth?" Skylan asked. "Why did Darius say the man could call me Taylor? That's not my name."

"No one goes by their real names all the time," she said. "You'll get used to that. Just go along with whatever Darius tells you." Skylan nodded her head and then said, "I'm hungry. Can we eat now?"

CHAPTER 20

There were no phone calls from Detective Martinez that next morning. Rachel was getting worried she had messed up to the extent that the story was no longer going to be hers. She focused on writing more of the filler stories her editor had requested. Her mind was not into it, though. She kept thinking about Maggie.

The woman that was with Darius didn't look harmed in any way. If it were Maggie, why had she stayed? Was she being threatened? Or worse, was she in love with Darius? All these questions were racing through Rachel's mind. She hated to think that Maggie had fallen in love with Darius. She pushed that thought from her mind. There had to be a good reason she hadn't tried to escape. Maybe she was protecting some other younger girls. That seemed to be the most logical reason.

The morning passed excruciatingly slow. Finally, just after 1:00 p.m., Detective Martinez showed up at her door. His mood didn't seem any better than it was yesterday, so Rachel decided she better tread lightly.

"Hi," she said. "I'm glad to see you. I was hoping I hadn't messed anything up."

"I've smoothed over the whole incident," he said. "I need you to come down to the precinct and help me with another cold case."

"Sure, let me get my bag."

Once at the precinct, Detective Martinez pulled the Lily Ashita file from the ever-growing stack on his desk. He let out an exhausted sigh and said, "I think you'll find this case of particular interest. A fisherman discovered a suitcase containing a body while fishing some years ago. The body was never identified. All the medical examiner could determine was that it was a child."

Rachel looked down at her lap and then said, "Is it Asia? The girl I told you and that other detective about?"

"That's why I want you to take a look. I'm not sure of anything at this point, but since you were an eyewitness and an unwilling accomplice, I need to see if this is the girl Asia you spoke of."

The photos of the suitcase were eerily haunting. The hard-shell of the suitcase was somewhat tattered and torn. Cement had hardened around what appeared to be clothing. There was nothing visible of a body until the last photo. The cement had been chipped away, and the bones were lying on the examiner's table. They were small, delicate bones. The skull still had some hair attached with a prominent crush injury to the back of it.

Rachel covered her mouth with her hands and let out a low, mournful cry. It was as if her entire body was rebelling against the sights she had just taken in. There was no stopping the cry. It was the very thing Rachel never wanted to relive. Time stood still as she tried to compose herself. It was as if a movie were playing the whole awful murder over and over in her head.

She shut the case file and looked over at Detective Martinez. "It's Asia. It's sweet little Asia," she said. "I killed her. I am no better than Darius." She put her head in her hands and began to cry.

"I think under the circumstances, you won't be tried for murder. You acted under duress, and besides that, you were a minor who was being held against your will at the time," he said.

"That doesn't make me feel any better. Asia or Lily is still dead."

"I understand," he said. "I'll need to get DNA confirmation. I'll speak to her parents about that. I know they'll be relieved to know what finally happened to their daughter. Darius will have another murder charge with all the evidence and your testimony."

Rachel needed to change the subject, so she wiped her tears. She sat up straight with a determined look and asked, "Have you got any leads on the Skylan Winslip case? My editor has been hounding me to get another story submitted."

"Not yet. I'm going to go undercover in a few days to pose as a potential customer on a website that promotes young girls for prostitution. I'm hoping to gather some damning evidence. I need you to lie low for a while and not get into any trouble. I'll have a story for you, but you just need to be patient. It may take a few weeks before I know anything."

"All right," she said. "You know where to find me. Please keep me informed."

Heading back to her apartment, Rachel decided to stop off at the local market and pick up a few things. Her refrigerator was empty, and she was in no mood to eat out. She hoped that the evening would be calm. She needed to recharge. A good meal and a hot bath should do the trick.

Putting away her things and starting her meal, Rachel poured herself a glass of wine and sat down to contemplate the day. The phone rang. She answered, "Hello, Rachel Denton."

The silence that greeted her was eerie. Finally, a woman spoke. "Skylan is safe for now. Please hurry and find her. Sophie is here too. Please hurry. I love you."

Rachel's heart skipped a beat as she said, "Maggie? Is that you? Maggie?"

The line went dead.

CHAPTER 21

Ruth had found the phone in the cubby behind the Pop-Tarts. She couldn't believe Sophie had stolen another one. Ruth had taken a big chance in calling Rachel. The phone was on its last bar of battery, and she knew she had to try something. These girls were going to wind up dead, just like the others if she didn't do something to save them.

Sophie had been listening by the bedroom door as Ruth was on the phone. She came in and sat beside her and said, "Was that someone who can help us?"

"I hope so," Ruth said. "I'm not sure why or where this phone came from, but I'm going to use it to help us."

"Why didn't you tell them where we were?" she asked. "How are they supposed to find us if they don't know where we are?"

Ruth instantly knew she had made a mistake. Rachel didn't know where they were. How could she have been so stupid? "I'll let them know when I call next time," she said. "Don't you tell anyone I have a phone! Darius would kill me for sure."

"Your secret is safe with me," Sophie said. "I want out of here, so please call that person back."

"I will," Ruth said. "But first, I have to get dinner and then get Skylan ready for tomorrow's customer."

"Do you think Skylan's God is real?" Sophie asked. "I'm starting to think she might be an angel or something. Her first customer didn't hurt her. Everyone gets hurt by their first customer."

"Her beliefs are real, Sophie," Ruth said. "I believe there is a

God too. I pray every night that He will watch over us and keep us safe. Now, get Skylan and tell her to help with dinner. And let's not talk about any of this with Darius, okay?"

Sophie gave Ruth the thumbs-up sign as she walked to the bedroom door.

Ruth hid the phone in the wall behind the refrigerator. Mice had carved out a nice hiding place for the phone. She needed to call Rachel back, but she knew now was not the time. Darius could walk in any minute if he chose to eat dinner with them tonight.

Just as she was standing up from the hiding the phone, Darius came walking through the front door. Ruth quickly acted as if she had dropped a spoon that she had been holding.

"Hi, Darius," she said. "Are you joining us for dinner tonight?"

"Depends," he said. "What are you having? I brought you over some chicken the other day, so I was hoping you would be making that casserole I like."

"Not a problem," Ruth said. "Casserole, it is. The girls are in the bedroom. Do you want to speak to them?"

"Not yet," he said. "Maybe after we eat."

Sophie heard Darius come into the house. She tensed and went over to Skylan's bed. She climbed up and sat beside her and whispered, "Don't say a word about you talking to your customer about Jonah. Darius will blow a gasket. Do you understand?"

Skylan understood so she gave Sophie the thumbs-up. She didn't want to speak because she was afraid for Sophie. She didn't want Darius to hurt her again.

When dinner was ready, Ruth came in and told the girls to go to the table. Darius was sitting there, dishing out his portion as they sat down to eat.

"Nice to see you girls again," he said. "How was today?"

"Good," they both said at the same time. Each was given a plate and began to eat. Neither girl looked at him. After finishing their dinner, Sophie asked, "Can we be excused?"

Darius was just finishing his food as well when he looked at Sophie and said, "Taylor can go to her room, but I want you to stay and talk to me for a little while."

Sophie swallowed hard and gave Skylan a look that said, "Go to the bedroom." Skylan walked over to the bedroom and shut the door.

"Come here. Sit on my lap. I need to talk to you about this new look you have. Short, blond hair is not what your customers want. Why did you change it?" His voice had lowered to an angry growl.

Ruth interjected. "I changed it after Sophie got back the other day from her outing with you. She said you didn't want her to bring attention to you. I thought this would be a good idea even though whatever sketch you saw was not her. She never leaves my side unless she's with you or another customer."

"Did I ask you?" Darius sneered. "I was asking this little gal here that's sitting on my lap."

Sophie didn't want Ruth in trouble, so she said, "I told Ruth it would be best. My regular customer will be fine with it as long as I do what he wants. Plus, he told me last time I was with him that he was dreaming about a cute, short-haired blonde."

Darius ran his hand up Sophie's shirt and pinched her nipple hard. Sophie gritted her teeth so she wouldn't flinch. She wasn't going to give him the satisfaction of knowing that it hurt. Next, he raked his fingernails down her belly over the knife wounds, causing a couple to break open and bleed again. Sophie sat still. She knew it would end soon. She just needed to endure this one more time. Darius thrived on hurting others, and when he realized he wasn't getting the effect he wanted, it would stop.

"Get outta here, you little bitch," he said. "I've got better things to do."

Sophie got down off his lap and walked to the bedroom. Once

there, she broke down and cried into her pillow. Skylan rubbed her back until she fell asleep. Skylan knew things were getting worse, and something or someone better come soon to rescue them.

After Darius was done with Sophie, he turned his attention to Ruth. He went over behind her as she was doing the dishes and ran his hands down her back and over her buttocks.

"I think we need to go for a drive," he said. "I want a woman's touch tonight."

Ruth's insides curdled at the thought, but she knew it was the only way she would stay alive and be able to help these girls.

"Give me a minute," she said. "I'm almost done."

Ruth went to let the girls know she'd be gone. Both girls were asleep on Sophie's bed. *Just as well*, she thought. *They'll never know I'm gone.*

Darius drove over to the warehouse. Ruth wasn't sure why they were going there because they usually went to Darius's place. Once inside the warehouse, he turned to Ruth and said, "Take off your clothes."

Ruth knew this wasn't going to be like all the other times. She had overstepped her boundaries when she had interjected for Sophie. She stripped off her clothes and stood naked before the man she had named "The Evil One."

Darius proceeded to inflict the most heinous sex acts upon her. Some he had never done to her before. It was intense, and the pain was excruciating. Ruth could feel the blood dripping down her legs. He beat her upper torso, and her breasts were swollen and red. Before the torture ended, he told her if she ever interrupted him again, he would kill her.

Ruth cleaned up the best she could, and Darius returned her to the house. He acted as if nothing had happened. Ruth was confident the next time would be her last. She was on her way out in Darius's eyes. Just like Leslie, she would wind up buried in an empty lot. She had to get help, if not for her, for the girls.

Sitting in the dark with the phone in her hand, Ruth dialed Rachel's number again. The one bar was fading fast on the phone.

"Hello," Rachel answered. "Who is this?"

The line went dead. The battery had died. Ruth closed her eyes and knew she had waited too long. She got up and hid the phone back behind the refrigerator and prayed that somehow, someway, she could get another phone.

CHAPTER 22

Detective Martinez got the call that his profile was ready for the website "Forever Young." His supervisor had permitted him to pursue this avenue in hopes that they could rescue Skylan Winslip before the unthinkable happened.

The Internet Crime Unit had already reached out for Detective Martinez. His screen name was "Smooth Operator," and he would be pursuing a good time with a young, blond-haired Caucasian female. The longer the hair, the better. His request indicated he was a wealthy businessman who wanted to remain completely anonymous—no face-to-face contact with the delivery driver. The girl would be delivered to the Metropolitan Gentlemen's Club. The doorman would be expecting her.

There was no response for over a week. Detective Martinez felt like they had hit a dead end. No other leads were turning up anything, either. Finally, on Monday of the following week, there was a response to his request. It was from someone called "Tiger's Blood." He stated that he had a young girl with short, blond hair, and she was a pleaser! She would not disappoint, and the short, blond hair was not going to be distracting. She would oblige to anything Smooth Operator wanted. The price was $1,000 for two hours. Delivery and pickup included. The protocol for pickup or return of the girl would be coordinated via text. No face-to-face contact with the driver was a problem.

Detective Martinez instructed the detective on duty to respond with a date of Tuesday, June 4th, at 6:30 p.m.

Darius was excited about the possibility of this new client that had reached out to him. $1,000 for two hours was good money. Sophie would be the perfect first girl for this very influential customer. For this client to remain anonymous most definitely meant he was a man of great importance and status. Some of his clients were politically connected, and if the girl pleased him, then there would be more customers. These types of clients were always good for the money, and if they had friends, they would recommend the services. He would let Ruth know to have Sophie ready.

Detective Martinez knew the owner of the club and made the arrangements to set up the sting. Even if it weren't Skylan that walked through the door, it would be a girl they could save by getting her off the street and out of the clutches of whatever sicko was making her do these jobs.

He felt good that things were starting to look up. Maybe they were nearing the end, and this prostitution ring could be broken up for good. All he had to do was wait at the club and hope the meeting would take place.

Tuesday evening arrived, and he sat just inside the door at a small table near the wall. The meeting time came—and there was no girl. Thirty minutes passed, and finally, the doorman led in a girl who appeared to be around eleven years old. The girl had short, blond hair and carried herself with an air of maturity that the detective hadn't seen in such a young girl. He started to get up when the girl noticed him and started walking his way. He stood there as she came over and sat down at his table.

"Good evening, sir. My name is Sasha. I'm here for your pleasure," she said.

Detective Martinez felt awkward. Her blond hair looked freshly cut and colored. Her facial features were somewhat familiar, though. She wasn't Skylan, but she *was* someone's daughter.

He had to get her to open up about her real name and who she worked for, but how was that going to happen? He quickly regained his sense of character and proceeded.

"Are you hungry?" he asked. "I've ordered a small snack if that's okay?"

Sophie looked over at this man and said, "Sure, it's your dime, and I am a bit hungry."

"Good," he said. "My name is Joe. What's your name again?"

"Soph—sorry," she laughed a bit, "my name is Sasha."

He realized her mistake and quickly ascertained that this might be Sophia Lepaste, who had been abducted two years earlier.

Her face flushed a bit with her rookie mistake. She knew she better play this customer right, or it might be the end of her. The last time she had been with Darius, she thought he was going to kill her.

"Sorry," she said. "I'm a bit nervous. I've never been to this place."

"No problem," he said. "This is my first time doing this sort of thing too."

Sophie looked across the table at this man, and something in her gut told her he was not like any of the other customers she had been with. This man was gentle; he had a kind face and a friendly demeanor. Could it be this guy was a cop? She would play the game and see where this went. She knew Darius said she would only be with him for two hours.

"So, Joe," she said, "I'm experienced, and I can lead you through this."

Detective Martinez looked down and smiled a bit. She was playing the part well. He looked back up at her and said, "Let's discuss that after we eat our snack. Here it is now."

Small sandwiches were placed on the table in front of them, and she instantly grabbed one and began to eat. She realized her mistake immediately and put the sandwich on her plate and apologized. "I'm sorry," she said. "I guess I was hungrier than I thought."

"No problem," he said, "go ahead and enjoy them."

"Thanks," she said as she once again ate with gusto.

"I don't really like the name Sasha," he said. "Is there another name I could call you while you're here?"

Sophie slowly swallowed the bite she had in her mouth and looked over at this man. Was this the one man that would save her? She thought about it for a moment, then said, "I guess you could call me Sophie. That's what my mom called me."

"I like that name," he said with a smile. "Sophie it is! How old are you?"

"Eleven and a half," she replied. "Why are you asking? Am I too old for you?"

"Oh, I was just wondering," he answered. "No problem with how old you are. Can I ask you one more thing?"

"Sure," she said, "like I said, it's your dime. Besides, I'm done eating, so we can get on with it."

"My name is Detective Joe Martinez. I work with the New York City Police Department. Does your last name happen to be Lepaste?"

Sophie's eyes widened with excitement. She was going to be saved! But just as quickly as the excitement came, the light went out of her eyes, and she became almost sad.

"What's wrong?" he asked. "I thought you'd be glad to see someone like me."

"I am," she said. "But what's going to happen to Ruth and Skylan?" She realized she had slipped up big time. She sat up with determination and said, "You have to save them too. I can't be rescued and leave them there."

Detective Martinez had heard her right. She had mentioned a Skylan. It was an unusual name, so this was an enormous stroke of luck.

"Just tell me where they are, and I'll make sure they're safe," he said. He was excited that he had finally found little Sophia Lepaste. Her parents would be ecstatic. After so many girls that he had found deceased, this notification was going to be a pleasant experience, not one filled with sadness and sorrow.

"No," she said with determination. "I need to show Darius that I had a good customer tonight and act like nothing's wrong. If I don't, then they'll end up dead, and so will I."

Her determination and pleading eyes convinced him she was right, but he didn't want to let her leave and return with Darius. It was his duty to act on her behalf since she was a minor. His supervisor would rake him over the coals if he let her go back with Darius . . . Especially after he had established that she was being held against her will and actively being forced to have sex with customers. He had to think fast. He had to save not only Sophia but also Ruth and Skylan too.

He decided she would be allowed to return with Darius. He would have a couple of unmarked cars follow them, and then he'd have the address where the girls were being kept. He would get a warrant from the judge and be breaking down the door before the girls were asleep in their beds.

"Tell me more about Ruth and Skylan," he said. "Are they young girls like you?"

"Skylan is younger than me. Ruth is older. She's more like our mom or older big sister. She cooks for us and helps us with our outfits."

"What about Darius?" he asked. "Does he live with you and the others?"

"No," she said. "I don't know where he lives."

With that answer, Detective Martinez was questioning his decision to let her return with Darius. He knew this was the only way he could find out where the girls were being held. He had to take the chance. His supervisor would just have to understand.

"Okay," he said. "I'm going to let you go back when our time is up. I want you to act like you usually do after a customer so that Darius doesn't suspect anything. Can you do that?"

Sophie nodded her head. "I'm a good actress," she said.

Time passed quickly, and now, it was time for Sophie to leave. Detective Martinez was nervous, but he had called for extra manpower so they could track Sophie back to the house where she was being held.

"Just act normal," he said. "We'll be right behind you. I'm positive this will be your last job you'll have to do for Darius."

Sophie gave him the thumbs-up sign and walked to the door. She looked back one last time and then exited the building.

Darius was there waiting on her. She climbed into the backseat, put her seat belt on, looked up at Darius, and said, "He was okay. Nothing unusual. Said he would like to see me again if it was okay with you."

Darius turned back to start the car. He smiled to himself as he pulled away from the curb. This was going to be a good client. His luck just might be changing. Skylan had a regular, and now Sophie was proving her worth even more with this new, powerfully rich client.

Nine blocks from the club, he was still basking in the glory of making more money when he saw the light turn yellow. He punched the accelerator and hoped he could make it through without drawing any undue attention to himself. Just as he entered the intersection, a trash truck barreled through, T-boning the car and shoving it across a lane of traffic into a streetlight. The car wrapped around the pole and came to a crashing halt.

Sophie felt the crushing pain from the seat belt as the glass from the windows flew over and around her. All she saw was the grill from the truck before she was violently tossed into the light pole. Her world went dark as she lost consciousness.

CHAPTER 23

The detectives and officers following the pair were on the scene immediately. They phoned Detective Martinez and told him about the accident. The status was critical, with one fatality.

When Detective Martinez arrived on the scene, he saw the ambulance and paramedics working on someone. As he got closer, he saw that the critical victim was Sophie. His heart sank. His mind was numb. What was he going to tell her parents? He took a deep breath and went over to the mangled car. Inside was the deceased body of Darrin Potswell, aka Darius. He had died upon impact. Any further information on any other missing girls had died with the only one who could have shed some light on the matter. Detective Martinez was frustrated, but he wasn't going to give up.

He followed the ambulance to the hospital and waited while the doctors worked on Sophie. Detective Martinez called the precinct and told one of the team to go and notify Mr. and Mrs. Lepaste of the whereabouts of their daughter. He would meet with them at the hospital. When the doctor finally came through the waiting room door, he glanced around and spotted the detective.

"Evening," he said. "I'm Dr. Edward Steinbruck. Are you the father?"

"Detective Martinez, New York Police. How is she?"

"She's critical, I'm not going to lie. She's in a coma. She has a broken arm, broken pelvis, and a shoulder dislocation. She has severe bruising from the seat belt. Her head trauma is our main concern with brain swelling. We're monitoring her closely."

Detective Martinez nodded and took a deep breath. At least she was still alive. "Thanks, Doc, I'll escort the parents in when they arrive," he said.

"I do have some other concerns to discuss with you before the parents arrive," Dr. Steinbruck said. "Other injuries this girl has are consistent with child abuse and molestation. Her vaginal and rectal region are very damaged. She has slash marks on her stomach and back that are in the process of healing. The burns on her inner thighs are healed but look like they were made with a cigarette. This girl has been through hell, Detective. I sincerely hope it is not her parents who are responsible for this."

"All I can tell you right now is that they are not. This girl was abducted approximately two years ago by a child prostitution ring, and we just found her today," he said. "I would appreciate you not saying anything to anyone as the case is ongoing. There are a lot of missing girls out there, and I want to find as many as possible. Her testimony and knowledge about where she was held and information on her abductor is critical in pursuing the other missing girls. Is she going to pull through this?"

"It's going to take some time," the physician said. "We'll do our very best to help her heal."

"Thanks, Doc. We're all praying for her recovery."

Mr. and Mrs. Lepaste came running though the hospital doors holding each other's hand for support. You could see the worry and relief of finally finding their daughter. Detective Martinez led them to a private waiting room where they could talk.

"Have a seat, Mr. and Mrs. Lepaste. I need to fill you in on the accident and your daughter." He cleared his throat, and his eyes focused on theirs as he began. This was not going to be an easy task.

"Your daughter, Sophia, was abducted by what we believe is a child prostitution ring that has been operating here in New York

City. We also believe they have ties to other major cities within a certain radius as well. Your daughter met me this evening while I was posing as a wealthy customer. She was in good spirits when we talked. She confided in me that she had been staying with two other girls. One of the girls is Skylan Winslip, who was abducted recently from the subway. I'm sure you've read about it in the newspaper and seen reports on television."

Both parents sat with silent tears streaming down their cheeks. Each was lost in their own terrible thoughts as the detective was explaining where their daughter had been. Their imaginations were running rampant with horrible thoughts of what might have happened to their daughter over two years. Mrs. Lepaste's hands were shaking as she clasped them together, trying hard to stop the shake. She looked to be a strong woman, and Detective Martinez immediately could see where Sophia had gotten her strength.

"Can we see her?" Evelyn asked. "I need to see her." She turned to her husband, Ed, and said, "Tell him, Ed. We need to see our daughter."

"We will see her, Evelyn. Let's hear out the detective first, and then we'll see her."

"When you see your daughter, she will not look the same," Detective Martinez said. "She has short, blond hair now. Some of her injuries from the car accident include a broken arm, broken pelvis, a dislocated shoulder, and head trauma. She has severe bruising from the seat belt as well. She is currently listed as critical and is in a coma. She also has other injuries from her time in captivity. There are slash marks on her stomach and back that are healing. She also has severe trauma to her vaginal and rectal regions. These injuries are consistent with the molestation and abuse she endured while being held."

"Oh my God," Evelyn moaned. "My baby, my girl!" She held her head in her hands and began to sob. Ed wrapped his arms around his wife and closed his eyes. He let out a mournful cry as he buried his head in her shoulder. They both sobbed and hugged each other, trying to comfort each other while absorbing the awful information they had just been given.

Detective Martinez sat while the couple worked through the grief with the information he had just given them. He knew this was going to be hard, but he also knew the next few questions would be even harder . . . The inevitable question of why he didn't rescue her while he had her in the club. The department was going to pay for this one. He might even lose his job over this.

The Lepastes wiped away their tears, and Ed looked over at Detective Martinez and said, "Thank you. Can we see our daughter now?"

"I'll let the nurse on duty know," he said. "I also need to ask you not to talk to any media. We need to find these other two girls before it's too late. Sophia could be the key to getting this prostitution ring shut down for good."

"Not a problem," they said. "We just want to see her."

The nurse led them back to Sophia's room. He would visit her later. He had to get back to the precinct and formulate a plan to find Ruth and Skylan. He had no idea if there were others out there that would take Darius's place and move the operation or even go underground for a while. They had to move fast if they were going to save these other two girls.

His cell phone vibrated in his pocket. He looked at the number and instantly knew it was Rachel. Yes, she would want a story. Right now, that wasn't possible. He let it ring. He would contact her tomorrow.

CHAPTER 24

Rachel's editor had called and asked if she would go and cover a horrific car accident near Manhattan. Getting the address, she got a cab and had the driver get her as close to the scene as possible. After walking the last block and a half, she saw the scene. A trash truck had T-boned a car and then shoved it until it wrapped around a light pole. It was a terrible scene. The ambulance and firemen were working feverishly to get out whoever was in the backseat. A sheet covered the front windshield and driver's-side door, which told her that the driver was deceased. She elbowed her way through the crowd to see if she could get closer.

As she got near, she recognized some of the detectives from the precinct where Detective Martinez worked. She took a closer look at the car and realized it was Darius's car. She wrote down the tag number and then pulled up the photo she had taken at the warehouse. It was the same car! Was Darius driving? Was he the one who was deceased? Who were they getting out of the backseat? Was it Skylan? She had to know.

She took some photos of the scene and was quickly recognized by one of the detectives. He came over, grabbing her elbow and forcefully escorted her to the far perimeter of the scene. He told her that Detective Martinez would be over shortly.

She decided she would wait for him, especially after the warehouse incident. She wanted his continued trust. She wanted the story, and she would prove to him that she could play by the department's rules. He never came. They wrapped up the scene, and she went back to her apartment. She called, to no avail. He was not answering. She had to know who was driving that car. She didn't want anyone else to get the scoop on this story.

After several hours, she decided she would go down to the precinct to see if she could get any firsthand information. When she arrived, Detective Andrews greeted her and escorted her back to his office.

"Have a seat," he said. "I was told you'd probably show up here. We don't have anything for you to go to print with yet. You're going to have to be patient. Detective Martinez told me to let you know that Darius won't be a threat to you any longer."

"He was the driver of the car?" she asked. "Who was in the backseat? Was it Skylan?"

"I can tell you it wasn't Skylan," he said. "We're still actively looking for her."

"And the driver?" Rachel asked again.

"Can't officially tell you until the next of kin is notified," he said. "But I *can* tell you that Darius will not be a threat to you any longer."

Rachel knew by the comment that the driver had been Darius. She was relieved to know he wouldn't be hurting any more girls. She also knew that there were girls out there that didn't even know he was dead yet. They were still being held. How could she help in getting the word out, so they knew it was safe to go to the police?

All these thoughts were going through her mind when Detective Martinez stuck his head in the door of Detective Andrews's office. He was a little surprised to see her. She started to stand up, but he put up his hand and motioned for her to sit.

"Detective Andrews, could I have a word with you?" he asked. "I'll be brief."

Detective Andrews left the office, and Rachel sat back in the chair. She closed her eyes and said a prayer for all the girls out there who were being held against their will. She said a prayer for the girl who had been hurt in the accident. She prayed that Maggie would somehow find out about the accident and get in touch with her.

Both detectives came back into the office. Detective Andrews looked angry; Detective Martinez looked worried.

"What's going on, guys?" she asked. "What's wrong?"

"Tonight was my undercover assignment I told you about," Detective Martinez started. "I met a young girl at the Metropolitan Gentlemen's Club. The girl turned out to be Sophia Lepaste. You've written a couple of pieces on her disappearance. She was adamant that she return with Darius to the house so we could help to rescue two other girls. She wasn't going to have it any other way. I relented and let her leave with Darius. I was having her followed by three detectives when the accident occurred."

"So, that's why I saw those detectives at the scene," she said. "Was Sophia hurt badly?"

"She's in critical condition," Detective Martinez said. "I've informed her parents and spoken to them about keeping away from the media until we can try to rescue the others that Sophia told me about."

"How can I help?" Rachel quickly asked. "I can do whatever you need me to do. Did she say who the other girls were?"

"She said their names were Ruth and Skylan. She mentioned that Ruth was like an older sister or mother to her and Skylan."

Rachel's heart skipped a beat! She couldn't believe the fact that Skylan was going to be found. "That's wonderful news for Skylan and her family," she said. "Do we know who this Ruth is?"

"Not at the moment," he said. "Plus, there's the problem of not knowing where they are. Sophia is the only one who can tell us, and she's in a coma. I've notified Skylan's parents, and they're anxiously awaiting any developments. I'm trying to find any missing girls named Ruth from ten years ago or so. It's a lot to comb through, so I need you to be patient and hold off on any story until I say."

Rachel was not happy about the complexities of this case, but she understood that there were lives at stake. One of those lives could be her sister's. Just like lightning, a thought raced into her thoughts. She sat straight up and said, "Maggie's middle name is Ruth!"

Detective Martinez glanced at her and raced over to his office to grab the file on her and Maggie. Sure enough, Maggie's middle name was Ruth. Could it be? It was too soon to say. Things were looking up, though. If he could find Ruth and Skylan, then they might be able to give him additional information on other girls being held.

"It's a possibility," he said as he looked at Rachel. "I'll still need to check the other missing persons' reports, though. Keep praying. We're sure to find them."

Rachel knew she had to do something, but what that something was she didn't know. She walked out of the precinct and hailed a cab. She decided she would have the driver take her down to the warehouse where all the clothing had been found. There had to be a clue there somewhere.

Getting out of the cab, she saw the door was slightly ajar. She walked up carefully, listening to see if anyone was actually in the building. Not hearing anything, she entered the dusty warehouse and made her way up the stairs to where the clothing was. Everything was quiet except for the wind whistling through the decrepit windowsills. It was an eerie sound that blended with the scene before her.

Endless racks of clothing hung, from dresses to jeans to fancy shirts made for children that mimicked adult styles. It was sickening. She browsed through the clothing admiring some but mostly just turning up her nose, thinking about the young girls who were forced to wear these outfits. She had been one of those girls. She had been forced to do things that shouldn't have been allowed. It disgusted her to think that after all these years, this type of business could still be going on. Where was people's decency? Had the entire world lost its moral code?

She was looking through the little coats when one caught her eye. It was a puffy purple coat with little pockets on the outside. Sticking out of the pocket, a small piece of paper caught her attention. She quickly took the paper out to see what it might be. As she unfolded it, she heard a sound behind her. Before she could turn around, she felt a smashing blow to the back of her head. She lost consciousness and crumpled to the floor.

She awoke with an extreme headache in a small, dark room that still smelled like the warehouse. She couldn't see anything, and her vision was blurry. She moaned and moved, only to find her feet had been taped or tied. Her hands were still free, so she reached to untie her feet when she felt the hand. She froze. Someone was there. The hand reached out again, and this time brushed Rachel's hair away from her eyes. Rachel could make out the outline of a female, maybe in her twenties.

"Hi, I'm Rachel. What's your name?"

"My name doesn't matter," she said. "Why are you here? Are you one of the house monitors? I haven't seen you around or heard about you."

Suddenly, the young woman gasped. "Did something happen to Ruth? She meets me here sometimes to talk. I haven't seen her in quite some time."

Rachel rubbed her head and said, "I am not sure who Ruth is, but I'm Rachel Denton. I work as a journalist with a newspaper. I'm investigating a child prostitution ring. I thought this place might be connected somehow."

The young woman glanced around as if expecting someone to come through the door at any moment. She was afraid, Rachel could tell, but who or what was she afraid of?

"Can you tell me why you're here?" she asked.

"We can't talk now—Mr. Kyle will be here soon to pick me up. I need to get my things."

"Wait!" Rachel said. "At least tell me your name."

"Stephanie," the young woman said. "Stay here until we're gone. I won't tell Mr. Kyle you're here. So, stay still and stay quiet. Do you understand?"

"I do," Rachel said. "Don't worry. Can we meet here again in a couple of days? Same time?"

"I'll see what I can do," Stephanie said. "No promises."

Rachel waited until they were gone. She did manage to see them exit the building through a dusty windowpane from the room where she had been dragged after being hit in the head. Stephanie was a young white female with an athletic build and long, brown hair. She had it tied back in a ponytail. She was wearing blue jeans and a white shirt. Mr. Kyle was a large, older man approximately fifty years old. He had thinning, grey hair and was dressed in blue jeans and a tan T-shirt. He looked to be in great shape, like he worked out every day. It occurred to Rachel if someone were to see these two together on the street, they would think they were a couple. Older man with a younger female. Classic midlife affair. The car they were driving was a small sedan with tinted windows. She couldn't make out the tag number, though.

Rachel dusted herself off and left the warehouse. The paper she had retrieved from the little coat was all but forgotten. She was on her way to the precinct to let Detective Martinez know what had just happened. He would not be happy with her, but he couldn't deny the fact that what occurred was relevant to the case. Rachel only wished she would have gotten a little more information from Stephanie.

As Rachel exited the cab at the precinct, she reached up to smooth out her hair. Her hand felt the stickiness of the blood that had oozed out of the cut on her head. She quickly dismissed it and went into the precinct.

"I need to speak with Detective Martinez," she told the officer behind the counter. "I need to speak to him now!"

"One moment," he said. "I'll see if he's in. Did you know you're bleeding?" He got up to come around to see to her wound.

"I'm fine," she said. "Is he in or not?" She was frustrated, and she sure didn't want some rookie officer fawning over her and her head wound.

"He's here. One moment."

Detective Martinez came out and escorted her back to his office. "What happened to you?" he asked.

"I was conked on the back of the head," she said sarcastically. "I was in the warehouse trying to find anything of value when I got coldcocked by some young woman named Stephanie. She was there to get some things with a man named Mr. Kyle. She said she would try to meet me there in a couple of days to talk some more."

"Wait a minute," he said. "What did you think you were going to accomplish? Do you want to end up dead?" He was furious with her. She was so damn independent and forward-thinking. She was on the right path, but she was going about it all wrong . . . or so he thought.

"I need a cup of coffee," he said. "Do you want anything? Maybe a cold compress for that head of yours?"

"That would be nice," she said with a smile. "Thanks."

After giving the descriptions to the detective and answering his questions about what she had found, she reached into her pocket to get a pen out. She wanted to ask him some questions as well, so she could get another piece to her editor. Inside her pocket was the piece of paper she had found at the warehouse. She took it out and unfolded it. All that was written on the paper was an address . . . 4298 Seventy-seventh Street, Brooklyn.

"Here's the paper I told you I found!" she exclaimed. "Stephanie must have put it in my pocket after she hid me in that little room."

"We'll check it out," he said. "Now, can I get you to go home and stay there for a while? I need to do some things before I can brief you on the Sophia Lepaste case. It seems we are all getting tied up in a much-bigger case than any of us could have imagined."

Rachel knew she was in no position to push it with her questions. She decided tomorrow would be a better day for that. She would complete her piece on the accident and get it turned in to her editor. He would have to be happy with it. She would fill him in on the progress and explain to him that while everything was pending, her story would have to be pending as well.

CHAPTER 25

Ruth was getting worried. Sophie and Darius should have been back hours ago. She had no way of getting ahold of Darius, so all she could do was wait. Skylan came out of the bedroom and asked, "What's for dinner?" Ruth had been so worried about Sophie and her return that she hadn't even thought about dinner.

"I don't know. There might be enough milk for some cereal," she said. Skylan bounced off toward the cabinet where the cereal was kept. "There's only enough for one person," Skylan reported. "Do you want to split it?" Ruth sat on the sofa and bowed her head and said a silent prayer. "Ruth, did you hear me?" Skylan asked.

"You can have it. I'm not hungry," Ruth lied. What were they going to do? Darius was supposed to bring her some more groceries after he returned Sophie. It was getting late. Had something happened?

After Skylan ate her dinner, Ruth put her to bed and listened to her as she said her prayers. When Skylan fell asleep, Ruth decided to take a chance and go for a walk. She knew Darius strictly forbade this, but she needed some fresh air and time to think.

Once outside, the cool night air was refreshing. She could hear the sirens in the distance. She wished she could talk to Rachel just one more time. She had never gotten to say goodbye to her and had always felt bad for leaving her. As Ruth walked, she began to pray. She hadn't prayed so fervently before. She prayed for the safety of Sophie. She prayed that somehow, she and the girls could be rescued. She wondered if God even listened to her anymore. It seemed that she had been forgotten, and her final fate would be in the hands of Darius.

After walking a few blocks, she decided to turn back and head back to Skylan. As she passed a small convenience store, she noticed the news was on. She stepped inside and listened. The reporter was saying something about a horrific car accident. As she watched the screen, she noticed the car in the story was one like Darius drove. Her heart started racing as the reporter said that the driver had been killed upon impact, and the child passenger was in critical condition at a local hospital.

She left the store in a state of shock. She had no definitive evidence it was Darius and Sophie that had been involved in the car accident, but her heart knew it was them. What was going to happen to her and Skylan now? Darius had always talked about his second in command but had never given her a name. She didn't like surprises. Maybe Stephanie could help her figure out who would be taking Darius's place. She prayed it wasn't Mr. Kyle. Stephanie had told her horrendous things about him. If anyone could be worse than Darius, it was Mr. Kyle.

Once back in the house, Ruth went in to check on Skylan. She was sleeping peacefully. She lay down next to Skylan and drifted off to sleep. She would address everything in the morning. Skylan's appointment with the new client was tomorrow, so they had to be ready, just in case someone showed up to get her.

Rachel awoke the next morning to the news that a second fatality was credited to the car accident that happened yesterday. The unnamed child passenger had succumbed to her injuries during the night. Rachel held back the tears. Sophia Lepaste was dead. She had never gotten to say goodbye to her parents. Her parents had never gotten to say goodbye to their daughter. The news was heartbreaking. She quickly dressed and caught a cab to the precinct. Had Sophia regained consciousness before passing? If so, had she revealed anything about the address where Ruth and Skylan could be found? She had to know.

Once inside the precinct, she was escorted back to Detective Martinez's office. She was left to wait on him as he was with someone else at the moment. She bowed her head and said a prayer for Sophia's parents, Detective Martinez, and all the other girls that were still out there. This madness had to stop. She was determined she would do her part.

Detective Martinez came in after about thirty minutes. "Good morning," he said. "I've been expecting you. I guess you heard the news. Sophia didn't make it."

"I heard it on the TV this morning," she said. "I'm sorry. Did she ever regain consciousness?"

"No, she passed quietly. She's at peace now." His voice cracked as he spoke.

Rachel knew this was not the end. She knew there would be other leads. "We will still find Skylan," she said. "I know we will."

Detective Martinez nodded and then said, "I know we will too. Now, let's get to work on setting you up to talk to this Stephanie. You said she would meet with you again. Is that right?"

"It is! She said in a day or two."

"Okay, so here's the plan. I'm going to send you down to get wired. You'll have a tail, and they'll be there for backup, if needed. I want you to talk to her and get as much information as you can. I need to know her handler's name, where they stay, and what areas they work. Is that clear? I don't want you meeting with anyone but her!"

Rachel knew this was her chance. She was going to be able to get firsthand information and help the girls who were left out there. "Yes, sir! I understand completely. You will not be disappointed," she said.

After getting wired, Rachel was sent down to an empty office where she could formulate her questions for Stephanie. The first try at meeting with Stephanie would be tomorrow afternoon. Rachel wrote down her questions and went over them with Detective Martinez when he came to check on her. He seemed satisfied with her line of questions and sent her home for the evening.

Rachel left the precinct and went home. She had a hard time focusing on her story to be turned in on the car accident. Her editor wanted details but understood that the details would be sketchy as this was an ongoing investigation. Rachel was able to use Sophia's name, but the reason she was in the car was not to be released. Darius's name had not yet been released, citing next of kin had yet to be notified.

CHAPTER 26

Skylan woke up to find Ruth asleep beside her. She stretched and then placed her hand on Ruth's arm. She shook her slightly and said, "Wake up, Ruth. It's morning!"

Ruth opened her eyes and squinted at this little angel she had been put in charge of. "Good morning, Skylan."

"What's for breakfast? I'm hungry," Skylan said.

Ruth made a face and said, "You ate the cereal last night. I don't think I have anything in the house."

Skylan smiled and said, "I've got some money. Do you want it?"

Ruth sat up, looking bewildered and asked, "Where did you get the money?"

"Sophie has it. She said to use it in case of emergencies," Skylan replied. She climbed out of bed and went to the closet. She pulled back the corner of the carpet and gathered up the ten dollars and some change.

"Here," she said. "You can go buy us something for breakfast."

Ruth couldn't believe her eyes. Little Sophie was a smart cookie. She prayed she was doing okay in the hospital. "Okay," Ruth said. "I'll go down to the little store and get a couple of things. Be right back."

Ruth stepped into the convenience store and selected a box of cereal and a half gallon of milk. The television behind the cashier was turned down, but she could see the car accident scene from yesterday's news. "Can you turn that up?" she asked.

The clerk obliged, and Ruth heard the news. The child passenger had succumbed to her injuries and passed during the night. This was now considered a double fatality car accident. She almost dropped her purchases. The shock was overwhelming. The clerk noticed her distress and quickly asked, "Miss, are you okay?"

Ruth recovered and said, "Yes, I'm okay. I just don't like hearing about children passing."

The clerk looked at her and said, "Yeah, me neither. Very tragic."

Ruth paid for her things and quickly walked back to the house. She was going to have to tell Skylan the news. It was not going to be easy for her or Skylan, but they would figure this out together.

Skylan was sitting on the sofa when Ruth came in. She looked up and smiled when she saw the cereal. It was the one thing that reminded her of home—eating cereal for breakfast.

After Skylan had poured her cereal and milk, Ruth sat down beside her. "I have some bad news for you, Skylan."

Skylan looked up and said, "What bad news?"

Ruth held back the tears that were threatening to spill down her cheeks and said, "Sophie has been in a car accident. Neither she nor Darius survived. They both are dead."

Skylan looked down at her cereal and then said, "I'm going to miss her, but she's with Jesus now." Her mature response took Ruth by surprise. She had expected her to break down in tears and be inconsolable. Ruth smiled and said, "Yes, she sure is."

Skylan continued to eat her cereal in silence for a bit; then she looked over at Ruth and said, "Mr. Darius is not with Jesus. He was a bad man."

Ruth sat back in her chair and said, "I think you're right, Skylan. He was a very bad man."

Ruth knew that this was probably going to be the easiest part of the day. She still had to get Skylan ready for her appointment. The man she was meeting wanted her dressed in an animal print of some kind. This client that Darius had acquired for Skylan was an unusual one, to say the least. Without Darius to take her to the warehouse, Ruth had to get creative.

"I'm going to go and get your outfit ready for your client today," Ruth said. "Finish up your breakfast, and then you can help me."

Skylan came into the bedroom and watched as Ruth went through the clothes. Finally, she asked, "If Darius is dead, then why do I have to go see a client today?"

Ruth stopped going through the clothes and looked at her. She was so innocent and yet so smart. "We have to be ready in case Darius's second in command comes to get you. I'm not sure who it will be, but we have to be ready," Ruth stated.

Skylan let out a sigh and said, "Okay, so what do I need to wear?"

"Your client wants an animal print. I'm not sure why, but I have to do what the client wants," Ruth said.

"Sophie has a leopard print shirt. I can pair that with a black skirt." Ruth said, "I think Sophie even had a leopard print bow for her hair."

Skylan shrugged her shoulders. "Sounds good to me, I guess."

After getting dressed, the two of them waited on the sofa for what seemed like an eternity. Skylan was quiet and subdued. She was thinking about who this client was. She was hoping it was the man on the boat. She could talk to him, and he wouldn't hurt her. Ruth was looking through her magazine that was two years old. They both jumped when they heard the knock at the door.

Ruth got up to answer it and said, "Who is it?'"

"Darius sent me," the voice replied. "I'm your driver today."

Ruth opened the door to see Mr. Kyle standing there. Her heart sank. She most definitely did not want to send Skylan with this monster. She knew she had no choice, though, so she said, "She's ready."

Mr. Kyle looked at Skylan and smiled. "I'm sure she is. Can't wait for the client to see her; she looks divine."

Skylan hated it when people talked like she wasn't in the room. She wanted to say something but thought she better be on her best behavior. She quietly walked to the car and got in the backseat.

Mr. Kyle turned toward Ruth and said, "I guess I'm your new handler. Seems Darius went and got himself killed. Little girl he was transporting was killed too, just so you know. Here's twenty-five dollars. Go and buy you and the girl some groceries. I'll take you two to the warehouse in a couple of days."

Ruth nodded and said, "Thank you."

Mr. Kyle got in the car and drove Skylan to the marina, where Darius had dropped her off two days ago. Skylan knew this client. She knew he wouldn't hurt her. As they pulled up, the blond-haired man was waiting on them. He opened Skylan's door and smiled down at her. "I'm so glad you were able to wear the animal print. My favorite!"

Skylan got out of the car and held the blond man's hand. Mr. Kyle said, "I'll see you in a couple of hours."

Skylan looked up at the man holding her hand and asked, "What's your name?"

The man looked down and said, "How about I tell you that when we get on my boat? I'm in a bit of a hurry to get underway today."

Skylan felt uneasy but knew God was walking beside her as well. He wouldn't let anything bad happen. She trusted Him.

As they boarded the boat, the driver smiled at Skylan. His smile was not a nice smile, and Skylan knew this man was not nice.

Once down inside the cabin, the blond-haired man sat down on the bed. He was wearing shorts and a T-shirt with sandals. Skylan could see a scar that ran down the man's lower leg. She wondered what had happened to him.

"Come here and sit on my lap, Taylor," he said. "I want to talk to you."

Skylan went over, and the man hoisted her up on his lap. Her black skirt was short, and when she sat on his lap, she felt very uneasy. She sat still, though, and pretended to be interested in what he wanted to talk about. He placed his hand on her thigh and said he wanted to play a little game. Skylan tensed and said, "What kind of game?"

"I'll touch you, and then you touch me," he said. "I'll touch you on the lower leg, and then you touch me on the lower leg."

Skylan slid off his lap onto the bed. "Okay," she said, "I'm ready."

He reached out to touch her when she said, "Wait, you didn't tell me your name."

"My name is Jeff," he said. He then touched her lower leg down by her ankle. "Your turn," he said.

Skylan touched his ankle. She saw the scar again and asked. "How did you hurt your leg?"

Jeff looked confused and then remembered the scar. "I cut my leg while I was working," he said. Then he reached out, and his fingers brushed over her lips.

Skylan looked at him and froze. She didn't want to touch his lips. Then an idea came to her. "Did you know that God shut the mouths of the lions so they wouldn't eat Daniel?"

Jeff smiled and said, "I wondered how long it would take you to start a conversation about a Bible story."

"Well, did you know that?" Skylan asked. "I don't know the whole story, but I do remember that Daniel was thrown in a lions' den, and the lions didn't eat him because God shut their mouths."

"That's right, God did shut the lions' mouths. I like your leopard shirt and hair bow," he said.

"Thanks," she replied. "Why do you like this game of touching?"

He looked at her and seemed to be confused. He didn't know how to answer her. She was so young and so innocent, and he wanted her more than anything. It was strange how, when he was in her presence, the urges weren't as strong, and he was able to restrain himself. She was always talking about Bible stories, and that reminded him of his childhood. Sunday school was a safe place for him. He didn't have to worry about his older brother bothering him then. His older brother, Brent, was six years older than he and had tortured him. Brent had forced him to perform oral sex beginning when he was eight years old. He raped him at the age of ten. He had hated his older brother. Now, sitting here talking to this little angel, he started to hate himself. He was forcing this girl to do things she didn't want to do. "I shouldn't like this game," he said. "Let's do something else."

Skylan knew she had successfully diverted the awfulness and thanked God for helping her. "What do you want to do now?" she asked.

"Let's go up on deck and watch the waves. Maybe we can talk about another story."

"Okay," Skylan said. "I really don't know that many stories."

Once they both got up on deck, they sat in the chairs and watched the waves break as the boat skimmed across the water. Skylan looked over at Jeff and asked, "What stories do you know?"

"I always liked the story about Noah," he replied. "Do you know that one?"

Skylan nodded and said, "I sure do! Noah built the ark and gathered up the animals two by two."

Jeff smiled. "That's right. Do you know why he told Noah to build the ark?"

"I don't remember," Skylan said. "I know there was a flood."

Jeff looked out across the water and seemed lost in thought. He said, "Yeah, the world was getting wicked, and they wouldn't change their ways, so God told Noah to build the ark and save the animals and his family. God was going to make it rain for forty days and forty nights. That's what I remember anyway."

Skylan sat in thought for a moment. She looked up at the sky and imagined what it would be like to have it rain for forty days and forty nights. "I wonder if God thinks the world is getting wicked again."

She watched as the man she knew as Jeff looked out over the water. She didn't know if he had heard her or not. Something told her just to be still, so she went back to watching the water.

Jeff knew this would be the last time he would see this little angel of God. He was convicted and knew he needed to straighten out his life. Funny how talking to a little girl can change your perspective on life. It was as if God were speaking to him directly. Who was he fooling? God *was* speaking to him directly! Two hours was almost up, so Jeff motioned for his driver to turn the boat toward the dock. Suddenly, a thought occurred to him. Could he save this little girl? He turned toward Skylan and asked, "What's your real name?"

Skylan was surprised. "My name is Skylan Marie Winslip."

"Nice to meet you, Skylan," he said. "I'm going to try to help you get back to your mom and dad. You need to be a good girl and not say anything to your driver. Just act like we had a normal day, and you'll be back to see me day after tomorrow. I'll act like normal too. We have a deal?"

Skylan was excited and knew she would need to act normal with her driver. Mr. Kyle looked mean, and she didn't want to make him mad. "Okay," she said.

As soon as the boat docked, Jeff escorted her to Mr. Kyle's car. Skylan acted normal and didn't say a word. Jeff looked at Mr. Kyle and said, "We had a great time! I want to see her day after tomorrow. Same time, same place. This time, I want her wearing a cowgirl outfit."

"Will do," Mr. Kyle said. "I'll have her here."

Jeff looked at Skylan and winked. Skylan wanted to smile, but she knew that was inappropriate. She bowed her head and said a silent prayer of thanks. She was going to see her mom and dad again!

Mr. Kyle dropped her off at the house and instructed her to have her cowgirl outfit on the day after tomorrow. Skylan nodded and said, "I'll be ready."

Ruth met her at the door with a worried look. "Are you okay?" she asked.

"I'm fine," Skylan said. "We talked about Daniel and the lions' den for a while, and then we talked about Noah."

Ruth looked confused. "He didn't do anything to you?"

"He touched my leg and my lips, and then we started talking about the Bible stories. He said he is going to help me see my mom and dad again."

Ruth was shocked. "How is he going to do that?"

"I don't know, but I know he is," Skylan said. "He said to come the day after tomorrow dressed in my cowgirl outfit."

Could this be the answer to prayer that Ruth had been praying? She would need to prep Skylan to be prepared for the worst, however. This man was probably just saying that to get her to do the things he wanted. Ruth thought she would also sew the address to the house into the cowgirl outfit on the off chance this guy was actually telling the truth. She wanted to be rescued too! She would sew the address into the underside of Skylan's skirt. The police would surely find it, and she would be saved as well.

CHAPTER 27

Rachel finished getting ready so she could meet with Stephanie at the warehouse. She was nervous, but she knew what questions she would be asking. As she left the apartment and hopped into the cab, her resolve was stoic. She was going to get the answers she wanted. She was going to help stop this prostitution ring.

The cab pulled up to the warehouse. Rachel got out and stood for a moment and found her backup. They would be listening and recording every word. The door to the warehouse was partially open when she approached. She listened at the door for any movement inside. She hoped Stephanie was already there.

Climbing the steps to the second floor, Rachel caught movement near one of the clothing racks. She stopped and called out softly, "Stephanie, is that you?" No response. She waited on the steps for a few more moments, and then a dove flew up from the floor by the clothing rack. The sudden motion startled her, and she froze.

After calming herself, she decided that there was no one else in the warehouse. She calmly walked over to the little room where Stephanie had dragged her the other day. The windows were covered in dust, and the room was dark. She stopped in the doorway and heard a sound. She waited. Suddenly, a muffled voice said, "Come in quick; hurry. I don't have much time."

It was Stephanie. Rachel recognized her the moment her eyes adjusted to the darkened room.

"Take this address," Stephanie said. "There are other girls there. I'm not supposed to be here. I'm supposed to be with them. Please help."

"Definitely," Rachel said. "Can I ask you who your handler is?"

Stephanie looked scared. "Mr. Kyle is the only name I know. That's it. I have to go."

Stephanie climbed out of the half-open window and went down the rickety fire escape that was still semiattached to the building. Rachel watched her go and gripped the paper that she had given her. All it contained was an address where girls were being held.

Rachel quickly exited the building and caught a cab to the precinct. Her backup followed as well. Detective Martinez would be very interested in this address.

The detective had been notified by the officers that had been listening in that Rachel was on her way. He met her at the door and ushered her back to his office. She gave him the paper and the information about Mr. Kyle. It wasn't much, but it was a start.

He looked at the address and said, "This is good. We'll get some units on this right away. I'll let you know what they find. I'm hoping Skylan will be one of the girls she mentioned."

"I hope so too," Rachel said. "Is there any way I can go with you to the house?"

"Sorry, Rachel, not allowed. I'll let you know what we find. You'll get the story, don't worry."

Rachel was disappointed but knew he was right. Not the time to go against regulations. She wanted the exclusive, and this was the only way she was going to get it.

A team was quickly assembled, and Detective Martinez went to the address that Stephanie had given them. He decided to approach the house in street clothes and pretend to be lost. When someone answered the door, then he would give a signal to the team to move in if this truly was a location that was housing child prostitutes. He hoped that he would recognize Skylan and be able to give the signal immediately.

Upon approaching the house, it looked quiet. He wondered if anyone was home. He knocked on the door. No response. He knocked again. He heard a shuffling noise within the home. Then a tall, slender girl in her twenties answered the door. "Can I help you?" she asked.

"Yes, thank you," Detective Martinez said. "I'm afraid I'm a little lost. I'm looking for the Williamsburg Bridge. Can you give me directions?"

"I'm not supposed to talk to anyone I don't know," she responded as she began closing the door.

"Wait, please," the detective said. "I'm new to town, and I'm truly lost. This house looked so inviting I thought someone nice surely lived here. Please help me." At that moment, he noticed a young girl walk past. "Hi, there," he said. "I like your T-shirt." The young girl stopped and looked at the detective, then bolted out of sight. "Is that your daughter?" he asked the young lady.

"No," she said quickly. "I'm her cousin. She's from out of town."

"My name is Joe Martinez," he said. "What's your name?"

"Steph—oh, I'm sorry," she said. "My name is Stormy."

She had almost said Stephanie, and Detective Martinez gave the signal. This was the house. His team rushed the back door and front door at the same time. Three girls were in the house. Stephanie, the housemother of sorts, and two twelve-year-old girls. All were very scared and wanted to leave immediately after realizing these men and women were the police. They didn't want to be there when Mr. Kyle came back.

The girls were taken back to the precinct, where they were all interviewed, each giving their real names and cities from which they were abducted. Stephanie had been abducted fifteen years ago at the age of nine from a small town just south of Washington,

D.C. One twelve-year-old was kidnapped four years ago at the age of eight from Hershey, Pennsylvania. The other twelve-year-old was snatched three years ago at the age of nine from Pittsburgh, Pennsylvania. All three were taken to the hospital to get checked out while their families were notified.

Detective Martinez called Rachel and told her they had rescued three females at the address she had obtained. Stephanie was one of the ones freed. Rachel was excited and started firing off questions. "Did they say where more girls were located?" she asked. "Have they seen or heard of Skylan? Have—"

"I'm going to stop you right there, Rachel," he said. "We're still in the preliminary stages. I just wanted you to know that three females had been recovered. I'll get the particulars as we go on. I'll keep you informed. If you want to break the story, write a generalized blurb, and I'll see if Detective Andrews will give it the green light."

"Will do," she said. "It will be a perfect breaking news story!"

Rachel set to work writing the news article. She knew her editor would be beyond ecstatic if he could see some progress being made by the police department in shutting down this prostitution ring. She had to be vigilant not to let too much be included in the piece because she did not want to jeopardize Skylan's life or Maggie's—if they were still alive.

Rachel's story was complete with praise for the New York City Police Department in their discovery of a child prostitution house. No names were included, but the article went on to say that this was still an active investigation and more abducted girls were expected to be found.

She handed her story over to Detective Martinez and crossed her fingers. Detective Andrews was a tough cookie, and she hoped her praise for the department would give her an edge on the story. She waited for approximately thirty minutes when the administrative assistant for Detective Andrews came through the door. "Miss Denton," she said, "I'm sorry, but Detective Andrews had to step out for a call. He said for you to come back in the morning, and he would have an answer for you."

Rachel was disappointed and frustrated. She had hoped to be emailing her piece to her editor within the hour. Now, she would have to disappoint her editor once again. "Is Detective Martinez coming back?" she asked.

"No, I'm afraid not," she replied. "He went with Detective Andrews."

Rachel knew she was at a dead end, so she gathered her things and went back to her apartment. Tomorrow would be another day, and hopefully, she would get the green light on her story.

CHAPTER 28

The call had come in from a man claiming to know where Skylan Marie Winslip was being held. Both detectives raced to get the information. This was a lead they couldn't let slip through their fingers. The caller had given Skylan's full name. He claimed to know things that hadn't been released yet to the press. This had to be the one lead that would bring Skylan home.

The man claimed that Skylan would be at the marina around 2:00 p.m. the next day. She would be wearing a cowgirl outfit. If the police wanted to rescue her before something terrible happened to her, then they would need to come in unmarked cars and plainclothes.

Neither detective slept that night. Both were excited and hopeful about snagging this man and rescue Skylan. Skylan's parents were not notified and wouldn't be until a positive identification could be ascertained. They would get the call then, and, hopefully, be meeting their daughter back at the precinct for a happy reunion.

Electricity was in the air the next morning. Both detectives gathered their teams and began to make preparations for the 2:00 p.m. meet at the marina. Each team wore plainclothes. They would look like they belonged at the marina. No one would know they were police.

All the teams were in place by noon. All they had to do now was wait.

Skylan was finishing up her lunch as Ruth fervently sewed the address into Skylan's skirt. She wouldn't tell Skylan because she didn't want Mr. Kyle to find out. It would be disastrous if he knew. Skylan came into the bedroom and saw Ruth sewing on the skirt. "What are you doing?" she asked. "Did I tear the skirt last time I wore it?"

"Just a little," Ruth lied. "I wanted to fix it so you would look nice for your customer."

Skylan looked at Ruth and smiled. "You're so nice. I know God is going to save us."

"I believe you just might be right," Ruth said. "Now, here, let's get you dressed."

The outfit was cute. Skylan's short red hair and the black cowgirl vest were quite striking. Skylan looked like a minimodel. Ruth fought back the tears as she twirled Skylan around. She prayed that this man who claimed to be the one that was going to save Skylan was actually telling the truth. She hoped this was not the day that Skylan would find out how evil and mean some customers could be. It would break her heart to have Skylan come back with the telltale signs of being raped by some savage man that was three times her size. *Please, God*, she silently pleaded, *protect this child*.

Mr. Kyle knocked on the door, and both girls jumped. Each had been praying silently, and the sudden knock had startled them back into the cruel reality in which they were living. "Now be a good girl and no surprises," Ruth said. "Just act like it's a regular day and a regular customer."

Skylan pressed her lips together in a little half smile. Her eyes showed the fear she was feeling, but she held her head high and finally said, "I will."

Mr. Kyle was pleased to see that Skylan was ready. He smiled at her and said, "You look very cute today. I hope your customer is pleased." Skylan felt her skin crawl with the syrupy tone in his voice.

She remembered what Sophie had told her about the things that these men had made her do. She didn't want that to happen today or any day too soon. She silently prayed for God's help.

The ride over to the marina took about forty-five minutes, and Mr. Kyle was silent the whole way. Skylan was secretly glad. She did not like him. He was old, mean, and really strong. She could only imagine what type of harm he could inflict upon someone. So far, he had not touched her, and she wanted to keep it that way.

They pulled up to the dock where Jeff usually was, and Skylan looked out the window to see if she could see him. He wasn't there, and her heart skipped a beat. What if he didn't show up? She started to feel panicky. Mr. Kyle turned in the seat and looked at her. He noticed some distress and said, "Don't worry. We're just a bit early. I'm sure he'll be here."

Skylan forced a smile and nodded her head. She noticed there were a few more people on the dock today. It was a sunny, warm day, so she deduced that the people just wanted to enjoy the sunshine and their boats.

After about fifteen minutes, Skylan noticed Jeff's boat pull into the marina. She sat up a little straighter and waited. He got off his boat and walked up the dock to where the car was parked. "Hi, Taylor," he said. "Sorry I'm a bit late. Had some business to take care of before I came."

"Hi," Skylan said.

Mr. Kyle leaned over and asked, "You want her the whole two hours today?"

"That I do," Jeff said. "We're going to have a blast today."

"It's your dime," Mr. Kyle said. "Just don't damage the goods too much."

Jeff looked down at Skylan and asked, "Are you ready? I've got cookies on the boat."

Skylan slipped out of the car and took his hand just like in times past. He squeezed her hand a little and smiled, then winked. They both started walking toward the boat. Jeff turned back and gave Mr. Kyle a small wave as the car pulled away and was gone.

Detective Martinez had been within earshot of the whole conversation. He knew this little girl had to be Skylan. The caller had indicated she would have on a cowgirl outfit. All the other children that he had seen were in shorts and T-shirts. This was her! He stepped off the boat and onto the deck directly in front of the two as they walked hand in hand toward him.

Jeff knew this was probably one of the police officers that would be there to rescue Skylan. He held her hand a little tighter as they approached the man who had stepped out in front of them. "Good day, sir," he said. "Pardon us as we get to our boat."

"Is that a little cowgirl you have there?" Detective Martinez asked. "My daughter loves to play dress up as well. I'll have to see about getting her an outfit like that."

Jeff stopped walking and said, "It sure is. She is quite the little cowgirl. Would you like to check out the outfit?" Jeff hoped the police officer would identify himself, and he wasn't disappointed. Before he could turn around, three other officers were pinning him to the railing of the dock. They informed him they were New York police and proceeded to read him his rights. Skylan had been scooped up by the officer that had stepped in front of them.

As Detective Martinez carried Skylan toward a waiting unmarked car, she pushed away from him a bit and asked. "Did God send you? I prayed He would send help."

The tears were forming in the detective's eyes as she spoke. He had never thought that God would send him anywhere, but this little girl had just touched a nerve. She was like a little ray of sunshine he was holding in his arms. The innocence and unparalleled sense of belief was a lot to take in. He answered in a voice that was raspy and full of emotion, "I guess He did."

Skylan hugged his neck and said, "Thank you so much!"

After she was tucked into the backseat of the unmarked car, Detective Martinez turned his attention back to the man his team had handcuffed on the dock. The man was being cooperative and seemed to be defeated as he answered their questions. Unfortunately, he didn't have a lot of information to share. He said the driver would return in two hours and be expecting the girl.

Detective Martinez told part of his team to stay at the marina until the driver returned. Hopefully, they could get him as well.

Ruth was nervous as she paced back and forth across the little living room. Was Skylan okay? Was she safe? Did the customer lie to her? Was he having his way with her? The questions were torturing her. She had to distract herself somehow. She set about cleaning the kitchen when she heard the front door fly open and bang against the wall. She closed her eyes and knew this probably wasn't going to be good.

Mr. Kyle came storming into the kitchen. His face was red with rage, and his fists were balled at his side. "Where is the phone?" he yelled. "I know you have one because the police were tipped off about Skylan's customer. I saw them take down the client when I circled back around on another drive at the marina."

Ruth nervously laughed, then said sarcastically, "Really? You think *I* have a phone? Darius forbid it, and I knew better than to go against him. I've felt his fury before."

"Well, Darius is dead! So why would you fear him now?" he yelled. "Where is it? You better cough it up quick if you know what's good for you. Do you know what I could do to you?"

Ruth knew all too well the sadistic things this man could do. She also knew she needed to be smart so that the police would have time to find the address sewn into Skylan's skirt. She did not want to die by this man's hand. She wanted to see her sister again. She *had* to see her sister again.

"I don't have a phone," Ruth calmly said. "I don't know how the police knew, but it wasn't from me."

Mr. Kyle walked over and stood in front of her. His hot and fetid breath assaulted her face. He grabbed her by the hair and slammed her head against the refrigerator. Ruth knew it was coming, but she had no idea this man could move so fast. The blow had caused a gash in her forehead, and blood was oozing down her face, stinging her eyes. She had no chance to say anything as the second blow came in hard. His fist came up, hitting her on the cheek as she tried to duck the punch. He connected, and Ruth felt her world going black. She prayed this beating would stop. As she crumpled toward the floor, she suddenly felt her body being pulled back up. He wasn't done. She groaned. He flung her over toward the living room, where she landed half on and half off the couch. She tried to get up to run, but he was on top of her before she could get her footing. As he straddled her, it seemed his fists turned into windmills as the blows came one after another. She lost consciousness at some point and welcomed the blackness.

Mr. Kyle proceeded to impose even more torture upon the unconscious Ruth. She was beaten within an inch of her life before he finally stopped. Her breathing was shallow, and her face was unrecognizable. He stripped her clothes off and saw the telltale signs of where Darius had had his way with this one. After raping her and cutting her so no one would ever want her again, he stood up and smoothed his clothes. He needed to change clothes and get back to business. It would not be good to show up at the next appointment covered with blood.

He went into the kitchen and turned on the gas. The house would go up in flames before this girl could ever tell her story. This was going to be the last time she messed up.

CHAPTER 29

Skylan was excited as she sat in the back of the unmarked police car. She asked the woman in the driver's seat, "Are you a police officer?"

"Yes," she replied. "My name is Officer Jane Stiller. Are you okay?"

"I'm fine!" Skylan said with enthusiasm. "Jeff told me he would help me. He wanted to be mean to me, but I would always start talking about Bible stories. He told me he liked the Bible stories when he was a kid."

"That's good to hear," Officer Stiller said. "We're going to go to the hospital now so the doctors can check you out and make sure you aren't hurt anywhere. Sound okay?"

"Sure," Skylan said. "I'm fine. Like I said, Jeff never hurt me. He just touched me on my leg and lip. He never hurt me, and he never did those nasty things that Sophie told me he would do."

At the hospital, Skylan was examined without incident. She was glad Officer Stiller stayed with her. They gave her new clothes to wear and a pair of new tennis shoes. After the exam, Skylan asked, "When do I get to see my mom and dad?"

"We're going to the precinct now," Officer Stiller said. "They should be there waiting for you."

The nurse came in then and handed the officer the clothing that Skylan had been wearing. As the nurse handed over the bag, she said, "There is some crude stitching on the skirt by one of the pleats. Seemed odd."

"Thank you," Officer Stiller said. "I'll check it out."

Once back at the precinct, Skylan was taken to a special room that had been set up by the area Child Advocacy Center. The room was child friendly and welcoming. Stuffed animals and game tables were carefully placed to give the child a sense of calm. Officer Stiller went into the room with Skylan and sat on one of the bean bags on the floor. Skylan sat on the other bean bag and hugged a stuffed teddy bear that had been placed there.

"Are my mom and dad going to be here soon?" she asked.

"They'll be here soon," Officer Stiller said. "First, we need to ask you some questions about what kind of things happened to you after you were kidnapped from the subway."

"Okay," Skylan said. "What do you want to know?"

"Do you know the person that took you from the subway?"

Skylan wrinkled her nose and said, "No, they had masks on, and I couldn't see all their faces."

"Where did they take you after you left the subway?"

"Not sure," Skylan said. "It was the house where Ruth and Sophie lived."

"Was there anyone else that lived there with you, Ruth, and Sophie?"

Skylan looked bored, then said. "No, but Darius would come and get Sophie and me to take us to see customers. Sophie was older than me, and Darius was a lot meaner to her. She told me what some of the customers would do to her. I told her and Ruth that God was going to save us. Ruth believed in God and prayed with me sometimes. Sophie believed but didn't like to admit it. She's dead now. Darius and Sophie died in a car accident." Skylan hugged the teddy bear and looked up at Officer Stiller with tear-filled eyes. "Do you think Sophie made it to heaven? I do."

"I have no doubt," Officer Stiller said. "She was a brave girl. From what you've told me, she was a pretty good friend to you as well.

"When did you find out about the car accident?"

"Ruth told me," Skylan said. "I guess she saw it on the news somewhere. We didn't have a television, so I think she saw it when she went for a walk."

"Did Darius ever hurt you?"

"He took me out one time and touched me in places he shouldn't have. He scared me," Skylan stated.

"Will you show me on the teddy bear where Darius touched you?"

Skylan looked up at the officer and then showed her the buttocks, chest area, and vaginal area. Skylan then attempted to change the subject. "Can I see my mom and dad now?"

"Just a few more questions, Skylan," the officer said. "Who is Jeff?"

"He's the man who helped rescue me," Skylan said. "He wanted to be bad to me, but I always started talking about the Bible stories I knew, and he would just talk to me about them instead of doing things to me. He said he liked Sunday school as a little boy. He said he would help me, and he did. Mr. Kyle didn't even know he was going to help me. Is someone going to help Ruth? She wants to be rescued too."

A knock on the door startled Skylan. She reached for another stuffed animal as the door opened. Another officer was standing there with a paper in her hand. "Sorry to bother you, Officer Stiller, but I have a memo here from the lab that there was some unusual stitching on the girl's skirt. They think you should take a look."

"Thanks, Officer Dorman. I'll be right there." She turned back to Skylan and said, "I'll have your mom and dad brought in to see you now."

Skylan's face lit up with the biggest smile as she jumped up and started dancing around the room.

As Officer Stiller entered the lab, the stitching was being

magnified up on the big screen. At first glance, it looked strange, but she focused and realized it was an address. She quickly wrote the address down and texted it to Detective Martinez. She hoped it was the address where Ruth could be found. She prayed it wouldn't be too late. She had seen the aftermath of some of the girls and women who had found disfavor with their handlers.

Detective Martinez read the text and quickly raced to his car. This had to be the address where Ruth was being held. As soon as he got in his car, a radio call went out. Seemed there was a house fire at the same address where he was going. He quickly radioed in and told them there was likely one occupant in the home.

He arrived on the scene to find the home completely engulfed in flames. His heart sank. He hoped Ruth had made it out alive. The fire chief saw him pull up and quickly went over and told him that one female victim had been found as soon as they had entered the home. She was brought out and was in critical condition. She had been transported to the hospital as a Jane Doe.

With a heavy heart, Detective Martinez thanked the chief and headed toward the hospital. If this Ruth was Maggie, how was Rachel going to take the news? He had to have definitive proof it was Maggie before he would bring in Rachel. She was going to be breaking the story of the rescue, and he wanted her to be prepared if this truly were Maggie.

As he entered the emergency room, one of the nurses met him with a pleading look. "Can you tell me who this Jane Doe is that was brought in? I have to enter her into the system and would like to know her name."

"We aren't sure at this point, miss," he said. "I'm working on getting that information for you as we speak. I'll need to get a hair and saliva sample, if possible."

"The doctors have already done that, and I have them ready for you," she said. "I was just hoping you'd make my job easier with a name."

"I'll take the samples to the lab immediately," he said. "Can I see her?"

"She's in surgery. She has internal bleeding that needed to be addressed. The girl is in pretty bad shape. Whoever did this to her is a monster. She was beaten so badly; her facial features are unrecognizable."

Detective Martinez gathered the samples and went directly to the lab. On the way, he called Rachel and told her to meet him there.

Rachel answered the phone on the second ring. She was hoping she was going to be given the green light on her story. "Need you to get to the crime lab ASAP," he said. "I have some news."

"I'll be right there." Rachel grabbed her bag and hailed a cab. She was nervous. She hadn't expected to meet the detective at the crime lab. She prayed little Skylan hadn't been murdered. Why else would she be going to the lab? The unknown was making her more nervous the closer they got to the lab.

She entered the lab where Detective Martinez was waiting on her. She looked at him curiously and asked, "Why are we here? Has something happened to Skylan?"

"I need a DNA sample from you," he said. "We believe we have found Maggie, but I want to be sure."

Rachel felt her world crumbling, "You found her? Dead?" she asked. "I want to see her!"

"She's in surgery right now at the hospital. The injuries she sustained have made her face unrecognizable, and I want to get a DNA test run to see if there is a familial match."

Rachel let out a sigh of relief. At least she wasn't dead. "How bad is it?"

"She's in critical condition. She was brutally beaten. They're addressing some internal bleeding right at this moment," he said. "Now, can I get that sample?"

Rachel put her bag down and said, "Of course! Let's do this!"

After the sample was taken, Rachel thought about Skylan again and asked, "What about Skylan? Did you find her? Is she safe? Was she hurt?"

Detective Martinez held up his hand and said, "Slow down there. Take a breath. We did find Skylan, and she's fine. It doesn't appear she was harmed or sexually molested at this juncture. We've done a preliminary interview with her, and she indicated there was only touching and no penetration."

Rachel sat back in her chair and said a prayer of thanks. She had hoped this little girl would not have to endure the abuse that she herself remembered all too well. Being kidnapped and touched was bad enough. "Thank goodness!" she said.

"Can I start on the breaking story now? Did you find out who was behind the prostitution ring?" she asked.

Detective Martinez shook his head and said, "No, we don't know who's behind the ring. We've managed to rescue a few girls, but we've not been able to find out who is controlling the whole thing. It appears there are splinter groups in different cities, and all the handlers answer to one person or place. Nothing is clear right now." He hung his head as if in despair.

Rachel felt terrible for him. She knew the cases had taken their toll on him, and he was no closer to shutting down the prostitution ring than when she first was assigned the case. "It's okay, Detective. I believe you'll find out who is responsible."

"Thanks for the vote of confidence," he said. "Let's go back over to the hospital and see if Ruth is out of surgery."

The Jane Doe was out of surgery and in the recovery room when they arrived. Rachel paced up and down the hallway until the surgeon came out to inform Detective Martinez of her status. The surgeon looked weary as he pulled up a chair and told them to sit down. "The surgery went well; we were able to stop the internal bleeding in the abdomen. There is extreme head trauma, and she will need to be seen by a plastic surgeon to address the broken bones in her face. She has been repeatedly raped and beaten with extreme damage to her vaginal and rectal areas. We were forced to perform a hysterectomy due to all the damage." He took a breath and looked at the detective, then asked, "Do we know who she is?"

Detective Martinez shook his head and said, "Not yet. I've got the lab running the DNA test now. We should know within a week or so." He looked over at Rachel, who was sitting there with her head down. He knew she had heard everything and was hoping that she wasn't going to break down. "Are you okay, Rachel?" he asked.

Rachel raised her head and looked directly at the surgeon. "Is she going to pull through? Is she going to be okay?"

The surgeon looked at the detective for an affirmation he could answer. Detective Martinez nodded his head in the affirmative.

"We are hoping she will be okay. There was a lot of trauma, and it will take time. But we are hopeful at this time," he said. "Do you know her personally?"

Rachel didn't answer and got up to walk down the hall. Detective Martinez looked at the surgeon and said, "She may be this young lady's sister. We're awaiting confirmation from the DNA test."

The surgeon nodded and said, "You can see her when we get her moved into the ICU."

"Thank you," Detective Martinez said.

Rachel was walking back toward the two as they shook hands. She looked at Detective Martinez with pleading eyes and said, "I need to see her. Even if it's not Maggie, I need to see her."

"The surgeon said as soon as she is out of recovery and in the ICU, we'll be able to see her."

Rachel sat down with a sigh and gathered her thoughts. She had to be strong. She had to make sure that this sort of thing never happened to anyone else. She knew from this day forward she would make it her life's goal to make a difference in the lives of the girls and women who had been abducted and forced into the ugly world of human trafficking. Somehow, someway, she would make a difference.

"I'll wait here until they get her moved," Rachel said. "I have nowhere else I need to be. If this is Maggie, I want to be with her."

Detective Martinez knew there was no arguing with her. "I'll go and grab us some coffee and a sandwich, then wait with you."

CHAPTER 30

After two hours in the waiting room, a nurse came and got Rachel and Detective Martinez. She informed them that Jane Doe was resting comfortably and was in a medically induced coma due to her facial fractures and broken bones. A plastic surgeon would be in to assess the damage within the hour.

Rachel stood up and turned to find the elevator. Detective Martinez followed suit. Once on the elevator, he asked. "Are you going to be okay if it turns out she *is* Maggie?"

Rachel looked at him and said, "I'll be okay either way. My goal in life now is to be there for those that have escaped the life or need to be rescued from the life. I'll finish this story, and then I'm embarking on a mission of educating the public and assisting those who will eventually be rescued."

Detective Martinez could see the resolve in her, and he was proud of the strength she was showing. He knew whatever she decided to do, that she would accomplish it with a purpose and a passion. First, though, she had to process the fact that this woman may or may not be her sister.

Walking into the Intensive Care Unit, they observed a very swollen and disfigured form in the bed before them. Tubes were hooked up to monitors, and the person before them was all but unrecognizable as another human being. Detective Martinez felt sick to his stomach upon seeing her, but Rachel walked right up to the bed and laid her hand over the woman's forehead. "I'm here," she said.

"No one will hurt you anymore. You have to stay strong so that you can get better."

Rachel pulled up a chair beside the bed and sat down. She held the woman's hand in hers and bowed her head. "Thank you, God, for rescuing this woman. Be her strength as she struggles to recover from this horrendous beating. I ask that you surround her with your love and be beside her every step of the way. I also pray that you will guide the detectives and show them the person that did this evil torture to this woman. Bring him to justice. I pray this woman's true identity be found, and her family informed. I ask all of this in Jesus' name. Amen."

Detective Martinez had not seen this side of Rachel and was taken aback by the power she displayed upon praying and being with this young woman. He believed in God, but he knew he didn't have the guts to pray to Him like that. He sat down in the only other chair and stared out the window. His mind went back to the marina, where Skylan had asked him if God had sent him. Never had he dreamed that he was an instrument in God's will. Skylan and Rachel were making him think differently about his job and his purpose. He would need to explore his relationship with God a little more closely. Maybe God was trying to show him something through all of this.

Rachel looked over at the detective. "Are you okay over there?" she asked. "You seem to be lost in thought."

"I am," he responded. "Guess I just need some time to think about some things."

His phone rang, and he quickly answered. "This is Joe; what do you have for me?"

After a brief conversation, he hung up the phone and said, "I need to get back to the precinct. The commissioner would like to speak with me. I'll check with Detective Andrews to see if you can go to print with your story."

"Thanks," she said. "That would be nice. I'll have another ready by this afternoon or evening also to give to him."

"I'll let you know," he said. "Are you staying long?"

"I'll be here most of the day," she replied. "I'm okay."

Detective Martinez knew she was more than okay. She was a warrior. He left, hoping the commissioner wouldn't be too hard on him. He knew he was going to have to face the fact that he let Sophia leave with Darius. This was likely going to be the end of his career. He hoped somehow the commissioner wouldn't be the nail in the coffin that seemed to be looming.

As he got in his car to leave, he stopped and bowed his head. "God, I haven't prayed to you all that much, but things in my life seem to be telling me I should. Please be with Skylan as she is re-united with her family. Please be with the Lepastes as they deal with the death of their daughter. Help me to find the people behind all this tragedy so that justice can be served. Thank you, God, for listening. Amen."

Somehow, he felt lighter as he drove through the incessant traffic to the precinct. He wasn't dreading the meeting as much. Was this the power of knowing and having a relationship with God? He hoped so.

The commissioner was waiting on him in the little office he shared with one other detective. Detective Martinez walked in and sat down across from his own desk since the commissioner was sitting in his chair. He felt awkward and uncertain but knew he had to be confident. He sat up straight and said with confidence, "Glad you could come in to speak with me today, Commissioner. What is it I can do for you?"

The commissioner was taken aback by the confidence this detective was showing in light of the fact that he'd let a victim who had been positively identified ride off with her known abductor. Did he think he was untouchable?

"I need to know the circumstances behind your decision to let Sophia Lepaste ride off with Darius Potswell. I've got attorneys both internally and externally breathing down my neck on this. A little girl has died, and it seems to have been at the hands of the New York City Police Department."

"I understand, Mr. Commissioner, and I'll be happy to explain. I am devastated over the fact that Sophia is dead, and I blame myself entirely," he said.

"Well, get on with it then, Detective. I have a meeting with Internal Affairs in exactly one hour."

One hour was not going to be enough time to explain the complexities of this entire case to the commissioner, but he was going to choose his words carefully and hope that the commissioner would see his side.

He cleared his throat and then began. "I set up a meeting under the guise of being a wealthy man who was interested in young girls. When Sophia showed up for the meeting, she was engaging and played the part. When I asked her name, she said, 'Soph, I mean, Sasha.' After talking a bit more, she seemed to warm up to me and knew I was different than her other customers. She revealed to me her real name and that she was being held with two other girls. Skylan and Ruth. She was adamant that she was not going to be rescued without those two. I relented and let her return with Darius with a plan in place where my team would follow them to the house. I would get the warrant, and then we would go in and rescue all three girls. Sophia indicated that Darius did not live with them, so I planned on going in after he had dropped off Sophia. I planned to track down Darius at a later date. I had no way of knowing they would get into a traffic accident. I feel terrible about it but want to follow this case to the end. We are on the verge of tracking down the main person or persons responsible for this prostitution ring or human trafficking organization, as you like to call it. I have reason to believe the people responsible are of influential status within our community and other communities where this is occurring. I'm hoping you will see the greater good here and afford me the opportunity to see this through."

The commissioner sat silently and stared at the detective. His experience was telling him to let this man run with the evidence and see it through, but his time spent as commissioner was also telling him to put a lid on this and hope the department wasn't sued for an exorbitant amount of money. He cleared his throat and then said, "For now, I'll let you be. Show me some hard evidence by tomorrow afternoon, or you will be put on desk duty. Do you understand?"

"I'll have your evidence," he said, "by tomorrow afternoon."

After the commissioner left the office, Detective Martinez let out a sigh of relief. This was his second chance, and he was going to make the most of it. He first had to see if Detective Andrews had given his blessing to Rachel's story.

Within a matter of minutes, he was told she could go to print. He phoned Rachel and let her know. He then picked up the phone and called the Internet Crime Division and inquired whether they had tracked down any of the IP addresses associated with the requests or responses of the "Forever Young" site. They informed him they should have something by the end of the day. It was looking promising.

He sat back in his chair and looked up at the ceiling. "Thank you, God," he said.

CHAPTER 31

Abigail and Eugene Winslip were beyond overjoyed to see Skylan. She did look quite different with her short, red, pixie cut. It didn't matter, though. She was still Skylan, and the three embraced and cried together. Their prayers had been answered.

Skylan pulled back from her parents and looked at them. "I missed you," she said.

"We missed you," they both said in unison. "Plus, we have a birthday to celebrate that happened the other day! Who was it that had that birthday?" they teased.

"Me!" Skylan exclaimed. "Can we have cake?"

"We sure can! What flavor would you like?" Abigail asked.

"Chocolate with sprinkles," Skylan answered. "Can I have the party at Sunday school?"

Abigail and Eugene looked quizzically at each other and then replied, "Sure, Skylan, if that's where you want to have it. Why Sunday school, though?"

"Because everything that saved me, I learned from Sunday school. I know God because of Sunday school, and I know some of the stories in the Bible," she replied. "I want all the other children and my teacher to celebrate with me."

Both parents smiled at each other and nodded their heads. "We'll celebrate this weekend."

Skylan was overjoyed at having the birthday celebration. She couldn't wait to see her Sunday school teacher and the other children. Her mood changed slightly, and she looked up at her mother and asked, "Can we go see Sophia's mom? I need to talk to her."

Abigail was uncertain and said, "I'll speak with the detective to see if that's possible."

This seemed to satisfy Skylan, and she danced around the room with excitement. "Can we go home now?" she asked.

"We sure can," they said. "Let's go."

Detective Martinez was informed of the request from Skylan to see Sophia's mom. His heart went out to little Skylan and wondered what on earth this little girl wanted to tell her. He made the arrangements after discussing the meeting with his supervisor. It was understood that the meeting would take place at the precinct. This would help both families meet on neutral ground, and in the event Skylan revealed any further details of her captivity or evidence that could help in finding out who was behind this organization, it would be recorded. Of course, all this with the permission of both sets of parents. Each set of parents granted permission, and the meeting was set for the upcoming Friday morning.

The forensic interview room at the precinct was staffed by the local Child Advocacy Center, and everything was in place for the meeting. Skylan and her parents were the first to arrive. Skylan was happy, and the whole ordeal hadn't seemed to affect her positive and bubbly outlook on life. Detective Martinez was thankful for that little bit of positivity and hoped this meeting would be a good one. Skylan busied herself with the markers and poster board that were available. She was patient and relaxed. This was something she knew needed to be done. She didn't know why, but she just knew she needed to talk to Sophia's mom.

Sophia's parents arrived a little later than planned and were very apologetic about their late arrival. The child advocate introduced Abigail and Eugene to Evelyn and Ed Lepaste. Skylan stood silently as the introductions were made. "And last but not least, this is Skylan," the child advocate said.

Skylan stuck out her hand and shook both Evelyn and Ed's hands. "Glad to meet you," she said. "I lived with Sophia for a while. I wanted to let you know she was a good friend of mine."

They were gracious as they listened. "Thank you, Skylan," Evelyn said. "I'm glad you were Sophia's friend." Her voice cracked with emotion, and she glanced away so Skylan wouldn't notice the tears welling up.

"It's okay to cry, Mrs. Lepaste," Skylan said. "I cried too when I found out Sophia died. It's sad because we won't be able to see her anymore."

Evelyn reached out to hug Skylan and said, "Thank you, Skylan. It is okay to cry. I shouldn't have tried to hide it from you. Was Sophia happy when you were living together?"

Skylan looked out the window for a minute and then turned back to Mrs. Lepaste and said, "We were happy as long as Darius didn't come by. He was mean and did awful things to Sophia."

Evelyn gasped and covered her mouth. The facts had been laid out for the Lepastes by one of the detectives after their daughter's death. They knew the awful things that this Darius had done. It still wasn't easy listening to this little eight-year-old girl reaffirming those facts. She uncovered her mouth and clasped her hands together. "What kind of things did you and Sophia do to have fun?" she asked.

Skylan smiled. "We talked. Sophia always teased me about God. Always asked why I believed He would save us. I know she believed too, but she wanted to act tough, so she never admitted it to me that she really believed. That's why I wanted to talk to you. I wanted to let you know that Sophia is with Jesus now."

Evelyn laid her hand over her heart and said, "Yes, she is. I truly believe that, Skylan. Sophia was a believer before she was taken. I never doubted that for a second. Thank you for letting us know. Is there anything else you'd like to talk with us about?"

"No," Skylan replied. "I just wanted to let you know."

To the astonishment of the adults in the room, the meeting was over. No new evidence was revealed except for the fact that Sophia believed in God. Detective Martinez walked the Lepastes out and told them the case was moving forward, and they were getting close to revealing who was behind this prostitution ring. Once again, he gave his condolences, hoping beyond hope that these parents wouldn't file a wrongful death suit against the department. Self-preservation was also the utmost in his mind.

Returning to the interview room, Detective Martinez spoke with Skylan's parents about the upcoming child molestation charges that were being filed on Jeff, the man who, in the end, had helped rescue Skylan. He informed them that Skylan would likely be called to testify about what happened each time she was on the boat. The child advocate could help with any preparation for the upcoming trial and would walk them through the process. Abigail and Eugene hadn't thought that far in advance and were apprehensive about having Skylan testify. The child advocate calmed their fears and told them they all would take things one day at a time.

Once everyone had left, Detective Martinez sat down at his desk. A file lay crossways on top of the many files he had on his desk that needed attention. He picked it up and saw it was from the Internet Crime Division. He quickly opened the file to the summary report, took a deep breath, and began to read. It seemed a couple of the IP addresses were coming back to a nonprofit organization called "At-Risk Youth—Untied." *What an odd name*, he thought to himself. After reading the summary, he flipped on the computer and googled the name of the organization. To his surprise, it was listed. He was confident the Untied was supposed to be "United," but there it was in black and white. It was an actual nonprofit organization. He clicked the link and was quickly presented with the organization's home page. It looked normal enough. Pictures of young children, both male and female. Nothing that would raise red flags yet. He scrolled down to find another link that looked odd. He clicked on the link, and the computer screen went dark. He reached for his phone to call the IT department to come and take a look at his computer. Then after a few minutes, the screen became a chat room with a live chat option. He quickly exited the site and called in the Internet Crime Division agent that had sent the report.

Agent Tomlinson arrived a few minutes later. "What can I do for you, Detective?"

"Can you tell me what I just got into on the internet?" he said. "It looked like a live chat room for customers wanting to solicit sex with minors."

"That's exactly what it was," he replied. "It's a public site with a backdoor into the dark web for those wanting to solicit sex with minors. They are operating under a nonprofit site they have set up for this particular business. This nonprofit is legally registered with the State of Virginia and accepts donations on its behalf. It looks all aboveboard . . . unless you click on the link at the bottom of their homepage. The link is inconspicuous, and most people probably don't know it's even there unless they're looking for it. And my guess is that if they unknowingly click on the link and their computer goes dark, they just quickly reboot their computer and think nothing of it. A person has to wait the entire three minutes before the chat room appears. The donations are being accumulated in a bank there in Richmond, Virginia. I haven't been able to access any names associated with the account yet. It appears the customers arrange their meeting with the minor and then back out and make the donation or payment on the public website—tax deductible and all."

Detective Martinez was sitting behind his desk, taking it all in.

This was far more complex than he initially thought. He asked, "So, is this tied to the 'Forever Young' site where we found Sophia?"

"It is," Agent Tomlinson replied. "The chat room directs its customers to one of three sites. The first site, 'Have Fun, Stay Young,' is for the average creep with an average budget. Prices are under the $200 limit. The second site, 'Forever Young,' appears to be for the more elite customers. The ones who can pay the big bucks. The third site, 'Young and Confidential,' seems to be for those who wish to remain anonymous and never have their faces seen except by the girls, of course. The 'Forever Young' site seems to be the most popular, although they allow you to remain anonymous at your request."

The detective rubbed his temples and held his head in his hands. Looking across the desk at Agent Tomlinson, he said, "Technology is making my job harder. Who thinks up these schemes?"

Agent Tomlinson shrugged and said, "Don't know. Hopefully, we'll find out soon."

"Thank you," Detective Martinez said. "That'll be all for now. This is a lot to wrap my head around. Call me if you get any names I can run down."

"Will do," he said.

CHAPTER 32

The hospital room was quiet except for the beeping sounds of the monitors. Rachel sat by the woman's side, holding her hand, secretly hoping this was her sister Maggie. She knew in her heart this had to be Maggie, but she hadn't voiced her thoughts for fear of being wrong.

The prestige of writing a breaking news front-page story wasn't even a high priority at this point. All she wanted was for this woman to be all right. Rachel thought of ways she could help the police track down more abducted girls and how they could be rescued. The beeping monitors reminded her of how dangerous that would be, but she didn't care. She wanted to help. She wasn't sure how she could, but she knew she had to. There had to be a way that she could help get the word out about human trafficking. She had to educate the general public so that they could help identify and alert police, who could rescue more girls. Who was she fooling? It was more than girls. Young boys had gone missing too. Although she didn't know any of the abducted boys, a coworker had written a piece on a couple of boys out of the Bronx who had gone missing a few years back. She wondered if they had been found. She made a mental note to follow up on the story of the missing boys when she had a chance. The problem of human trafficking seemed insurmountable, but she knew she would have to try to make a difference.

Rachel leaned back in the chair, closed her eyes, and began to pray. The hand she was holding suddenly twitched ever so slightly.

Rachel sat up and looked at the woman, trying to see past the swelling to see the young woman she was. "Are you awake?" Rachel asked softly. "My name is Rachel. I'm going to be here right by your side until you're better. You have to fight, though. I know you are strong. I can sense it. You have the strength of a lion." Rachel waited, but there was no movement. She let out a breath and sat back in the chair once more. Maybe she had imagined the movement.

The nurse came in to check vitals and looked at Rachel. "Can I get you anything, miss?" she asked.

Rachel shook her head and said, "I'm fine. I thought her hand moved a little bit ago. Is that possible given her condition?"

The nurse looked at Rachel with weary eyes and said, "Sometimes, patients will twitch in their sleep or while they're in comas. I'll consult with the doctor when he makes his rounds. I'm sure he'll want to know."

"Thank you," Rachel said. "I should be here when the doctor comes by. I'll speak to him directly."

The nurse nodded and left the room. Rachel was left with her thoughts once more. She removed her laptop from her bag and began writing the story. She was so focused on her story that she never heard Detective Martinez walk in. He stood watching her from the doorway for a good ten minutes before she looked up. She was startled to see him at first but quickly composed herself and asked, "Did you get the results back from the DNA test?"

"I did," he said. "You'll be happy to know you have helped to rescue your sister."

Rachel shut the laptop and sat in stunned silence. She looked up at the detective with tears in her eyes and said, "We rescued Maggie. We rescued Maggie!" She stood up beside the bed and leaned over her sister, stroking her forehead and spoke softly, "Maggie, I'm here, Maggie. I won't leave you. You're going to get better, and we're going to have a wonderful life together after all these years. Nobody is ever going to hurt us again." Maggie moaned slightly and tried to move her hand. "Don't try to move," Rachel said. "You need to rest. I'm not going anywhere."

Detective Martinez looked at Rachel and said, "I'll sit with Maggie if you'd like to go home and get a shower, pack a bag, and come back. If you're going to stay, then you'll need some personal things from home, I'm sure."

"Thank you," Rachel said. She leaned in close to Maggie and said, "I'm going home to get some clothes, and then I'll be back. This is Joe. He's the detective that helped to find you. He'll be here until I get back."

Rachel hurried to the front of the hospital, where she hailed a cab. As she sat back in the seat of the cab, she silently sent up a prayer of thanks. She had found her sister. She knew life would never be the same for Maggie, just as it had never been the same for her. She was confident, though, that her sister would survive this beating, and she would thrive in the next chapter of her life. They were strong girls, who had matured into strong women, and they were stronger when together.

"Here we are, miss," the cabdriver said. "Would you like me to wait?"

"Thank you," Rachel said. "I won't be but a few minutes."

The cabdriver nodded and sat back to wait on his fare.

Rachel raced up to her apartment, threw a few clothes in a bag, along with her toothbrush. As she was leaving, she stopped to look at the whiteboard, the corkboard, the coffee table that had become her desk, and thought to herself. *We did it. We found Skylan, Sophia, Maggie, Leslie, Stephanie, Lily, and many more.* "Thank you, Lord. Guide my path in this next phase of the investigation and lead my sister and me in our newfound life together. Amen."

Getting back in the cab, Rachel silently wished Sophia hadn't been killed in the accident. She said a silent prayer for Sophia's family. It hurt to know that Sophia was on the verge of being rescued when the accident had happened. She sat quietly as the cab drove her back to the hospital. They passed one of the NYPD precincts on the way, and one of the child advocacy vans was parked out front. Rachel prayed for whomever they were there to see. The cruelty of this world was everywhere.

Walking back into the hospital room, Rachel was surprised to find the doctor was already there. Joe was talking to him about the movement that she had observed earlier. The doctor was saying that Maggie was in a drug-induced coma to keep her calm and to let the swelling go down. Movement was possible but was most likely just muscles twitching.

"I will have to disagree with you respectfully, Doctor," Rachel said as she set her bag down. "I know my sister, and she knew I was here. That is why she tried to move earlier."

The doctor looked at Joe, smiled, and said, "You must be Rachel. Nice to meet you. My name is Doctor Frentmore. I'll be one of the doctors taking care of your sister."

Just then, Maggie moaned and moved her right hand ever so slightly. The doctor turned back toward his patient and called for a nurse. As he was examining Maggie, she moved her right hand again after the doctor prompted her to do so. "Well, I'll be," he said. "She's coming out of her coma. We will need to keep her quiet as she continues to heal. If that isn't possible, then I'll have to insist on giving her more medication to keep her relaxed. The plastic surgeon will be in tomorrow to formulate a plan for the facial repair after more of the swelling subsides."

"I'll keep her calm," Rachel said. "I won't be leaving her side."

Detective Martinez looked at the doctor and said, "I think you have your 24/7 nurse on duty now. Rachel will make sure her sister rests."

"I hope so," Doctor Frentmore stated. "This girl has a long road ahead of her. I'll check on her later."

"Thanks," Rachel said. "I'll make sure she rests." The doctor nodded and left the room.

"Thank you, Joe. I really appreciate you sticking up for me with the doctor."

"You're welcome," he said. "I'll be checking in on you as well. Let me know if you need anything. We have some pretty good leads on the people who are in control of the prostitution ring. I'll keep you informed. Sounds like it might get a bit messy before we finally catch the big fish. Then again, he or she may be too slippery, and we may never know who is behind this ring. I can assure you, though, we are trying our level best to get to the bottom of the organization."

"I know you are," Rachel said. "I have all the confidence in the world in you and your investigative team. Just keep me updated so that I can run with the story when it's time. My editor is breathing down my neck to get something in."

"Will do," Joe said. "See you tomorrow."

CHAPTER 33

D etective Martinez headed back to the precinct and hoped the Internet Crime Division had some names for him. He wanted a list so he could start eliminating people. Although by the way the organization was described to him, it might not be possible, but the time had come to clamp down on this scourge.

Agent Tomlinson met Detective Martinez at the door to his office. "Can I speak with you?" he asked. "I think I may have a pretty good list of donors to start checking out."

"By all means. Let's see what you've come up with," he said.

The agent took out a folder that appeared to have a lot of paper. Detective Martinez looked at the agent quizzically. "Is that all names? If it is, I think we need more manpower."

"I think you need to look at the list first," Agent Tomlinson said. "There are some names on here that we'll need to tread lightly around."

Detective Martinez looked the agent directly in the eye and said, "Do you think the people you are talking about tread lightly on their child victims? Do you think they cared how they hurt these children?" His voice was rising with each question, and he knew he needed to put a lid on it before others in the office heard his frustration. He needed to keep his composure and attack this giant with all the professionalism he could muster. He didn't want anyone to think he couldn't get the job done by being hotheaded and impulsive.

Agent Tomlinson looked at Detective Martinez and nodded. "I

know, Joe. I understand where you're coming from, and I didn't mean—"

"Leave the folder on my desk," he said. "I'm going to get some coffee, and I'll look at it when I get back."

"Sure thing, Joe," Agent Tomlinson replied. "There is also a better description in there about how the organization works and how they portray themselves to the public. They have quite a stellar reputation with helping some children. They donate to afterschool programs and even have a scholarship for high school seniors to apply for if they want to major in social work. This will be a tightrope of a case."

Detective Martinez let out a sigh of frustration and walked out of the office. The idea that this organization, through this website, was actually helping some people was disgusting to him. He had seen firsthand the torture, beatings, and aftermath of their handiwork. The two didn't jive!

After getting his coffee, he walked back to his office. As he sat down, he looked at the folder on his desk. That folder would hold names of people he probably would not recognize, but there would be those that he would. Before reaching for the folder, he set his coffee cup down and bowed his head.

"God, it's me again. I know you don't hear from me much, but I think I need to change that. This case has gotten to me, and I need you to help me. I pray that you would guide me in the direction to shut down this prostitution ring effectively. Help me, along with my fellow officers, to stop this awful crime of human trafficking. I know we won't stop it all but help us to make a difference. Amen."

As he lifted his head, he saw Agent Tomlinson standing in the doorway. "Amen!" he said. "Thought you could use some help going through the list. I didn't know you were a praying man."

"I guess I am," Joe said. "Come on in. I'd love the help."

The list was pretty straightforward, with donors listed by their level of donations for the year. The Platinum level was for donors of $100,000 or more. The Gold level was $50,000 plus. The Silver level was $25,000 plus. The Fellowship level was $10,000 plus, and Basic Member was $5,000 plus. The introductory level was $1,000 plus. It sickened them to know that each donation represented the molestation of a child.

They started with the less influential names. One of the names they recognized was Jeff Calista from the marina. He was a relatively new member since he was listed on the introductory level. The detective knew this didn't mean much, because he could have been using other sites to satisfy his fantasies, along with this one. The next name was one that surprised him. It was the police commissioner's nephew, Andrew Stigliani. He was listed as a Fellowship level donor. Detective Martinez quickly scanned the rest of the names on the first list. Then he picked up the second list and was hit with a name he had seen in the news for the philanthropic events he sponsored—Gary Beltrone, the "giving" governor of Virginia. He sat back in his chair and looked at Agent Tomlinson. "How many more big names are on this list?" he asked. "I don't know if I want to see anymore."

"I told you this was going to be a rough go," Agent Tomlinson replied. "There are names here from New York, Virginia, Pennsylvania, Ohio, West Virginia, and Washington, D.C. The names coming out of D.C. are the ones that floored me. Representatives and senators. How do we attack this beast?"

"Not sure," he said. "But we have to start somewhere. Let's bring together members from each state and make this a multijurisdictional task force. We have to vet each member carefully, making sure no member is involved in the business of human trafficking. If Stigliani is involved here in New York, then who are his associates within the NYPD? We have to make sure our task force members are clean. We don't want any moles. I hate to think it, but there will be members of law enforcement on this list or at the least associated with someone on the list."

Agent Tomlinson let out a sigh. "You're right, Joe, but how do we get the evidence we need to prosecute?" he asked. "Right now, all these men are guilty of is donating to a nonprofit organization that is known to help children. How are we going to prove they are soliciting minors for sex?"

"First things first," he said. "We need to talk to Mr. Jeff Calista from the marina. He may prove to be more helpful than we realized. He appears to have some sort of a conscience. After all, he did help to rescue little Skylan Winslip. Maybe we can get him to help us."

"I'll get to work on getting the task force formed. It may take a few weeks," he said. "I'll also set up a meeting with Mr. Calista. He's out on bond. I'm sure he's holed up in his fancy house by now."

"Great, let me know. Thanks."

Tomlinson walked out of the office, only to return a few minutes later. "Joe, you are *not* going to believe this, but Jeff Calista is waiting in the lobby to speak with you." This was news that neither officer was expecting. "Well, escort him back," Joe said. "By all means, this makes my job easier."

Jeff Calista walked into Detective Martinez's office, looking like he'd lost his childhood puppy. He sat down in the chair opposite the desk and lifted his head to look at the detective. "I bet you didn't expect to see me," he said. "To tell you the truth, I don't understand myself right now. I just felt I needed to come and talk with you."

"Well, I'm glad you came in. I have some additional questions I'd like to have some answers to. I believe you could be of some assistance in the rescue of more missing girls."

Jeff hung his head. "I'll do what I can," he said. "After meeting Skylan, I'm a changed man. She made me realize what I had been doing was wrong."

"How did you find out about Forever Young?" the detective asked.

"A friend introduced me to the site," he said. "I believe you are familiar with Andrew Stigliani?"

"I am," he said. "How long have you and Andrew been friends?"

"We went to college together. He introduced me to the dark web then," Jeff said.

Detective Martinez picked up his coffee cup and sipped the now lukewarm liquid. This was not going to be pleasant by any stretch of the imagination. "So, were you both into little girls in college too?"

The bluntness of the question hit Jeff hard. He bowed his head and took a few deep breaths. "We were," he replied in almost a whisper. "We would often book our fantasies from the same site. He liked his girls a little older than me."

"When was the last time you spoke with Andrew?"

"About a month ago. I ran into him at the marina, and he just started talking about this site where he could book a fantasy, plus get a tax deduction for his 'donation.' The donation was counted as payment for services. I'm always looking for tax breaks, so it sounded very appealing to me. I decided to give it a try. Never thought I'd meet an angel that would change my whole perspective on what I was doing."

"Do you know anything further about the website that would be helpful to our investigation?"

"I remember Andrew saying something about it being around for fifteen years or so, and they had the particulars down to a science. He said this was a grassroots site that started small and grew in increments so as not to give off any suggestions other than it was a nonprofit organization that helped children around the area. His words exactly were that 'It was foolproof! No chance of getting caught.' That's why I tried it. The other site I used was getting shut down, and it was harder to book fantasies, so I wanted something that wouldn't lead to my spending my days in jail. I know I'm a terrible person, Detective Martinez, and I know I need to pay for what I've done to all the girls."

"How many girls are you talking about?" he asked.

"I would book one every week. That is, until I met Taylor, I mean Skylan. I booked her every other day. I just had to be around her. She was so pure. My intentions were sinful, but when she would come, those intentions would get squashed, and we would start talking about the Bible stories she liked. She was the only girl I ever saw more than once."

Detective Martinez calculated the number of possible victims this man had violated. He was thirty-two years old, so one victim a week from the age of twenty onward would come close to 650 girls approximately. It was hard for him to wrap his head around that number. He rubbed his temples and looked across the desk at this monster sitting before him. He wanted to jump over the desk and strangle him. He wanted to stop this man from ever hurting another human being. *God, help me*, he said silently. *Show me how to proceed.*

"Mr. Calista," he started, "is there any way we can get you to help bring this website down and expose it for what it truly is? I need information on how to get to the origin of the website . . . The head person, the one who truly is the evil one, who never cared for any of these girls."

"I-I," he stammered. "How would I do that? I just started using the site. I don't know anything other than they had the types of girls I wanted."

"I'll let you know, but for now, I want you to face your charges and lie low. Can you do that?"

Jeff swallowed hard and sat up straight in the chair. "I can," he said. "Will I be put in danger?"

"Not if I can help it," the detective said. "I'll call you in when I have something for you to do. Thanks for coming in."

After Mr. Calista left his office, Detective Martinez started formulating his plan. He had to know who Gary Beltrone knew fifteen years ago. His hunch was that this had all started in Virginia about the same time that Rachel and her sister Maggie had been abducted. The now-governor seemed to stick out like a sore thumb on the list, and the fact that he was now a governor was disconcerting, to say the least. It seemed like a good place to start.

CHAPTER 34

Rachel had been staying at the hospital full time since finding out that Maggie was the woman so severely beaten. The hospital administration had given her a roll away bed and said she could take showers in the room. Rachel was grateful she could stay with Maggie. Her editor had even understood and let her work remotely. She wrote several stories on human trafficking, and Rachel was beginning to understand the complexity of the problem with each story. Detective Martinez had been instrumental in getting her in touch with several organizations that dealt with human trafficking. Their knowledge and goal of helping anyone involved in the life was more than commendable.

Maggie had had plastic surgery on her face and was healing nicely. Her internal injuries had all but healed over the last several weeks. Rachel was thankful her sister was healing and even talking about getting out of the hospital. She knew her apartment would be a little small with Maggie moving in, but they would make do until they could afford something larger. There was time for that, but now, they had to focus on getting Maggie well enough to leave the hospital.

Rachel lay her head back on the chair and took a few deep breaths. Maggie was sleeping peacefully. Rachel thought about the progress Detective Martinez had made as well. His multijurisdictional task force had been formed. He wouldn't reveal any names they were investigating, but Rachel knew he would share when the time was right. As she started to drift off to sleep, she heard the door to the room open. She sat up and saw a young woman standing there with long, brown hair.

"Can I help you?" Rachel asked. "My name is Rachel."

The woman looked nervous as she said, "Hi, my name is Stephanie. I came to see Ruth. I hope that's okay?"

"Oh, of course, it is," Rachel said. "I'm so sorry I didn't recognize you. How are you doing?"

"I'm fine," Stephanie said. "I heard that Ruth was here, and I wanted to come and see how she was doing."

Rachel smiled and said. "She's doing fine. Healing nicely."

"Hey, you talking about me again?" Maggie said sleepily. "I can still hear, you know. Who's here? Who are you talking to?"

Rachel laughed and said, "You caught me, sis. Sorry. Stephanie came by to see you."

"Stephanie? Oh yeah, hey, Stephanie! I'd get up but still a little sore, and these bandages over my eyes are the pits," Maggie said.

Stephanie came over to the bedside and held Maggie's hand. "I'm so glad Mr. Kyle didn't kill you!" Tears spilled down her cheeks as she continued. "Mr. Kyle is no longer around. I don't know where he went, but he's gone underground. I was rescued too!"

"I'm so glad, Stephanie," Maggie said. "Please call me Maggie. I don't want to go by Ruth anymore. That was Darius's name for me. I don't ever want to hear that name again."

"I understand," Stephanie said. "Maggie, I'm so glad you're going to be okay. I won't stay long. I know you need your rest. I'm staying at a women's shelter for the time being over on Houston Street. I'll come back to see you."

"As soon as these bandages come off, and I get the green light, I'll be out of here," Maggie said. "I'll be staying with my sister. I promise we'll stay in touch. Thanks for coming by."

Stephanie kissed Maggie on the forehead before she left. "Bye, Maggie. I'll hold you to that promise."

Rachel was watching the interaction between these two and knew there was a history that couldn't be ignored. There were understanding and comradery that no one could understand but them. They had been in the same roles within the organization. Housemothers to the girls who were being bought daily. The cruelty that these two must have seen over the years . . . Rachel could only imagine. Leslie had seen the same things. Rachel had never had to take care of the younger girls, but she knew the pain she and they had endured. She also knew Leslie had endured many beatings and sexual abuse at the hands of Darius. She could only imagine what her sister, Maggie, and Stephanie had had to do.

Maggie was unusually quiet after Stephanie left. Rachel knew she was lost in her thoughts and left her to them. She didn't want to pry and ask too many questions at once. She wanted Maggie to initiate whatever conversation about her past that she wanted, not what Rachel wanted to know. Rachel knew from her own experiences that she had never wanted to talk about any of it until she had been assigned this story opportunity. She did understand the benefit of talking, though, and would encourage it when the time was right.

"Rachel, are you still here?" Maggie asked.

"I am. Is there something you need?"

"Just to hold your hand. I need to hold your hand."

The tears welled up in Rachel's eyes as she took her sister's hand and held it tenderly. The two stayed sitting side by side, holding hands until they both fell asleep.

Detective Martinez walked in and found the two sisters hand in hand two hours later. He pulled up the spare chair to the foot of the bed and sat down. He didn't want to disturb them because they looked so peaceful. He knew their lives had been anything but peaceful, and he would let them enjoy the rest. He wondered if these two had any idea how big the organization really was. His team had been doing a lot over the last few weeks. The information they were compiling was proving to be very beneficial.

Fifteen years ago, about the time these two girls had been abducted, a man had started the so-called business. He was an outlaw biker who wanted to set himself up in his old age so he wouldn't have to worry about money. He had started by prostituting out his own children to wealthy businessmen whom he had associations with through the drug runs he made with the biker gang. His side business of child prostitution was growing, and he knew he had to do something different. He estimated that selling girls for sex was going to bring him considerably more money than running drugs, so he left the gang. His home base was in Manassas, Virginia, and he partnered with a local businessman who had shown him the ropes of setting up a 501(c)(3) organization online that could serve as his legitimate website helping numerous children through private donations.

Once the backdoor was initiated and the word on the street was out, donations started coming. The backdoor provided a dialog between the customer/donor and the one who would set up the fantasy dates, i.e., the pimp. The biker-turned-underground-prostitution-pimp was none other than Harold Beltrone, father of Gary Beltrone. It seemed that Gary was Harold's oldest son and had not been one of his dad's victims. He was already in his twenties when his dad started the business. His younger sisters, Alisha and Carol, had been the victims. Gary had watched his dad sell his sisters to different businessmen and local politicians from the beginning. He knew his dad was particular in who he let his daughters see. There were unwritten rules for the customers, like, not messing up their faces by hitting them, cutting them, etc. All the abuse was to be "undercover," as his dad had put it, away from the prying eyes of the public. As Harold successfully cultivated his business, Gary was introduced to the business side of things when his dad suddenly got sick. Gary was given a "district" to oversee. The "district" he was given was his dad's home turf, Manassas, Virginia, and Washington, D.C. Harold never recovered from his illness and eventually passed away. Gary stepped into the role of overseer at that point.

He graciously let his sisters out of the business, and fortunately for the task force, one of the detectives had found Alisha living a somewhat normal life in a small town in Virginia. She had proven to be a wealth of information on the organization and was currently in protective custody, along with her family. She had stated her older sister, Carol, had been killed in an automobile accident shortly after Gary had let them leave the business.

Rachel stirred in her sleep and then suddenly sat up, sensing someone else was in the room with them.

"Joe? What are you doing?" she asked.

"Came by to see you two, and you both were asleep, so I was letting you sleep," he replied.

"Who's here, Rachel?" Maggie said sleepily as she struggled to sit up straighter in the bed.

"It's Joe. He came by to see us."

"Hi, Joe," Maggie said. "I wish I could see your face. I'm due to get these bandages off in a couple of days. I can't wait."

"All in good time," he said. "I just wanted to come by and let you know the task force has made some progress, and we're hoping we can soon start formulating a plan to take down this website, Forever Young. Thought you two could use some good news."

Rachel was beyond excited. She knew her big article for the paper would come soon, as well. "Can you give me any information I can go to print with?" she asked. "I would really like to get something to my editor soon."

"Not yet," he said. "You'll be the first to know. I promise."

Maggie reached her hand toward Rachel and said, "You'll get

your story, sis. Just be patient."

Rachel knew she was right. The story would come once all the players were identified, and the operation had come to a close. Then the story would be hers.

"Anything I can get you girls before I leave?" he asked.

"I want to know if there are any organizations out there that can help these girls get out of the business," Maggie blurted out. "I really want to help, and I think if there were a way to help these girls and women, then we all could make a difference."

Joe smiled and said, "There are organizations out there who are doing their best to educate the general public and law enforcement about human trafficking. In fact, your sister, here, has been writing a series of articles for the paper that have highlighted a lot of what they're doing. You'll need to ask Rachel about some of the organizations she has been writing about."

"Thanks, Joe," Maggie said. "Guess I need to ask my little sister what she's been up to while I've been lying here in this hospital bed." She laughed a little and then stopped because of the pain to her face when she tried to smile.

"I'll be glad to tell you all about my articles, Maggie," Rachel said. "I've wanted to talk about them with you, but I didn't know if you were ready."

Joe waved goodbye as he walked out the door. He rubbed his head and smiled to himself. These two girls were going to make a difference. He didn't know how, but he knew they would.

Maggie pushed the button to raise the head of the bed more. She crossed her legs and sat there and looked at Rachel, or at least where she had heard her voice last.

"Okay, little sister, start talking."

Rachel looked at her sister and said, "OK, so, there are three organizations within the city who educate the public on child prostitution. They call it 'human trafficking' now. The term encompasses all humans, not just one gender or age range. The problem is much bigger than I initially thought. I've learned there is sex trafficking and labor trafficking. I also have discovered that 80 percent of all trafficked individuals are female, about 50 percent of those are children. Some 70 percent of those female victims are trafficked for sexual exploitation." (www.InOurBackyard.org)

"Go on," Maggie said. "Are any of the three organizations actively helping the victims get out of the life?"

"They have a hotline number people can call," Rachel said. "But I know in our case, we never had access to a phone, and we were never allowed out without our handler."

"Sophie was allowed out. I let her go," Maggie said. "I told her of the risks she was taking, but she didn't care. She would panhandle and shoplift so we wouldn't go without at the house, sometimes. I even found out she had a stash of money in her closet just for emergencies. She stole someone's cell phone, and that's how I reached out to you after Skylan was taken."

"Why didn't you ever go out and try to get help for the girls?" Rachel asked. "Leslie helped me escape."

Rachel immediately regretted the question as Maggie leaned back in the bed and took a deep breath. "I know she helped you, and I am grateful for all she did. Darius found her in Pittsburgh one night, and when he told me, I was fearful you were still with her. Darius had another house girl come sit with the girls I was watching at the time, and we went to Pittsburgh together. Leslie was at a local clinic when we found her again. She was sick or something. I'm not sure. We waited until she came out, and then we forced her into the car. She was adamant that you had died in a freak accident. She said you had stepped out in front of a city bus and were hit. You died on the street. I was beside myself. I mourned your death for weeks after that. Darius was mad. He told Leslie that her punishment was going to be harsh. It was. I had to watch him beat her into a bloody pulp. Then he did unspeakable things to her—"

"Stop!" Rachel said. "I know what happened to her. It was awful. You were there?"

"Yes, I was there. I helped to bury her after Darius was done," Maggie said. "I knew then I was never getting out. I would someday end up like Leslie. I could only pray to stay on Darius's good side and hope he didn't grow tired of me. Especially since I was getting older."

"When did you find out I was alive?" Rachel asked.

"I read your byline in the paper one day. Darius accidentally left a paper at the house when he left. I knew it was you. I never said anything to him. I didn't want him to know," Maggie stated. "I'm so proud of you, Rachel. Now that Darius is gone, and I'm out of those clutches, I want to help others like me who don't know there is help out there."

"I understand," Rachel said. "I want to help too. In fact, I know we will help. I've been doing a lot of thinking these past few weeks. I'd like to start a nonprofit group that will assist women and girls like us. I want there to be a way that they can find the help they need. I want there to be a safe place for them to go, if need be. I don't know how we'll accomplish all this, but I know we will."

Maggie yawned and said, "I know we will too. I'd like to name the place after Sophie. Maybe 'Sophie's Place'?"

"Sounds like a great name," Rachel said. "I'll see what I can find out about getting something rolling. I need to go and talk to Joe. You going to be okay here by yourself?"

"I'll be fine, little sister. Get outta here."

Detective Martinez entered the precinct and sat down at his desk. The day had been a good day. He had some great information from the task force, information they would be able to use while building a case. Now, he had to determine how he could use Jeff

Calista to infiltrate the group once more. They knew he had been arrested, and now, they needed to know that somehow, the charges hadn't stuck. He wanted them to get a false sense of security so that he and the task force could get the man behind the website . . . shut it down for good. He picked up the phone to call the district attorney's office. There had to be some cooperation and coordination. The time to begin was now.

Jeff was set to go to court two weeks from today. He had to convince the district attorney to drop the charges or something to send a message to the trafficking site administrator to convince them that Jeff was still a good customer/donor.

According to one of the agents, the site was being monitored from within the Governor's Office in Virginia. This was indicative of the governor wanting to keep a tight lid on his extracurricular revenue stream. The Richmond Bank was where the donors' funds were being deposited. An account for "At-Risk Youth—Untied" was the name of the account. People named on the account were: Sybil Langly, executive director for the fake organization, Ty Hagger, administrative assistant, and Gary Beltrone, the board of directors' chairperson.

The phone rang for what seemed like an eternity. Finally, a very tired but authoritative voice answered the phone. "Hello, DA Karris Finnigan speaking."

"Answering your own phone these days?" the detective asked. "This is Joe Martinez. I'd like to talk to you about the Calista case in the morning. The task force has the information we need, and I'd like to see if we can have Mr. Calista infiltrate the website in hopes of us shutting them down for good. I'd like to strike a deal."

"I'll see you tomorrow morning," he said. "At 9:00 a.m."

"Thank you. I'll see you then."

Rachel walked into the office about the time he was hanging up the phone. "Hi, again," she said. "I'd like to get some additional information on the nonprofit organizations you told me about the other day. Plus, I'd like to know how to start a 501(c)(3) myself."

"Wow," Joe said, "that's a lot for being so late in the day. You think we could take it a bit slower and maybe talk tomorrow? I'm beat, and I need to get ready to speak with the DA tomorrow about this case."

"I guess," Rachel said. "I was just hoping for a little more information to give my editor in the morning. I'll catch you tomorrow sometime."

"Thanks, Rachel," he said. "I'll have you some information. I promise."

He watched her walk out of the office and knew he had disappointed her. She wasn't deterred, though, because she would be back. She had proven she was as persistent as a dog with a bone when it came to getting the information she wanted.

CHAPTER 35

D A Karris Finnigan was a gentle giant, standing well over six feet tall with broad shoulders that told the story of being a boxer in his younger days. His abilities in the courtroom were extraordinary. His voice boomed throughout the courthouse on days he was working a trial. Detective Martinez knew he was a no-nonsense man and would listen to reason. There were numerous victims out there that were depending on them to bring down this ring and bring those responsible to justice.

"Good morning, Detective. How are you this fine day?"

"I'm good. I'll be better if we can come up with a solution to my problem, though."

"Ah, yes. You wanted to strike some sort of deal for Mr. Calista?"

"I do. I believe that he can infiltrate the website where all the solicitation and appointments are made. It's called 'Forever Young.' I've made some progress into who is behind the website, and some *very* influential people operate under its disguise of being a legitimate nonprofit site."

"I've been keeping up with the investigation. I'm surprised how long this website has been in operation and hope we can shut it down for good. Are you certain about the one or the ones behind the website? I haven't seen any names cross my desk yet."

"There's a good reason for that. We have tried our best to vet all persons investigating the case. We didn't want any leaks or anyone out there who could jeopardize this case. I hope you understand?"

"So, I assume you have looked into my background as well?" he said with a smirk. "I'm sure you've found nothing of interest there."

"I wouldn't be speaking with you if we had," Joe said.

"Good to hear," Karris boomed. "So, what kind of deal are we talking about here?"

"Based on our investigation, we have determined that the governor of Virginia, Mr. Gary Beltrone, is responsible for the website. He appears to be operating the website from an office in the Governor's Mansion. The funds being collected under the guise of donations are being funneled into an account at a Richmond, Virginia, bank. We believe Mr. Calista could play the part of a very wealthy customer/donor who has beat our system. If your office were to drop whatever charges you were going to file, then Mr. Calista could easily go back to his normal routine. Except for this time, we would be writing the script for him. We think if Mr. Calista cops an attitude of beating the system and goes in with a large monetary donation/payment for services, he could be back in their good graces."

DA Finnigan sat back in his chair and looked at the ceiling. "It's like putting the lion back in his den. I'm afraid Mr. Calista will go back to his molestation and abuse. Can you guarantee me he won't hurt any young girls or women if we put him back in business?"

"I can't guarantee you, no. But I have confidence in him and feel if we can keep him on the path he is on now, it could work."

"And what path is that, may I ask?"

"He genuinely seems to regret all his past discretions. He acknowledges he has done wrong and would like to help make things right. I'm hoping that he can work with a partner that we would assign him. Maybe portray them as a team. Let them book fantasies of the higher-dollar caliber and see where that takes them."

"Sounds very risky. I'll need to think on this awhile. I'll let you know by the end of the day."

Detective Martinez walked out the DA's office, hopeful. He knew he hadn't given him the whole background on the case, but he hoped that the DA would see the benefits far outweighed the risks. All he could do was pray he would get the green light.

The task force was set to meet the day after tomorrow, and he wanted to be able to go ahead and get the permissions he required to move forward before then.

Rachel was sitting in his room when he returned from the DA's office, notepad in hand and looking very much the professional. "Hi, Rachel," he said. "You are out and about early today."

"Wanted to get a jump on the day. Get me any information yet?"

"Slow down. I've got you the packet from the state on how to form a 501(c)(3) organization. That's a start, right?"

"You mean this one I downloaded last night off the internet?" she smirked.

"Okay, you got me. I downloaded the same thing," he confessed. "What else can I help you with?"

"For starters, I need some background on the website, 'Forever Young.' I believe you can at least fill me in on how the site works and maybe why the general public is unaware of its nefarious side."

"It's an ongoing investigation, Rachel. You know this," he said. "I'll let you in on all the details once some arrests have been made and the website shut down."

"Can you at least let me know where the investigation stands?"

"Rachel, I appreciate your tenacity and drive. You know you have the exclusive on this investigation. I will tell you that there will be some things that are going to happen. You may not understand them in the beginning, but you will have to trust me when I say it will be for the better. Do you understand?"

Rachel sat there feeling like she was being put off again. Heck, she *was* being put off. It didn't make her feel any better that he had stated she wouldn't like what was going to be happening. She wanted desperately to know but knew she had pushed the envelope as far as it was going today. She would have to back off and wait. Patience was not her most aspiring characteristic, but she'd have to play the game.

"Sure, Joe. I'll give it some time. You better not burn me on this."

"I won't, Rachel. I promise."

Rachel headed back to the hospital to be with Maggie. There had to be a way she could look into this simultaneously without causing harm. She would talk to Maggie about it. Two heads were always better than one. Plus, they both had been in the life. Maggie would have some details, she was sure.

The phone rang as Rachel was leaving Detective Martinez's office. Looking down at the phone, Joe prayed it was the DA before he picked up.

"Detective Martinez, may I help you?"

"Detective, you have a deal," DA Finnigan stated into the phone. "I was having a hard time with the charges I was going to file anyway. Seems Mr. Calista may have solicited a minor for sex, but no other crime was committed while the girl was in his charge. He never molested her or abused her the times he saw her. He would be better suited to help your task force and stop this website, in my opinion. I want a task force member with him at all times so that he is not tempted to molest or hurt anyone while doing this. Do I make myself clear?"

"Crystal!" Joe said. "I'll get on that right away. We'll keep you informed on our progress. Thank you."

Hanging up the phone, Joe bowed his head and said, "Thank you, God. Guide us in this next level of the investigation."

"Who you talking to?" Detective Ray Lochna asked as he stuck his head in the office.

"God," Joe said. "He's going to get us through this."

"Never really talked to God," Ray said. "Guess maybe I should start. You seem pretty sold."

"You work this job long enough, and you'll be sold too," Joe said. "What can I do for you today?"

"I was told to report to you. I guess I'm your new assistant."

"I didn't ask for any assistant. Who told you to report to me?"

"The commissioner's office sent my command a notice. I'm just doing what I was told. Detective Ray Lochna at your service."

With the multijurisdictional task force already formed and working, this sudden assignment of an assistant had Detective Martinez curious, to say the least. Was this an attempt by the commissioner to keep his nephew's name out of the dirty pool? If he had to guess, it probably was. He knew the game, and he'd keep his new assistant, but as for the task force, not all information would be available to Detective Ray Lochna. Hell, he didn't even know this detective.

"Okay, Detective, welcome," he said as cheerfully as he could. "If you'll go down to records and start pulling all prostitution arrest records from fifteen years ago, that would be helpful. Focus on the ones with younger girls, if you could. That will cut down on the number, I'm sure."

Detective Lochna looked disgusted with his assignment, but he quickly regained his composure and said, "Sure thing. I'll get right on that."

This day was proving to be very interesting. He wondered if he could trust anyone inside the office with any information. He called Agent Tomlinson from the Internet Crime Division and asked to see him. He knew this agent was trustworthy and maybe his only chance at having a stream of information that would only come to him and not through Detective Lochna.

It took all of ten minutes for Agent Tomlinson to arrive at Detective Martinez's office.

"What can I do for you, Joe?" he asked as he came in.

"Shut the door. I want to speak with you about this new assistant that I was assigned today."

"Wouldn't happen to be Detective Lochna, would it? I've already had the pleasure. Met him in the hall as he was headed down to records."

"Really? Yes, that's the one. He'll be working with me on this case. I'm not sure about him yet, so I want to find out all I can concerning him. Which precinct he is from, years on the job, past arrests, acquaintances on and off the job, etc. Get my drift?"

"Sure, but why me? Your secretary could do that just as easily."

"I want discretion. I want someone who knows the internet and can really look at someone. Plus, I want someone who is going to be loyal and trustworthy."

"Will do. I'll get back with you in a couple of days. Soon enough?"

"It will have to be. I want it done right."

Agent Tomlinson left the office a bit bewildered. Never had he been singled out to do such a thing. This had to mean that Detective Martinez was getting close. His trust level within the office had shrunk once he determined that the commissioner's nephew, Andrew Stigliani, was involved with the website. He couldn't blame Detective Martinez. He wanted this website shut down as well. He felt honored to be trusted with the task and information he would uncover.

Detective Martinez sat back in his chair and contemplated how he was going to proceed with this new assistant by his side. He would have to be on his A-game. Slipping up or giving the wrong person information was *not* going to happen.

CHAPTER 36

The bandages came off, and Maggie touched her face gently. Everything seemed to feel normal. She tried opening her eyes, but the doctor quickly told her to wait. They would need to clean the protective gel away first. After the nurses finished wiping her face, the doctor said, "Open those eyes and let's find out what you can see."

Maggie slowly opened her eyes. Everything was a blur. Shades of light and dark only. She couldn't make out a single thing. She panicked and started to cry.

"No need for tears, young lady," the doctor said. "I should have told you that things would appear blurry for a while. Your vision should clear up after a bit. Now, can you see me?"

"I can see your shape in front of me," Maggie stated, "but I can't see details."

"That's normal," the doctor said. "We had to do some extensive facial reconstruction. Within a few days, things should start clearing up for you. I don't want you to worry too much about it. I want you to continue to rest. I'll check back with you tomorrow afternoon."

"Thanks, Doc, I'll do my best."

Rachel looked at her sister and admired the way she was handling everything. She pushed her chair beside the bed and asked, "Maggie, how can you be so brave after everything you've been through?"

Maggie was shocked. She looked toward Rachel's voice to see her sister's shape sitting in the chair. "I guess I don't honestly know," she said. "I've always tried to make the best of things. If I let myself get down, then I wouldn't have been of any help to the girls I watched over. I prayed some, especially after Skylan came to live with us. She always seemed to have a direct connection with God. He watched out for her. Made me hopeful again about being rescued or possibly even escaping."

"Skylan *is* special," Rachel said. "She does seem to have that direct connection with God. I prayed some too when I was with Leslie. I didn't know where you were, and she was all I had left. I was never really close to any of the other girls that came and went."

"Rachel," Maggie started, "I need to know if Darius hurt you badly. He was a very mean man. I knew if I didn't do what he said, I would end up at the bottom of the river or buried in an empty lot."

Rachel was quiet. She didn't want to upset Maggie by telling her of all the awful things Darius had done. "I had to do some of the things you told me about before you left," she said. "I was careful not to make him mad or do something he didn't like. I was glad when Leslie figured out a way to escape. She never let me go back to that lifestyle. I thank God for that every day."

"I'm glad of that too," Maggie said. "Leslie was a good person. She was just in a bad situation. I'm guessing she was abducted at a young age, like us. I never got to know her."

"She told me once she was abducted too. She even showed me the little troll doll she was holding when it happened," Rachel said. "She had it with her to the very end. They found it hidden in her purse."

Both girls sat quietly for a few moments. Rachel wanted to ask her sister more questions and keep the conversation going, but she could tell it wasn't the right time.

"Get some rest, sis," Rachel said. "I'm going to work on my story for the paper. My editor wants it soon." She got up and kissed her sister on the forehead. "Love you."

"Love you too, Rachel."

Rachel's phone rang, so she stepped out into the hall to answer. It was Detective Martinez.

"Hi, Rachel. Any chance you can come down to the precinct? I've got some information I need to discuss with you."

"Sure, Joe. I can be there in about an hour. Need to make a quick stop by the newspaper first."

"See you soon," he said.

Rachel stopped by the newspaper and spoke with the editor about the next story. Rachel knew she needed to keep her job at the paper, but she also knew that these fluff stories weren't what she was called to do. She wanted her editor to let her do a more extensive series on human trafficking education. She wanted the general public to know what to look for and how to report. She wanted to write something that would make a difference! Luckily, her editor agreed. The stories would start next week. Rachel was thrilled. This was something she could do in conjunction with the three organizations that were already out there trying to educate others on the crimes of human trafficking. It was also the kind of story that she could put a personal touch on since she had been one of the girls for hire. It was also the story she could involve her sister, Maggie, in. Things were looking up.

As Rachel arrived at the precinct, she saw numerous television setups and wondered what was going on. Had they finally put together enough evidence to start making arrests? She slipped by the media and went straight to Joe's office. He was sitting at his desk looking through the open blinds at the media frenzy starting to form.

"Hi, there," she said as she entered his office. "What was it you wanted to speak with me about?"

He took a deep breath and said, "I need you to sit down and keep an open mind. I don't want you to speak until I'm done. Is that clear?"

She sat down and pulled her notepad out. "I'm ready."

"DA Karris Finnigan has decided not to pursue charges on Jeff Calista. Mr. Calista will become an informant for my task force, along with another undercover officer. They will be tasked with infiltrating the website we have identified as the doorway to this child prostitution ring. You won't be able to write anything on this until the investigation is complete. Do you understand?"

Rachel slowly put the notepad back in her bag and sat there quietly for a few seconds. The detective could see the wheels turning in her head. She was a smart girl, and she would see the benefits of this action. "I have one question," she said. "Will Mr. Calista ever be charged with anything?"

"He will not," Joe said. "He will be the main catalyst in bringing down the entire child prostitution ring."

Rachel looked at the detective, and he could see the frustration in her eyes. He could also see the understanding behind the disappointment. "I see," she said. "I'm assuming you have a pretty good idea who's behind the website?"

"We do," he said. "I can't tell you anything else about the case, though. I wanted you to hear about this deal from me, not the media. The commissioner will hold his press conference in about an hour, and I didn't want this to be a shock to you."

"Do Skylan's parents know?" she asked.

"They do," he said. "They agreed this is the best way to bring this ring down."

Rachel nodded her head in agreement and said, "Okay."

"I have to tell you something else as well. I was assigned an assistant. His name is Detective Ray Lochna. You won't need to talk to him. I'm not a hundred percent sure he's not a plant from the commissioner's office. Everything I tell you is in confidence and vice versa. I don't want him jeopardizing the investigation if he is a plant. I'll introduce you, so you'll know who he is, but I don't want you talking to him about your past."

The door to Joe's office quickly swung open . . . and in walked Detective Ray Lochna.

"Oh, hey, Joe. Didn't know you had someone in your office," he said. "I can come back later."

"No, stay," Joe said. "I'd like to introduce you to Rachel Denton, an investigative journalist for the *New York Times*. She's quite the writer. Have you read any of her articles?"

"Nice to meet you, Rachel," Detective Lochna said. "I've read a few articles, and you are pretty good."

"Thanks," Rachel said. "Nice to meet you too."

Rachel looked over at Joe and said, "Thanks, Detective Martinez. I appreciate your help and the compliment. I'll be seeing you."

She gathered her bag and left the two men standing in the office. She had felt the tension as soon as Detective Lochna had entered the room. She felt Joe was being cautious, and if her feelings were right, he had due cause to be. It would be a shame if something went wrong now. This ring *had* to be stopped.

Detective Ray Lochna made a mental note of the girl's name. He would need to speak with her privately if he could arrange it somehow. He knew her sister had survived the attack by Mr. Kyle and was currently in the hospital. This could be the long lost little girl that Mr. Kyle had spoken about with Darius one evening. He had to keep a low profile, though—he didn't want anyone to know about his "other" life. This was going to be a tightrope walk, for sure.

After speaking with Martinez, Ray left the precinct and went to meet with the commissioner's nephew, Andrew. They met at the marina on Andrew's yacht.

"Hey, Andrew," Ray said as he boarded the yacht. "I have some news. I met a Rachel Denton today from the *New York Times*."

"Yeah, so what?" Andrew asked. "Was she a looker?"

"Well, to be honest, yeah, she was. But more importantly, I think she may be that long lost little gal that Leslie escaped with way back when. Supposedly, her sister is the one who survived the attack by Mr. Kyle. Didn't she have a younger sister?"

Andrew poured himself a drink and sat down in one of the chairs on the deck of his million-dollar yacht. "Yeah, I think so. I remember Darius telling me about that abduction. Cute girls, tough as nails. Darius fell for the older sister hard."

"What's my next move?" Ray asked. "Heard through the grapevine that DA Finnigan isn't going to charge Calista. He's being cut loose."

"We don't have to worry about him," Andrew replied. "He'll go back to his old ways. He'll be molesting little girls before the ink dries on the release papers."

"What if they use him in a sting operation?" Ray asked.

"My uncle will clue me in if they do. All I have to do is buy the old guy dinner and chat him up a bit. I'll get the story," Andrew said confidently.

"It's in your hands," Ray said. "I'll see if I can get some answers from Mr. Kyle on why his latest victim survived."

"That won't be necessary," he said. "It's already been dealt with by the powers that be."

Ray shrugged his shoulders and got up to leave. "I'll make friends with the girls then. Getting them back to work could prove lucrative. Especially with Rachel. Quite the looker! She could bring in some high-dollar players."

CHAPTER 37

Rachel left the precinct and headed back toward the hospital. She had to warn Maggie about Detective Lochna. She knew by Detective Martinez's tone of voice this was one man that neither of them needed to talk to. Her senses had told her this man was somehow involved with the prostitution ring. She didn't know how she was going to prove it because she had been out of the business for so long. She did know the feeling she got when she looked in his eyes, though. She had seen that look many times when Darius would set her up with a customer. It was a look she had never wanted to see again.

"Hi, Rachel," Maggie said. "I wondered when you were coming back. I've been thinking about the place we're going to open. You know, 'Sophie's Place.'"

"Hey, Maggie, I need to talk to you first about some things. Detective Martinez called me into his office this morning and told me they're going to initiate their investigation into the website that's controlled by the people who were trafficking us. They'll have an undercover going in with Jeff Calista. He's the one who was seeing Skylan. The DA has dropped the charges on him so that he can help to bring down this ring."

"Wow," Maggie said. "You come bearing news, that's for sure. I guess if his cooperation and help bring down this ring, then I'm all for it."

"I know; made me angry. I wanted him to pay for his crimes," Rachel said. "But I'm with you. If it brings down the website and those behind it, then they've saved some lives and prevented future crimes. I have something else to tell you, though. There's another detective that's been assigned as Joe's assistant. His name is Detective Ray Lochna. He seems familiar, but only in the sense that he has that same vibe as all my customers had when I was set up by Darius. Joe asked that we *not* confide in him anything about ourselves or our pasts."

"Okay, then," Maggie said. "What does this Detective Lochna look like? I'll need to know since I'm seeing things a bit clearer today. By the way, the blue highlights in your hair are kinda cool."

Rachel smiled and laughed. "As you can imagine, I had to change my appearance so Darius wouldn't find me. I chose blue highlights a while back, and I've grown to love them."

Maggie smiled and said, "You look like a million bucks! I'm so glad to see you finally."

Rachel hugged Maggie and said, "I love you, sis."

"Love you too, now, what does this detective look like?"

"He is midforties, average build, with short salt-and-pepper hair. He wears khakis with a suit coat and looks like any other detective on the force. His tone of voice tells me he thinks rather highly of himself. You know, like some of the guys we met for Darius. His complexion is medium with a few acne scars. I'd say he's not married."

"Okay," Maggie said. "I will tell you there was a man that fits that description that Mr. Kyle would see once in a while. I saw them talking one day outside the house. Mr. Kyle had come over to see Darius, but he wasn't there. This guy showed up about the same time. He and Mr. Kyle went outside to talk. I couldn't hear what the conversation was about."

"I'll snap a photo of him with my phone, and then we'll know if it's the same guy," Rachel said. "Joe will need to know. I know he doesn't want anyone messing up this investigation."

"Sounds good," Maggie replied. "Now, about Sophie's Place. I need to figure out how this is all going to work. Number one, I don't have any money. Two, I don't have an education, and three, I have no idea where to start. All I know is I want Sophie's Place to be a resource for girls and women like us. I want them to feel safe. I want to provide them the counseling and opportunity to heal. I'm even envisioning an offsite facility where they could learn life skills that would propel them into a productive and viable future."

"Slow down, sister," Rachel said. "I know you're excited about starting Sophie's Place. I am too, but we have to go about this logically and with education. I've made arrangements for us to shadow the director at one of the organizations I was telling you about. She has agreed to informally take us under her wing once you are out of the hospital and have gone through counseling. I'll be right by your side because I haven't been to counseling either. I've spoken to Joe about my life but not a professional therapist. Once we complete the counseling and feel strong enough to proceed, then we can start making more permanent plans. It doesn't seem difficult to start a 501(c)(3), but we'll need to know that we aren't duplicating services. I feel we should be an entirely different resource for these girls and women while working in conjunction with the existing organizations that are already established."

"You are so smart," Maggie said. "I thank God that you made a success out of your life. Going to college, graduating, and securing a job at the newspaper . . . I'm proud of you."

"I can help you get your GED if you'd like," Rachel said. "Then you can go to college too. It's never too late."

Tears rolled down Maggie's cheeks. "Thank you. I just might take you up on that offer. Is it possible to start studying now? I need a distraction."

"I'll get some books from the library this afternoon," Rachel said. "We can start this evening."

The doctor came through the door smiling from ear to ear.

"Hi, Maggie," he said. "How would you like to go home? I've reviewed your chart, and it seems that everything is in order. Your vision is improving, and there is no need for you to stay if you don't want to."

"Woohoo!" Maggie exclaimed. "I'm ready! Where do I need to sign?"

The doctor laughed, "I'll have the nurses get the paperwork started. You should be out of here this afternoon sometime."

"Thanks, Doc!" both girls declared simultaneously.

Maggie looked at Rachel and said, "What am I going to wear home? Am I staying with you? What does my hair look like?"

Rachel smiled. "I'll go out and get you some clothes. Yes, you're staying with me. I wouldn't have it any other way. Your hair will be fine. I'll be back within the hour with everything you need. I can't let my sister leave looking like a ragamuffin."

"Thanks, Rachel," Maggie said. "You're the best."

Maggie sat back into the bed and leaned her head back against the pillow. She was really getting out of here. She couldn't believe it. She was worried about Mr. Kyle, though. Joe hadn't mentioned anything about the police having him in custody. He hadn't tried to find her at the hospital, but would he try once she was released? She was worrying, and she couldn't help it. She couldn't take another beating.

The nurse came in to take her vitals one last time before discharge. She smiled down at Maggie and said, "You are one tough cookie. I admire your strength."

"Thanks," Maggie said. "Guess I never caught your name."

"My name is Celia. I've worked here for twenty years, and I've never seen anyone so strong. You have beaten all the odds."

"Nice to meet you, Celia," Maggie said. "I guess you could say I have had to stay tough. I wanted to see my sister again."

"Sisters are the best," Celia said. "I wish I could see my sister again, but she died when she was fifteen. They found her body in an alley three blocks from our house. I was eleven at the time. The police said she had been abducted, raped, and then murdered. They say she fought, though. There were skin cells under her nails, but no DNA matches have ever been found."

"Oh my goodness, Celia. I'm so sorry."

"It's okay," she said. "I've come to live with the loss. That's one reason I became a nurse—to help people heal from whatever ailment or tragedy they've endured."

"Well, I'm glad you've been one of my nurses. You all have been so kind. Thank you," Maggie said.

"All right. You're ready for discharge. I'll go and complete the paperwork, have the doctor sign it, and you'll be on your way," she said as she turned toward the door.

"Up for one more visitor?" the man said as he entered the hospital room. "I come bearing gifts."

Maggie sat up and looked at this man. The hair on the back of her neck stood up, and all the warning signs were there. This was a man she did not want any part of. She didn't quite recognize him, but she was sure she had seen him before.

"And who might you be?" she asked.

"Detective Ray Lochna. Thought I'd swing by and see how you were doing. Sounds like you're headed home. So, where is home going to be?"

"Not sure," Maggie said. "Haven't thought too much about it."

This was the man Rachel had told her about and warned her not to give him any information. She would keep the conversation light. Hopefully, Rachel would be back soon.

"Well, here's a magazine," he said. "Thought you might like to have some reading material. I'm assuming you have most of your vision back?"

"Still a bit fuzzy," she said. "Thanks, though. I'm sure I'll be reading it soon."

The detective stood fidgeting at the door. It was like he didn't know what to do next. Finally, he pulled up a chair beside the bed.

"Mind if I stay and visit a bit?" he asked.

"The nurses are getting my discharge papers ready, so suit yourself," she replied.

"What's it like . . . to survive such a beating?" he blurted out.

Maggie looked at him and wondered what kind of man would ask such a thing. She determined he was a monster, one very much like Mr. Kyle. She did not doubt that this man would do things to a woman or girl that would be irreprehensible. She prayed Rachel would return soon. Until then, she had to come up with a way to get him to leave.

The nurse call button was beside her. She knew she could push it, and a nurse would come running. She didn't want to do that, though. She just wanted him to leave on his own. If she were to fake a symptom to get the nurses in here, it would delay the discharge. She decided to play along.

"It's painful," she said. "I don't think anyone knows the pain quite like a beating victim."

He leaned in closer and whispered. "Maybe your next beating you won't live to tell about it."

She closed her eyes and pushed the nurse call button. The voice came over the intercom and asked if there was something she needed.

"My chest!" Maggie yelled. "My chest! I can't breathe! I need help!"

As predicted, the nurses came running, and Detective Lochna excused himself, saying he'd visit with her later.

Maggie lay there as the nurse hooked her up to a heart monitor and prayed for Rachel to get there.

"What's going on here?" Rachel asked as she came through the door.

Maggie sat up and tore off the sticky tabs from her chest and reached out to Rachel.

"He was here! Detective Lochna. He was here! He brought me a magazine and started asking me what it was like to survive a beating. He also told me the next time I wouldn't live to tell about it."

Rachel was texting Joe before Maggie had finished telling of the incident. This was not going to happen. She would make sure they were safe, and Joe would help them.

"Are you listening to me?" Maggie all but shouted. "I'm talking to you!"

"I heard you. I'm texting Joe to let him know. We're staying here until he gets here. Understand?"

Maggie calmed down and filled in the nurses about the incident. They understood there was no medical emergency. It was forty-five minutes before Detective Martinez arrived. When he entered the room, he looked concerned and a bit disheveled.

"All right, tell me what happened," he said. "I'll need you to start from the beginning."

Maggie told her story while Joe listened.

"You said he looked familiar," Joe said. "Did you recognize him?"

"All I know is he is the same man that was talking to Mr. Kyle one day outside of the house," Maggie stated.

"I'll have an officer assigned to you two before you go home," Joe said. "I don't want to take any chances. If he is here to disrupt this investigation—or worse, harm you—then I want to stop that from happening."

"Thanks," Rachel said. "I'm sure this is all going to get pretty wild before it's all said and done."

"I'm afraid so," Joe replied.

CHAPTER 38

Detective Martinez went back to the precinct, where he called in Agent Tomlinson from the Internet Crime Division. "Give me some news," he said. "I need to know who this Ray Lochna is and where he's from."

"You're not going to like this. He's from the DC area where he was working homicide the past few years. He got a transfer to the New York City Police Department a couple of months ago. Seems he specifically requested the Internet Crime Division. His request stated he wanted to help with the growing sex crimes against children."

The detective sat back in his chair and contemplated his next move. He had to be careful.

"Thanks, that's all I need to know. He'll be kept busy. Not on this case, though," he said.

"Can I ask who your undercover is going to be?" Agent Tomlinson asked.

"Haven't decided yet—need someone who hasn't been in the field. A relatively unknown."

"I'd like to help, if you think I could do the job," he said.

Detective Martinez assessed Agent Tomlinson and decided he would fit the bill. He was knowledgeable on police procedure and damn good at all things internet. The advantage would be that he hadn't been in the field in some time because he'd been stuck behind a computer for years tracking down solicitors and whatever else he did.

"You just might be the person I'm looking for. You think you can play the part of a rapist and child molester?" Joe asked.

Agent Tomlinson swallowed hard and knew he had asked for this. "I think I can manage," he said.

"Good," the detective said. "I'll get the necessary paperwork ready, and you meet me here day after tomorrow. Don't shave either. I want you to look a little scruffy. Between you and Jeff Calista, we're going to shut this website down."

"Will do," Agent Tomlinson said. "See you then."

Detective Martinez called Jeff Calista and told him when the meeting was going to be. They would come up with a plan.

Detective Lochna came in the office looking like he'd lost his puppy.

"What's got you so down?" Detective Martinez asked. "Looks like someone died."

"I went to see the girl in the hospital this afternoon. I was there to introduce myself and let her know I was working with you on the case. She freaked out on me and went into some sort of cardiac arrest or something."

Detective Martinez was furious. Who did this guy think he was? He took a deep breath before replying. "Why would you do that? I'm not sure you are working on this case with me. I haven't given any blessing to that effect, and I'm not inclined to either if you sent her into cardiac arrest!"

"I didn't mean too," he said. "I just wanted to get to know our victim."

"I think you'll be better suited to work in the office. I need those files I sent you to research on child prostitution. Do you have them?"

"I'm not done yet. There are a lot of files to go through," he stated. "Why are those files so important anyway? Not sure they have anything to do with the current case."

"I'll decide if they are important," Joe said. "I won't know unless you get your butt down there and get back to work. I expect you to have them on my desk by the end of the week."

"Yes, sir," Detective Lochna said. "I'm on it."

After the detective left the office, Joe sat back and thought about how he was going to keep this man out of his way until the investigation was over. He wished he could send him somewhere out of state to investigate. He would have to call a couple of the other task force members and see if he could get some strings pulled or at least have a viable lead he could send this guy on. With the possibility he was involved with Mr. Kyle, it made it all the worse. They would have to keep tabs on Detective Lochna *and* keep him at arm's length at the same time. This case was getting more complicated by the minute.

Maggie was dressed and ready to leave the hospital. Rachel looked at her and admired her big sister. She was a strong woman. She hoped the next step of getting her settled into the apartment wouldn't be a big deal. It was small and barely had enough room for one. They would make do, though. They were resilient.

"Ready to go?" Rachel asked.

Detective Martinez texted Rachel's phone. He had sent an address of an apartment where they could stay until the investigation was over. He also stated they would have police protection 24/7.

"Wow!" Rachel exclaimed. "Guess we're getting the red-carpet treatment. We have a special apartment we'll be staying in until the investigation is over. Seems Joe wants us under police protection as well. Hope it's nice. Says a uniformed officer will meet us downstairs with a key and instructions."

Maggie rolled her eyes. "Guess we'll make do. Maybe one day we'll have our own place."

"Oh, we will," Rachel said. "I can guarantee you that."

Both women made their way down to the elevators. As they

reached the bottom floor, and the doors swung open, a uniformed officer met them and escorted them to a waiting car. He instructed them they were to go to the apartment on the third floor when the car arrived at their destination. They were to stay in the apartment until Detective Martinez arrived later that evening.

Maggie looked down at her hands as they sat in the backseat of the car. "Do you think Mr. Kyle will be coming after me again?" she asked Rachel.

"Not on my watch, sis. I know that's why Joe wants us to hide out for a while. He wants us safe so he can get these guys."

"I know. I'm just scared," Maggie said.

The apartment was in a pretty nice neighborhood. Rachel hadn't been in this part of the city much. As they got out of the car, she wondered how the police department could afford such a nice place. She also wondered if this was maybe a safe house of sorts.

Rachel opened the door to find an immaculate apartment. Two bedrooms, one bath with a chef's-style kitchen, open concept living/dining room. As she explored, she noticed there were already clothes hanging in the closet, food in the pantry, and towels in the bathroom.

"Hey, Maggie, looks like we're set for a while. There's everything we need for a few days," Rachel said.

Maggie was still standing in the living room when Rachel walked back in from the bedroom. The officer that had walked them up explained that Detective Martinez had supplied the apartment for them and would be by later that evening. Rachel thanked him and then locked the door behind him when he left.

"Are you okay, Maggie?" Rachel asked.

"I'm okay," she said. "Just thinking about how this is different and the same from where I came from. We can't leave. Everything is supplied for us. I guess I'm just scared."

"It's nothing like that, Maggie," Rachel said. "Detective Martinez will get these guys, and he'll rescue countless girls that need help. We'll never have to do any of those things again. Do you hear me? We're free! *You're* free!"

"It doesn't feel like I'm free," Maggie replied. "I still feel trapped."

"Let's get settled," Rachel said. "We can talk over a nice cup of tea when we're done. I want to talk more about your ideas for Sophie's Place."

Rachel knew she had to distract Maggie from her thoughts. It was the only way she was going to be able to get through these next few days. She remembered being a bit stir-crazy after moving in with her friend, Kori, and her husband. It was a blessing that she was able to get her GED and start thinking about college. She would help Maggie do the same. There was plenty they could do while they were lying low.

Detective Martinez arrived around 8:00 p.m. with lots of books and items that would keep the girls busy while staying in the apartment. He could smell they had already had dinner, so he was happy to see that they were settling in nicely.

"Hi, girls," he said. "Smells good in here. Glad you found everything to your liking. I know it's not the ideal setup, but I hope it works for you."

"I think we'll be fine," Rachel said. "I appreciate you bringing the books and stuff. We can sure use them. By any chance, can I get you to bring some study aids for someone who will be taking their GED before long?" she said as she motioned toward Maggie.

"Sure can," he said. "Be glad to. I'm going to be unavailable next week, so I'm going to give you a coworker's cell number. If you need anything, please let him know. His name is Ed Traviston. He's in charge of your protection.

"I think we'll have this website shut down within a month or two. Hoping to have things buttoned up where we can move you girls back to your apartment within a week or two if everything works out."

"Sounds good," Maggie said. "Does that mean you're getting close to getting Mr. Kyle off the streets?"

"You'll be the first to know," he promised.

"Thanks," Rachel said. "I have all the confidence in the world with you and your task force."

"Oh, and if you girls need to go somewhere, just text this number, and an officer will escort you wherever you need to go," he said.

"Well, I guess that means we aren't housebound," Maggie said sarcastically.

Rachel looked at her sister and understood all too well. "No, we aren't housebound, Maggie," she said. "We'll get through this. You just wait and see."

CHAPTER 39

Joe had successfully gotten the girls squared away in the apartment without Detective Lochna's knowledge. He was thankful the detective seemed to be licking his wounds and sticking to his latest assignment. There was something shady about that guy, though. He would have to make a call to his D.C. contact on the task force. Maybe he could shed some light on his suspicions.

Detective Lochna made a call to the organization once he left the marina. He wanted to speak with Mr. Beltrone but was told he was out of the office on business. He was disappointed. He thought he had enough information that would propel him up the ladder and secure him a place within the organization that would net him some hefty profits. He might even be able to leave the detective gig behind.

He had been an "enforcer" for a while, and moving up would make him district superintendent. This would net him 20 percent more for each girl delivered by the district administrators. It would be a substantial pay increase.

He decided to grab something to eat at the local diner. He was tired and hungry, and a burger sounded divine. While waiting on his burger, he wondered if he had made a mistake by going and talking to the girl in the hospital. The enforcer was ingrained into his DNA. It came naturally to play the part. He knew this girl wasn't going to be allowed to live. He had made threats to her. Had she told Detective Martinez? Most likely. He had to figure out a way to get to the Beltrones and tell them his grand plan.

Before he had a chance to eat, the diner door swung open, and Andrew Stigliani came strolling over and sat opposite him. "Got a proposition for you," Andrew said. "I think you might like it. Come on, my new yacht just docked, and I want you to see her."

The waitress brought the burger, so Ray grabbed some napkins and wrapped it up for later. This proposition sounded promising. Maybe the Beltrones were thinking of an advancement for him after all. Perhaps Andrew had made a call on his behalf.

As they were pulling into the marina parking lot, Ray noticed a black sedan parked a few spaces down from where Andrew's yacht was docked.

Andrew was excited and said, "Park this thing already. I'm excited to show you my girl."

As they were getting out of the car, Mrs. Beltrone exited the black sedan. All of Ray's senses were on high alert now. It was not commonplace for Mrs. Beltrone to be out with the help.

Andrew quickly adjusted his jacket and said, "She's here to take the maiden voyage on the yacht."

"Sounds good," Ray said. "Can't wait." Maybe Andrew had her come in person to tell him about the promotion. He hoped that was the case, anyway.

"Hi, Ray," Mrs. Beltrone said as she walked up to the two. "Here to take the maiden voyage too?"

"That's what Andrew told me," he replied. "She sure looks like a nice one."

After boarding the yacht, they set sail for open waters. Andrew had dinner provided, and all seemed to be going well. After dinner, they sat on the top deck with their drinks, reliving the "good ole days." Ray felt this was the perfect time to bring up the promotion he so desperately wanted.

"Mrs. Beltrone," he stated, "I'd like to inform you I've found the girl that ran away with Leslie all those years ago. You remember the girl Darius had that escaped?"

"I'm familiar," she said. "It's been many years, hasn't it?"

"Yes, I know," he said. "But the young girl that was with Leslie is alive and well. She's right here in the city. I'd like the opportunity to introduce her back into the organization. I'd like to be made district superintendent with control over, let's say, six or more districts. I would promote this girl to our wealthier clients. I know she's older, but she'll bring in the money. I can guarantee you that."

Mrs. Beltrone got up and started pacing the deck. Ray knew this was how she contemplated any offer, so he let her be. He knew she'd walk around until she had figured out her response. She would be back with an answer; he was sure of it.

Olivia Beltrone had seen some bold characters in her time, but this Lochna fellow was pushing too hard. She knew when he had been transferred to New York, that she would probably have trouble with this one. Why couldn't she trust people just to do their jobs and be content with the salary, plus bonuses she provided? This business of selling little girls had become a million-dollar business in the course of just a few short years after her husband had become governor. She was not going to let these two sniveling bottom suckers try to one-up the organization by calling the shots.

As Andrew and Ray sat on the deck, they chatted more about the old days and all the good times they remembered. Both were drinking heavily, and the effects of the alcohol were starting to show. As the two toasted each other one last time, two men silently appeared from below deck behind them. Neither Andrew nor Ray were aware of their presence. Olivia nodded in the affirmative when the taller of the two men looked her way. Without a sound, bullets hit the two men simultaneously in the back of the head. Both died instantly.

She had watched the entire scene unfold. She walked up beside the two dead men and saw the blood pooled beneath them. "Get this mess cleaned up!" she stated. "And make sure there's nothing for anyone to find. I'm not going down for anything these two may have screwed up."

The dead men were wrapped in sheets from below deck and weighted down with an anchor. Their bodies were dumped overboard in the open ocean. No one was going to find them. A plausible story would have to be spun to keep the cops from snooping around. She had done it before, though, and she would do it again. Andrew's uncle, the police commissioner, would believe his freeloading nephew had taken off on some voyage on his new yacht with his new friend, Detective Lochna.

Her ruthless attitude and greed for the almighty dollar overshadowed any speck of compassion or sympathy she had for her fellow man, woman, or child. This business had become her lifeblood, and she didn't care how many girls were hurt or killed to maintain the lifestyle she enjoyed.

CHAPTER 40

Detective Martinez and Agent Tomlinson formulated a plan of action before they met with Jeff. They were enjoying a cup of coffee when Mr. Calista arrived.

"Hi, guys," Jeff said as he entered the office. "Reporting for duty."

"Have a seat," Joe said. "We've got a lot to hammer out today. First things first, this is Agent Tomlinson. He'll be your partner in crime. He'll go by the name of Sam Sorensky. He'll be your partner, and you'll be bragging that you got off scot-free. You're bringing him into the website for business and pleasure. You will want to see young girls together. Do you understand?"

"I do," Jeff said. "How will I be paying for these services?"

"We've acquired a credit card for you with a limited amount of funds. It's in your name. It will appear to be yours. In all reality, it is NYPD property," Joe said. "You'll pay for the services just like you did before, and if they question why you're using a different credit card number, you can explain that you canceled your other one. It's highly unlikely they will ask, though."

"What sort of girls are we looking to book?" Agent Tomlinson asked. "I need to get my head wrapped around how I should act with certain age groups."

Jeff looked at Agent Tomlinson and said, "Well, Sam, you'll need to act natural, not creepy. The girls will pick up on creepy. The nicer you are, the more fun you can eventually have."

"Whoa, wait a minute," Joe said. "You and Sam will *not* be having fun with *anyone*. You will play this off like you did with Skylan. Or rather, how Skylan played it off with you, Jeff. You will get the girl talking and not harm or touch her at all. Do you understand? If you don't think you can handle that, we can call this off right now."

"I understand completely," Jeff said quickly. "I just wanted to let my partner know how to act was all."

"Okay, now that that is understood, I have this laptop you can use to book your client. I want you to log on and see if they'll let you back in," Joe said.

Jeff picked up the laptop and started typing. Once in the chat room, he typed a braggadocios message to the site administrator claiming the virtual "slap on the wrist and don't do it again" attitude he received from the NYPD. He went on to explain how he had acquired a partner and that they needed a girl around the age of eleven with blond hair. She would need to be comfortable with two men. He stated they would be willing to pay $25,000 for two hours with this girl.

It wasn't long before his message was answered by someone with the screen name of 2Gs. 2Gs stated he would look around and get back with him.

"How long does it usually take?" Joe asked Jeff. "Will they get back with you within the hour?"

"Pretty sure they will. Our $25,000 is a lot for two hours," Jeff said. "That should have gotten their attention."

Sure enough, after thirty minutes, the screen was active with the reply. It stated they had found a girl from the Virginia area and would be willing to meet with the donor day after tomorrow. They wanted to know where the gentlemen would like to meet.

Jeff quickly replied they could meet at the private gentlemen's club at 11:00 a.m., where he was a member. It was in downtown Richmond. The girl could come under the guise of being his daughter. Payment would be sent ASAP.

2Gs replied and stated that would be fine. The girl's name: Tamara, a white girl with blond hair. She's had experience with twos and was willing to accommodate.

Seeing the reply on the screen made Detective Martinez and Agent Tomlinson sick to their stomachs. They hoped this meeting would be beneficial in infiltrating the ring at a higher level than Joe had tapped into when meeting Sophia.

"Okay, we're set. Now, what are you two going to talk about with this girl?" Joe asked. "We need to have a plan."

Agent Tomlinson sat back in his chair and cleared his throat. "I think we wait and see what the girl is like. I mean, they say she's experienced with twos, but how do we honestly know? How do we know she is truly eleven years old, for that matter? She may be older. I'd like to talk to her first and ascertain what direction the conversation should take at that point."

"Sounds good for you," Joe said. "But Jeff will need to know options for conversation. He's not used to doing this as an investigative tool."

"I'm pretty versed in a lot of subjects," Jeff stated. "I think I can hold my own."

"Here's what I want to happen. You two will both be wired. We'll be listening in on all conversations. I want you to see if this girl is familiar with the business. If she doesn't seem to be, then it's small talk until the two hours are up. Make sure the girl knows not to let on that she didn't engage in any sex acts. If she is anything like Sophia, she'll be glad for the reprieve. She will also be a good actress. Keep on your toes, gentlemen!"

"Will do," Jeff said. "Sam, I'll let you take the lead."

The two left Detective Martinez in his office. Joe bowed his head and said a prayer. "Lord, help us to put a stop to this website and the people behind it. Amen."

The next two days were spent researching possible suspects

that might be tied to the website. It was looking more and more like the governor of Virginia had some high-powered people that may be pulling strings from D.C. It didn't surprise any of the task force. They expected heads would roll when things started falling into place.

Detective Martinez found a viable case that Detective Lochna could work on and not suspect he was being put off. There was a missing teenager from the Bronx, and it was closely tied to Mr. Kyle or at least someone who fit his description from some chatter the task force had received from their informants on the street. This was something Detective Lochna could focus on without being too far removed from the current case that Detective Martinez was working. He thought it was strange, however, that he had not seen Detective Lochna yet today. Maybe he had called in sick. He would speak with HR and see if they had heard anything from him.

Detective Martinez had his team assembled and ready. There was one team parked behind the gentlemen's club and one parked in the front. The two teams were comprised of Virginia police, state troopers, and a couple of FBI members. Joe was sitting in the van behind the gentlemen's club with the team, earpiece in and ready to see if this plan was going to work. He hoped it would.

"A black SUV is pulling up to the building now, blond girl getting out," the front team reported. "Can't see the driver. Windows are tinted too dark. Girl has now entered the club."

Detective Martinez sat and listened intently for the introduction to take place.

"Mr. Calista, your daughter has arrived," said a gentleman with a smooth and otherworldly voice.

"Thank you, Trent, that will be all," Jeff said.

"Hi, there, Tamara. How are you doing today?" he said as he

looked at the girl. "Are you ready to spend some time with your dear old dad?"

"I'm okay," she said with a flippant preteen attitude. "What are we going to do today?"

"I think we'll head back over to the house and watch a movie," Jeff said. "What do you think?"

Agent Tomlinson cleared his throat and got Jeff's attention.

"Oh, I'm so sorry, Tamara. I want you to meet a friend of mine. His name is Sam. We went to college together. He's spending the day with me as well. Hope you don't mind?"

"Hi, Tamara," Agent Tomlinson said. "How old are you now? I haven't seen you since you were a baby. What's it been? Eleven years now?"

"I'm four . . . I mean, twelve," she replied. "I'm ready to go when you are, Dad."

"You know, I'm pretty hungry," Agent Tomlinson said to Jeff. "You think we can grab some lunch here before we go?"

Jeff shrugged his shoulders and said, "Sure, I'm a bit hungry myself. How about you, Tamara? Are you hungry?"

Tamara looked at these two men and knew this was going to be a different sort of so-called date. She had been prepared to be groped and raped by these two men, but if they were hungry, she was going to play along. Maybe they would forget about her and just spend their time eating. The plus side of this whole thing was that she was going to eat a good meal as well.

"I am a little hungry," she said. "Do they have good food here?"

"Excellent food," Jeff said. "Desserts are the best."

They ordered their food and made small talk until the food arrived. Agent Tomlinson had caught the slip by Tamara when she stated her age and asked, "So what grade are you in now?"

"I'm homeschooled," she quickly replied. "My mom says I'm an excellent student and doing eighth-grade work already."

She hoped that would cover the slip she had made earlier. She didn't want Lonnie, her handler of sorts, to know she had made any mistakes with this job. He had told her this was a big-time gig and to be on her best behavior.

"I bet your mom is so proud of you," Agent Tomlinson said. "I can't believe she has time to homeschool with her job and all."

"She finds the time," Tamara replied. "I'm a great self-studier, and she appreciates that tremendously."

"Her name is Carol, right?" Agent Tomlinson asked Jeff. "It's been so long, and you've dated so many after your divorce years ago, I can't remember."

Tamara looked at Sam and wondered why these two men were playing this whole father/daughter/family thing to the hilt. It was strange to be having this conversation when Lonnie had told her she would be pleasing two men today. She wasn't going to complain by any means, but it was highly unusual to be sitting here like this.

"Her name is Melanie," Tamara stated. "I think she goes by Melanie Thorenson." She secretly hoped these two were cops. Maybe they would look up Melanie's name and rescue them.

Their food finally arrived, and Tamara started eating immediately. She looked up and realized her mistake and put the fork down. "Sorry," she said. "Guess I was hungrier than I thought."

"That's okay, Tamara," Jeff said. "Enjoy your food. This is a five-star restaurant."

An hour had already passed, and the meeting so far had only netted the investigation one name: Melanie Thorenson. As the three ate their lunch, the team was running the name through the system to see if they could find anything relevant.

Detective Martinez's cell phone rang. "Hey, Joe, this is Special Agent Vicki Forsythe. We have a hit on that name the girl gave the guys. She was reported missing eight years ago out of the DC area."

"Thanks," Joe said. "This is the break we've been waiting on. I'll let my guys on the ground know."

Agent Tomlinson was wearing an earbud and was quickly informed about the news. "Hey, Tamara, you mind if we just finish our food and skip the movie today?" he said. "I'm really enjoying talking to you and Jeff. I'd like to hear more about what you've been up to these past few years."

Jeff looked over at the agent and understood. He quickly agreed and settled in to enjoy his T-bone.

"Fine with me," Jeff said. "I might enjoy a slice of the triple chocolate cake for dessert if we're staying."

Tamara couldn't believe her ears. These two would rather talk about pretend things and eat! Was she dreaming? She was going to get a free meal, dessert, and a pass on the horrible things that Lonnie told her she would have to do with these two men. Miracles *did* happen. She wondered if these two were actually cops. She decided to test the waters a bit more. She had to know.

"Ooooh, I'd like a piece of that chocolate cake too," she said. "I mean, I wanted to watch a movie this afternoon, but the chocolate cake sounds great!"

She began to eat voraciously again and forgot all about how this job was supposed to end. Between bites, she kept looking at the two men. One of the men, Jeff, seemed to be like all the other men she had to meet for jobs, but Sam was different. He didn't seem the type to hurt girls. She had a hunch he was a cop. Who was the other guy, though? Her instincts told her to play it close to the cuff. If Lonnie found out about her not doing the job, then she would be in for a beating she wouldn't soon forget. Melanie, her caretaker of sorts, had always told her and the other girls to be extra nice to the men they met, and nothing bad would happen. Of course, Melanie was wrong. There were men out there who were very evil, and they did hurt girls, no matter how nice they were.

"So, where are you living now?" Agent Tomlinson asked.

Tamara looked at the bite she was about to take and decided she would take a chance. She would tell him the street name of where the house was that she stayed. There was no house number, but she had guessed by the neighbors' house numbers a few blocks down. She hoped she'd get it close. Maybe close enough that if he were a cop, she and the others might be rescued.

"Over on Clay Street, 400 block, not far from downtown," she said. "Old brick, two-story walk-up. It's okay."

Detective Martinez could sense she was testing the waters. So, he cued Agent Tomlinson on a few more questions. Before Agent Tomlinson could say anything, Jeff started talking.

"Oh, you must be over there where they are redeveloping a lot of things," Jeff said.

"Yeah, I guess you could say that," she replied. "I can see them working on buildings just down from the house."

Agent Tomlinson was impressed with Jeff's knowledge of Richmond. Joe was talking to him in his ear about winding things up and not letting on about being a cop.

"So, let's order that dessert," Agent Tomlinson said. "I'd like some of that apple cobbler. You two want the chocolate cake?"

They both nodded and continued eating while Agent Tomlinson waved a waiter over to the table.

"Two chocolate cakes and an apple cobbler with ice-cream, please," he told the waiter.

"Yes, sir. I'll have it out shortly," the waiter replied.

Tamara finished her plate and sat while the two men finished their meal. She couldn't wait for the chocolate cake to arrive. She hadn't had cake in forever!

She looked over at the wall clock and saw she only had thirty minutes left on this job. She was having a nice time for a change. She didn't want it to end. She decided she would ask Sam if they could do this again. She didn't want to be forward, but if all the jobs with these two ended like this, she wanted to do it again. It was risky because she knew sometimes, the men would be nice one time, and then the next time, be awful. But she didn't care. She liked this guy Sam. She had to take the chance.

"So, Dad," she started, "you think we could do this again sometime? I like talking with you, and I really enjoyed the lunch."

Jeff looked over at Agent Tomlinson and saw that he agreed, so he replied, keeping in character, "Sure thing, honey. When would you like to do this again? You'll have to ask your mom. I'm free most any day."

"Oh, I'm sure she'll let me. I'm getting older now, so she doesn't worry as much," she said.

Detective Martinez knew they had received some useful information from Tamara. He knew Tamara most likely wasn't her real name, but she had given Melanie's real name. He was confident that the neighborhood in Richmond where she gave the vague address was real as well. He would have the front team follow the pickup car and verify she had been telling them the truth.

He didn't like not telling her they were law enforcement, but he needed to know where the house was, and then, they would set up surveillance while he did the paperwork to get a warrant. They would pick up the driver and see what he could tell them. He had a feeling this was going to be like swimming upstream, but he was determined to bring this ring down.

The front team followed Tamara in the black SUV as the driver delivered her back to the house. It was the very house she had described at the lunch date. As the SUV parked in front of the house, the driver rolled his window down and blew smoke from the driver's window. The team was able to get a good photo of him as they watched.

Lonnie sat there, feeling proud that he had just delivered to a customer who had seemingly, enjoyed the company immensely. Jeff was the type of client he liked. He didn't mess up the girls and delivered them back with bruises. This might prove to be a lucrative arrangement. His money had been good, and he was ready if the request came in again.

Detective Martinez went to work on getting a warrant for the house. He wanted to get in there and see if Melanie Thorenson was there.

Detective Lochna had not come in for work, according to HR. Nobody had heard from him. Dispatch texted Detective Martinez and told him a patrol unit had found a jacket that belonged to the missing teen in the vicinity of an old warehouse district. They wanted to know how to proceed. Joe called dispatch and told them to tell the officer a detective would be in touch. Hopefully, they would find this girl soon. He prayed she would be found alive.

CHAPTER 41

Rachel spent the week helping Maggie study for the GED test that was scheduled for the last Friday of the following month. Maggie was a quick study and knew most everything she needed for the test. Rachel found herself teaching more math than she wanted but was content to have her sister with her.

The two talked for hours on end about how Maggie had managed to survive all these years. Rachel saw a side of Maggie that made her proud. She knew her sister was a strong woman, but she hadn't thought about just how strong she had managed to be.

There had been numerous girls that had come and gone from the home. Darius had moved them several times as well. Maggie knew most of the girls didn't make it out and were most likely murdered because of their ostentatious attitudes. She had warned them, but they hadn't listened. They cried over all the ones who didn't make it. It was a week of in-home therapy that needed to happen between the sisters.

As the two discussed their past, a future started to materialize. Both wanted to form an organization with a safe house for those wishing to start a new life. They wanted these girls and women to know there *was* another life, a *better* life awaiting them. Rachel took copious notes as the two discussed their plans.

Detective Martinez received his warrant within hours of the request on the house on Clay Street in Richmond, Virginia. He was surprised at the quick turnaround since he was one of the out-of-state officers on the task force. The judge was ready to execute the warrant and get these girls rescued, if at all possible.

The black SUV had been stopped after leaving the residence for a traffic violation. The driver, Mr. Lonnie Pershing, unfortunately, had a Failure to Appear Warrant on a drug charge. He was taken to the precinct, where he was waiting on a member of the task force to interview him. After that, he would see the judge on the warrant.

Detective Martinez gathered the team, and they made their way to the house on Clay Street. Approaching the home, they saw the curtain move in the front window. A small face peered out at them with innocent curiosity. The girl appeared to be very young. Maybe three years old.

As an officer knocked on the door, someone appeared to grab the little girl away from the window rather harshly. The curtains swayed from the motion. The officer knocked again. This time, a female, appearing to be in her late teens to early twenties, opened the door slightly.

"Can I help you?" she asked as she looked past them out onto the street. She acted as if she were looking for someone that might be watching her.

"Hi, my name is Detective Joe Martinez. I'm here to see a Melanie Thorenson," he said.

The girl's face went white as she realized this was her day to be rescued. She stepped back slightly and leaned on the door for support. "My name is Melanie," she stated weakly.

"We have a warrant to search the home," Joe stated as he showed her the warrant.

"Come in," she said as she stepped farther back and opened the door wider. "You can search all you want."

As the team entered the home, they observed two young girls around the age of ten and then the three-year-old they had seen in the front window. As they were entering the kitchen, Tamara came out from behind the closet door where she had been hiding. She saw the officers and ran over to Melanie and began to hug her.

"I told them where to find us," she told Melanie. "I told them. We won't have to do this anymore!" There were tears of joy running down both Melanie's and Tamara's faces.

Detective Martinez quickly ascertained there was no one else in the home, and all were taken down to the local station. It felt good to have rescued these girls, and it would feel even better when they were reunited with their families.

At the precinct, it was determined that the two ten-year-olds were from the Pittsburgh area. They were cousins who had been playing in a local park when they had disappeared approximately six months ago. It was believed they had wandered off by the creek and had been lost. The search team had looked for the girls for three weeks before giving up. The parents had continued their search efforts and had recently been in touch with an organization for missing and exploited children. Their names had been added to their list of missing. The two girls would stay in protective custody until their parents came. Forensic interviews would need to be conducted as soon as the parents arrived.

Tamara was found to be a missing girl from the Nashville area. Her family had been on vacation when she had vanished from a hike in the Smoky Mountains. Her real name was Teresa. She had been missing for two years.

Melanie had been missing for eight years. She had been ten when she disappeared. While in the clutches of the man she referred to as Lonnie, she had become pregnant by him. She gave birth to the child two and a half years ago. The little girl's name was Lindsey.

All the parents were notified, and Detective Martinez was confident he would glean more information from Melanie in the days to come.

As Detective Martinez exited the office where the girls were, he was called down to the interrogation room by one of the task force members. It seemed Mr. Lonnie Pershing was willing to talk.

"Okay, let's get this ball rolling," Joe said as he poured a cup of coffee and sat down opposite Mr. Pershing.

"I want a deal," Lonnie stated. "I'm not telling you anything unless I can have a deal. I have a child now, and I don't want anything to happen to her."

Detective Martinez smirked at the irony of that statement. Here this guy was delivering girls to men who would do unspeakable things to them, and he's worried about his little girl? A little girl who was living with other girls who were taken from their families and made to live this life? The two things didn't mesh, but he decided to play along. Who knew what this guy could deliver!

"OK, Mr. Pershing, let's start at the beginning. How did you get involved with this organization?"

"It all started about five years ago. I lost my job with the city, and I started dealing drugs to get by. I moved to Richmond because of the job with the city. I was the maintenance supervisor for all the city offices. They ran a random drug test one day, and I turned up hot. Lost my job. Didn't have many friends here, so I did what I knew would make a quick buck, and I wouldn't lose my lease."

Detective Martinez looked bored. "And . . .?"

"Well, I met this guy that worked for the governor's wife doing errands and such. He said he would try to hook me up with a job. After about a week, he said he had a job for me. I was going to be the chat supervisor for the website, 'At-Risk Youth—Untied.' I would receive donations, answer questions about the organization, and do general office work. Never could get them to correct the 'United.' Anyway, I did that for about two months when I realized there was a backdoor on the website. Naturally, I wanted to take a look. So, I got into the backdoor and realized this was a child prostitution site.

I was getting paid good money, so I didn't say anything." He took a long drink from the water bottle on the table before he continued.

"I watched the site and was intrigued by that side of the business, so I started poking around to see who was in charge. I wanted in on some of the action. I noticed that there were quite a few entries on the donor sheets from very reputable businessmen and figured I might learn something if I played my cards right. One day, the governor's wife came in and caught me in the backdoor. She quickly shut the door and told me I couldn't say anything. I told her I wanted in on that part of the organization. I could do most anything they needed me to do."

He took a deep breath and then continued. "She told me they always needed district administrators, and she would look into getting me a district. She informed me of the job qualifications and responsibilities. She said I would need to be on top of my district from day one, no exceptions. Job paid double what I was making and more if I recruited recurring donors. I was definitely interested. After about a week, she came back to my office and told me I'd be shadowing a Mr. Kyle, and he would show me the ropes."

Now, Detective Martinez was getting interested. He didn't want to push this guy too much because, so far, he was singing like a canary. So, he pushed back from the table and said, "I need a break. Can I get you anything?"

"I'd take a sandwich and soda," Lonnie said. "If that's what you mean anyway."

"Be back in a few," Joe said. "I'll see what I can do."

Detective Martinez returned with a vending machine sandwich and soda for Lonnie and an oversized cup of coffee for himself and a granola bar. "Bon Appétit," he said as he put the items on the table.

"Thanks," Lonnie said. "I'm starving."

"Let's keep this rolling, Lonnie. I want to hear the whole story."

"Well, I started shadowing Mr. Kyle. He was in charge of a

district out of Pittsburgh, Pennsylvania. He had four houses he controlled. He was making good money too. He was pretty ruthless and cruel. If the house girls or house moms didn't do what he asked, then they got a beating. I didn't much care for that part of the job. Anyway, he taught me the ropes, and they assigned me a district here in Richmond. I learned from Mr. Kyle if I ever wanted to party with any of the house moms or girls, then I could, but it would need to be kept from the higher-ups. I was down for that. I had seen some really nice girls."

Detective Martinez sat looking at this monster with disgust. This was not a pleasant interrogation to listen to, but this guy and his mouth just kept on going.

"So, did you take advantage of that part of the job?" the detective asked.

"I did a couple of the younger girls, but I liked them just a little older. When I was assigned to Melanie and her girls, I was attracted to Melanie. She became my girl. I have a daughter with her. Her name is Lindsey. She's two and a half years old. I mainly just drove the girls around to clients after Melanie became pregnant. I don't even think the higher-ups even know Melanie had a baby. She had her at home, and luckily, there were no complications."

"When you talk about the 'higher-ups,' who are you talking about? Do you have names?" the detective asked.

"Governor Beltrone and his wife Olivia, for sure. I know he meets with Senator Bushwater from Tennessee a lot. I know the bank where the money goes is in Richmond. I also know that Mr. Kyle won't be found. I helped the governor take care of him."

He stopped talking and looked down at his half-eaten sandwich. He acted as if he had said too much and regretted his last statement.

"What's wrong, Lonnie?" the detective asked.

"I didn't kill him or anything, you understand? I just drove the truck."

"Tell me what happened to Mr. Kyle."

"He committed suicide from what Governor Beltrone told me. I guess he messed up big time with one of his houses. He was supposed to take care of the girl that called the police. I guess the girl lived. Anyway, Mr. Kyle is dead. I helped to bury his body in a field outside of town. I was warned never to speak of this to anyone, or I'd end up beside him."

"How did Mr. Kyle really die?" the detective asked. "Doesn't sound like suicide to me. What were his injuries?"

Lonnie looked at Detective Martinez and said, "You know I'm a dead man for talking to you. What's in this for me?"

"I'll talk with the judge and see what I can do. We can start with solitary confinement. Sound good?"

"Yeah, I guess," Lonnie said. "Mr. Kyle had been shot. Execution style. His hands were tied behind his back, and he was shot in the back of the head. I guess you could say he went quickly—unlike his victims."

"How did you keep your daughter a secret from the governor?"

"I soundproofed a closet in the house, and we would hide her in there if I was at the house and received a call from the organization, or if someone would stop by."

"Who would stop by?"

"Mr. Kyle would sometimes stop by just to make sure I was keeping everything on the up-and-up with the organization. Told me he would be their enforcer if anything went south."

"Who actually pulled the trigger on Mr. Kyle? Was it the governor?"

"Don't really think so. Mr. Kyle was dead when we got there. The governor wasn't sure where to take the body after we got him loaded in the truck. He was nervous. Like it was his first time to be this close to a dead body. He kept texting someone, and finally, we ended up in that field. The governor sat in the truck the whole time

I dug the hole and dragged Mr. Kyle's body over to it. Said he didn't want to get his hands 'dirty.' Started acting all uppity after I dug the hole."

"Could you tell us exactly where this field is located?"

"Sure, it's approximately fourteen miles west of Richmond, off Highway 64. Somewhere around Bryan Park. I'm not sure, but I could drive you there."

Detective Martinez arranged for a field trip. Lonnie was going to show them where Mr. Kyle came to rest. He knew Maggie could put her fears to sleep as soon as they verified the body was Kyle's. The task force was working feverishly, getting all the evidence for the arrest warrants.

CHAPTER 42

Verification of Mr. Kyle's body was quick. He had indeed been shot in the back of the head. Fingerprints were a match to the set on file with the Pittsburgh PD. He apparently had spent a few nights in jail for a DUI. Mr. Kyle was actually Mr. Kyle Edwards. Lived in Pittsburgh but maintained apartments in Richmond and New York. He apparently was quite the traveler. His role within the organization was yet to be determined. By the sounds of everything, he had been promoted to enforcer and had multiple districts under his thumb.

Lonnie was charged and held in solitary confinement. A victim's protection order was placed on him by Melanie at the urging of Detective Martinez. He knew Lonnie would be in prison for a long time, but there would be a day when he would be released. He would make sure Melanie was informed of options when it came to Lonnie. It was evident she wanted nothing more to do with him.

The task force was issued warrants for Governor Beltrone and his wife, Olivia. There were search warrants for the Governor's Mansion. There would be other arrest warrants issued after researching the evidence. All were confident this would be a major bust and, hopefully, a significant blow to the underworld of child prostitution.

The missing teenager from the Bronx was found alive and well at a boyfriend's house. She had wanted her disappearance to appear to have been an abduction. One more found alive. Another victory for the department.

Agent Tomlinson returned to the Internet Crime Division and was happy to do so. Jeff Calista was never charged. His involvement in taking down the prostitution ring was concealed, and he was free to do as he pleased. It would be learned later that Jeff had flown overseas to France, where he allegedly committed suicide in a remote town south of Paris.

Rachel kept a close eye on the news while staying at the apartment with Maggie. She had ascertained the task force was making headway since the local news was stating that a prominent member of New York society and a member of a child trafficking ring had been found dead. The cause of death was still to be determined, according to the news reporter. Rachel knew the task force wouldn't be giving out much information until they were done. She was left to guess who this prominent member of New York society might be.

Maggie found solace in studying for her GED. The test date was fast approaching, and she wanted to get this under her belt so she could enroll in some college classes. She wanted to fast-track as much as she could because she was more than ready to start helping other girls who found themselves in the same position she had been.

Rachel had inquired through the precinct how little Skylan was doing. The report had come back from Detective Andrews. She was more than a bit surprised that he would be the one sharing the information. He stated Skylan was doing well. She had started school again and seemed to be adjusting back to normal life. Her parents were in counseling as well as Skylan. All were doing fine.

Detective Martinez pulled up in front of the apartment where Maggie and Rachel were staying. He had news for them, and he was glad it was finally time to let them know.

Rachel opened the door and said, "Hi, stranger! It's good to see you. Maggie, come here. It's Detective Martinez."

"Hi, girls. It's been a long few weeks. The investigation is all but over. I can tell you that you can leave the apartment and go back to yours anytime. There is no danger to either one of you."

Maggie looked anxious as she asked, "Did you get Mr. Kyle? Is he behind bars?"

"He won't be bothering anyone ever again. His body was found outside Richmond, Virginia," he said.

Maggie let out her breath in a sigh of relief. "I'm finally free."

"Rachel, I've put together a summation of the investigation. Some details have been purposely left out, but I think you'll be able to put together a story from what I've given you. Detective Andrews and I would still like to approve anything you write before it goes to print. As you'll see, the tentacles of the organization are far-reaching with some *very* influential players. I trust you will write the story in a way that will help the community and be informative at the same time. There may be future arrests, so I would like this story to be more informative than revealing. I feel like I'm talking in circles. Do you understand what I'm trying to say?"

"I do," Rachel said. "I've been thinking about my final story, and what I have decided to do is write about the facts but also inform the readers of the immense problem we have nationwide. I want to provide the readers with information that will empower them to notice what's going on in their communities and neighborhoods. Give them tips to look for and help them identify when someone needs help. Finally, I would like to provide them with phone numbers that they can call if they know of someone who needs help. I hope we're on the same page."

"I think we are, young lady," he said. "I'm proud to say you are right on target."

Rachel smiled and said, "Thanks for everything. We'll be going back to my apartment until we can find something bigger. Don't be a stranger."

Detective Martinez smiled and said, "Not a chance. See you soon."

The next day, the girls moved back to the apartment, where Rachel still had her makeshift investigation laid out. They walked in, and Maggie laughed at the sight.

"I think you need a housekeeper," she said. "This place is a mess."

Rachel laughed. "It will tidy up quickly. Don't you worry. Now, help me with these groceries."

After cleaning up, Rachel set down to start the article. The summation that Detective Martinez had given her was perfect. It gave just enough details to let the readers know the task force had taken down a major child prostitution ring tied to the governor of Virginia, Mr. Gary Beltrone, and his wife, Olivia. It was clear the website was shut down, stating other sites would soon follow suit. The data provided was incomprehensible. The task force had rescued a total of 173 girls from Pennsylvania, Virginia, and New York, collectively. They also arrested 142 people who had ties to the organization, including some prominent names out of the DC area, New York, Virginia, and Pennsylvania.

After getting all the pertinent information for the article included, Rachel ended the article with an indicator list of how to identify human trafficking. She included the National Human Trafficking Resource Center hotline number and a list of things the reader could do to help fight human trafficking.

She closed her laptop after she sent the copy over to Detective Martinez. She felt good about the article and was confident it would pass the review with flying colors.

Maggie was sitting opposite Rachel, watching her write.

"You looked so intense when you were writing," she said. "It's fascinating to see you at work."

"I do tend to get into a zone when I'm writing," Rachel said. "I guess you could say I like what I do."

"I can tell," Maggie said with a smile. "How about calling it a night? Hit the ground running tomorrow morning with a plan for Sophie's Place."

Rachel yawned and said. "I'll take the sofa. You take the bed."

"Suit yourself," Maggie said as she got up to go to the bedroom. "I knew being the older sister would come with some perks."

Rachel lay on the sofa, closed her eyes, and started praying. "Dear Lord, I know I haven't been the best at talking to you. I just want to say how happy I am that my sister, Maggie, is here. Thank you for allowing all the circumstances to fall into place so Detective Martinez and his team could rescue Skylan, Sophie, Maggie, and all those other girls. I don't know how this type of crime can go on in America, but I trust you will help all the law enforcement personnel across the country to put an end to it. Help us as we go down this path of creating Sophie's Place. Guide us as we begin the process. In Jesus' name I pray, amen."

Maggie had got up when she heard Rachel praying and stood at the bedroom door. She silently prayed with her sister. When the prayer was finished, she said. "Amen. Thanks, Rachel. Good night."

"Good night, Maggie, I love you," Rachel replied.

The next morning, the girls were eating their breakfast when Rachel's phone rang. "Hello, Rachel Denton."

"Hi, this Evelyn Lepaste. I'd like to meet with you today if you have time."

Rachel was surprised, "Sure, I can meet you around 10:00 a.m. at the library if you'd like. Do you mind if my sister Maggie tags along?"

"That would be fine," Evelyn said. "My husband will be with me. See you at ten."

"That was strange," Rachel said. "I wonder what they want to meet with me about."

"It might be they want to speak with me since I was with Sophie for a couple of years."

"You might be right," Rachel said. "I guess we'll find out."

They both finished breakfast and got ready to catch a cab down to the library.

Once inside the library, they spotted Mr. and Mrs. Lepaste sitting in one of the research rooms toward the back of the library. Both were sitting straight with somber looks on their faces. Maggie held back slightly as she spotted them. Rachel turned toward Maggie and said, "I'm right here with you, sis. It'll be okay."

"Good morning, Mr. and Mrs. Lepaste," Rachel said as she entered the room. "This is my sister, Maggie. I don't think you all have met."

"Nice to meet you," they both said. "We would like to talk to you about something, something that is very near and dear to our hearts." Both seemed to take a moment before continuing. "We've been thinking about what happened to our Sophia, and we want to make sure that sort of thing doesn't happen to anyone else. Detective Martinez told us that you and your sister were thinking of starting an organization to help girls and women who find themselves involved in this human trafficking. We would like to help too."

Maggie was listening intently, and when there was a pause, she said, "We'd love for you to help. We have tons of ideas, but we haven't put any of them into play yet. We want to provide the community with ways they can help identify victims of human trafficking and how they can get help for these victims. We also want to provide an avenue for girls and women like me to get their life back on track once they have been extricated from that life. I would personally like this to be a faith-based organization because faith in God is what got me through it day by day. I didn't realize how much I relied on God until Skylan came to live with us."

Maggie took a breath and looked at Rachel. Rachel was staring at her with all the admiration a younger sister could have. It gave her the courage to continue.

"I'd like the organization to be a nonprofit with satellite offices throughout the country. Of course, we would need to get established before we could start branching out nationwide."

Mr. and Mrs. Lepaste smiled and looked as if they had found a new best friend. They were sitting in awe of Maggie and her ideas for the future.

"We would love to help with all of that. We have a trust fund that was set up for Sophia that contains around $400,000. Her uncle set up the fund when she was born. We always hoped the police would find our Sophia, and she would be able to use it one day," Mrs. Lepaste said. "We would like to help you set up this organization and be active directors on the board. My husband has the background for setting up nonprofits and can expedite the process."

Rachel and Maggie were shocked. Neither had ever even considered asking Sophia's parents for help. This offer was staring them in the face, and they knew they had better accept immediately if they ever wanted to make a difference for the victims of human trafficking.

Maggie cleared her throat and said, "We would love to have your help. The trust fund will go a long way in helping to establish a brick-and-mortar storefront, plus resources to distribute within the community. I will have to insist on all of this going through an attorney for the proper paperwork and end results. The other thing I want is to name the organization. I think it should be named 'Sophie's Place,' in honor of Sophie. She saved my life, and I want to help save others in her honor."

Mr. and Mrs. Lepaste were both in agreement with Maggie's requests. They looked over at Rachel and asked, "Are you in agreement with your sister on this name?"

"I am," Rachel said. "I wouldn't have wanted to name it anything but Sophie's Place."

"Then it's settled," Mr. Lepaste said. "I'll get to work on the paperwork right away. Do you have a building you have looked at in the city yet? If not, I have a rental we just purchased as an investment property, and we would be glad to rent it to you for ten dollars per year. It's a 10,000-square-foot, two-story building."

Rachel sat across the table and was in awe. These two had just answered her prayers. Sophie's Place was really going to happen. She and Maggie were going to make a difference!

She thought about their mother suddenly. Would she be proud of her two daughters? It was hard to believe that she and Maggie would be facing this world alone. She hadn't thought too much about it until now. She kept noticing the sadness in Mr. and Mrs. Lepaste's eyes and wondered if that sadness would ever diminish with time. It wasn't fair that Sophie had to die.

Maggie was busily talking when she looked over at Rachel, who seemed to be lost in thought. "Are you okay, Rachel?" she asked.

"I'm fine," Rachel replied. "I was thinking about all the girls who never got to say goodbye to their parents and all the parents who never got to say goodbye to their girls."

Mr. and Mrs. Lepaste looked at each other and smiled as tears streamed down their cheeks. Maggie sat silently, remembering the girls and young women who had been killed. Mrs. Lepaste looked at Rachel through the tears and said, "That's an excellent start on a mission statement for the organization. I can tell you Sophie would be proud and excited about this new venture!"

PERMISSIONS AND ACKNOWLEDGMENTS

I would like to thank the organization In Our Backyard for allowing me to use their Freedom Sticker with the National Human Trafficking Hotline number and their Indicator Informational Sheet. www.InOurBackyard.org

Statistics and information on the neighborhood of California-Kirkbride (Pittsburgh) provided by Wikipedia.

A special thank-you to my daughter-in-law, Michaela, who meticulously read the rough draft and helped in the editing process. Your suggestions and comments were welcomed.

CPSIA information can be obtained
at www.ICGtesting.com
Printed in the USA
JSHW040000010520
5437JS00001B/1